Each and Every Summer

Consistently Inconsistent
One Motion More

EACH AND EVERY SUMMER

L A TAVARES

Each and Every Summer
ISBN # 978-1-83943-985-8
©Copyright L A Tavares 2021
Cover Art by Louisa Maggio ©Copyright May 2021
Interior text design by Claire Siemaszkiewicz
Totally Bound Publishing

Published in 2021 by Totally Bound Publishing, United Kingdom.

EACH AND EVERY SUMMER

Dedication

Mom & Dad,
There isn't a Thank You card out there that could encompass how grateful I am for every laugh, every lesson and all the love you've given…so I wrote it. This story is my Thank You for everything you've done and everything I am because of you.

Acknowledgements

Stephanie, my agent, and Jamie, my editor, thank you, once again, for building the ladder that got me here. I wouldn't be doing this without either of you. Cheers to another story completed and hopefully many more to go.

Carrs, Clarks and Sandonatos, for being main characters in the most important stories of my life, I thank you. This book is for all the laughs and all the magic we shared during our many years of leaving our mark on our favorite vacation spots.

Brenda C and Ginny K, I can't express enough gratitude to you both for your love and support as I worked on this novel. Your feedback and encouragement helped write these pages. Love you!

Resha, you've always been one of my biggest fans, even well before I became an author. Thank you for always cheering the loudest and investing yourself in this story and in me.

My 'Flohana', I'm so happy I'm 'home' and able to share these experiences with each of you. Thank you for celebrating all the good times with me and tolerating me during the bad.

Makenna, I see so much of you in the younger version of Lyla. Like her, you are adventurous, bold and beautiful. Stay wild, pretty girl. Thank you for all your encouragement.

Tyson, much like Achilles and Weston, you rescued me too. I always needed you far more than you needed me. Your paw prints are all over this story and my heart.

And, as always, Brad and Jacoby, for inspiring me every day, keeping me on my toes and supporting me endlessly. I love you to the moon and back.

Chapter One

Weston

The campground was quiet. Not silent, but quiet. Silence on the grounds was a rarity. Birds chirped and critters snapped twigs and crunched leaves as they ran through the abundant foliage, sounding off their small, happy-to-be-out-of-hibernation squeaks. The fire Weston Accardi kept lit continuously, day and night, crackled and popped as it chewed into the pieces of wood he fed it.

Soon the soundtrack of the campground would transform from its current nature-inspired sounds to a blend of noises that belonged to the incoming camping families. Children would run and play, shrieking at decibels specific to summertime. Their laughter and yells would echo through the plush pine trees as parents unpacked the camping gear and essentials from the overloaded trucks to prepare the site that they would call home for the duration of their stay. Music — both played through Bluetooth speakers and strummed on old guitars—would travel from the dirt driveways beneath each RV and become one with cloudless blue sky above.

Each currently bare site would have a tent or RV secured on it, and every available rental trailer or cottage would have people occupying them. *Every single one*, Weston thought as he thumbed through countless pages of reservations. He'd requested the bookings be printed and delivered to the site he'd claimed as 'The Owner's Headquarters' during the off-season renovations. The rest of the employees had WiFi access within the offices and laptops or tablets to view the information and spreadsheets, but Weston found nostalgic peace of mind by holding the printed reservations in his hand the exact way his father before him had done while sitting in the very same chair. A half-grin slid onto Weston's cheeks. He was pleased with the turnout of reservations for the grand reopening of Begoa's Point Family Campground. His father would have been too, had he been alive to see it.

Weston tucked the most recent reservation listings into the worn-out openings of the accordion-style folder and tossed it inside the door of his RV, which was situated in a wooded area well away from the hustle and bustle of the main grounds. When his parents had owned the campground more than fifteen years before, they had chosen a site at the center of the grounds directly within earshot of anything and everything going on within their property's perimeter. They'd preferred it that way—involved, hands-on. In many ways, Weston liked that too, maintaining full control, but when the sun went down, he preferred a hushed space to retreat to in order to separate himself from his work and enjoy the serene nature that surrounded him.

"Achilles." Weston followed the call with a quick, wet-lipped whistle and a pat of his palm against the thigh of his cargo shorts. He grabbed a leather leash from the picnic table with a clink as the metal clasp sounded against the tabletop. The dog's ears perked up like antennas receiving a signal. His tail picked up speed, wagging in long, swift motions that swept the sand off the patio mat that covered the land just outside the RV. "Want to go on a run?"

The dog leaped from the shaded dirt area he could usually be found in — a spot he'd claimed to hide away in from Maine's hot summer rays. He darted toward his owner and pushed his large head into Weston's hips with a force that almost knocked him over.

"I'll take that as a yes." Weston used his palm to ruffle the fur between the German Shepherd's ears. Achilles bounded around in circles with an impressive agility comparable to that of a show dog. With his energy and antics, no one would guess he was missing part of his hind leg. Then again, like pup, like owner. Most people hardly noticed that Weston was an amputee as well. He was a man who ran multiple miles per day, every day, with his dog stuck to his side. He walked all over the campground and was hardly ever seen in a golf cart unless there was an emergency that he needed to handle sooner rather than later. He maneuvered around using his left leg prosthetic as if it were his own natural limb.

Weston stretched out his back and his existing leg before clipping the dog's leash around his waist. The dog usually ran free, but the leash stayed on Weston's person in case the need arose for him to use it. Weston took off down the winding dirt path into a long trail of cookie-cutter cottages — empty now but soon to be filled with families ready to embark on their summer camping adventures. There would be some newcomers, but most of the reservation list was composed of returning families from his parents' time of owning and operating the same campground prior to its untimely closure.

He and Achilles ran uphill, turning a corner to jog past the recently updated tennis and basketball courts, as well as a newly renovated shower and bath house. A custodial worker waved as Weston came around the bend of the road and jogged past.

"Good morning, Larry!" Weston called. Larry tipped his hat in Weston's direction. Weston had made it a point to learn the name of every employee — a rule of his father's that he'd inherited and valued. He continued his journey down the pathway toward the beachfront bar and restaurant, stopping where Mark Jenson was readying the place for the upcoming grand reopening. The outdoor bar itself was a new addition, built while the cabins and sites were being remodeled, but Mark was an original employee. A longtime friend of Weston's father, Mark had run the bar and restaurant during Begoa's Point's first run and had agreed to come back to manage the new facility.

"Morning, boss." Mark moved large boxes of glasses from the ground to the bar top as the sun beat down on the tiki-themed hut while he worked. He wiped his brow on his forearm. His sweat-soaked shirt clung to his skin at his chest and back. "What are we having today?"

"The usual will be fine." Weston slowed and came to a full stop. Achilles followed suit, coming to a halt, then lying down in the small bit of shade the bar provided.

Mark grabbed a silver bowl from a below-bar cabinet and filled it with water before stepping out from the service area and coming around the bar to serve it to Begoa's Point's most prominent VIP. Mark stayed on one knee for a moment, scratching below the dog's chin. Achilles stood and started lapping water from the bowl, leaving more water on the ground in a messy puddle than he'd swallowed.

Mark returned to his position behind the counter, filled a cup with ice and water and slid it across the bar into Weston's hand.

"Where are you headed to today?" Mark leaned into the bar.

"All over the grounds, I think. The usual path." Weston paused to take a sip of the ice-cold water. "At least as far as the marina. I just want to make sure everything is ready to go for the opening."

"That's what you said yesterday." Mark raised an eyebrow. "Then again, it's what you will probably say tomorrow and the day after that too."

"I like to be prepared." Weston sent his now-empty plastic cup back across the bar.

"You will be. You are your father's son, after all. I wouldn't expect anything less."

Weston looked at Mark, analyzing the new lines that sank into his skin, but other than a few signs of aging, Mark looked almost the same as he had when Weston's parents had owned the campground before its closure, leaving Mark and many others without a job.

"Thank you for coming back, Mark. This place wouldn't be the same without you, even after all these years. I'm sorry we ever put you out of a job in the first place." Weston turned his eyes downward in sadness.

"It's not your fault, Weston—"

"It is, actually," Weston interrupted, adjusting his ballcap, with his gaze still glued to the floor. He watched the dog, if for no other reason than to avoid Mark's eyes. "You know it and so do I."

"It's not. You knock that off right now." Mark's voice teetered on scolding, and he wagged one aging finger in Weston's direction. "You know that your dad used to come down to the old bar every night for last call. *Every* night. He sat on the same barstool each time, and you know what he told me?"

Weston shook his head. He had been only seventeen when his parent's ownership had come to an end, so he'd not reached the legal drinking age where he could spend those waning nighttime hours with his dad, occupying Mark's bar stools. His 'no' wasn't an entirely honest answer to Mark's question, however. He knew what Mark was going to say—what his dad had used to say—but he wanted to hear it. If he couldn't hear it from his own father, Mark's affirmation was the next best thing.

"He said it was his dream to see you run this place. So maybe it didn't happen as he'd expected, but it's happening, and you should be proud of that. You're not a kid anymore, Weston. You've grown and should be so proud of who you've become. Your father would be."

"I remember that. He used to come down here every night but never had a sip of alcohol." Weston smiled at the seemingly small memories of his father, but they were anything but insignificant. They were everything.

"I remember watching you run around these grounds, from learning to walk all the way to chasing after the girls on the beach in your teenage years." Mark continued to speak, but Weston's mind was elsewhere, time-traveling down a winding path to his childhood.

It was a humid day, the kind where it was too sticky to do anything except sit around and complain about how hot it was.

"Give me your change," Charlie said, reaching across the table for Weston's quarters.

Weston grabbed the coins off the table and held them in his sweating palm, pulling them out of his best friend's reach. "You just had two ice creams. What do you need now?"

"Fried dough, of course. I'm just fifty cents short. Come on. I'll share it with you."

Weston handed over his quarters begrudgingly, but he couldn't resist fried dough any more than the next kid could. Charlie sprinted to the ordering window.

Charlie returned to the table, but just as he did, his mother beckoned from the beach.

"Be right back, Wes. We're number one forty-eight." The red color of his skin peeking out from the edges of his tank top led Weston to believe it was time for Charlie to reapply sunscreen.

"Numbers one forty-seven and one forty-eight," the snack bar attendant yelled from the pick-up window. Weston stood and headed toward the counter. Just as he did, a young girl with a mess of deep brown curls made her way there. The attendant handed two large, golden-brown fried doughs out of the window and they both headed toward the table where the cinnamon and sugar — the best parts — were kept.

The girl waited, rocking back and forth.

"Go ahead." Weston slid the shakers toward to her. "You ordered first."

She smiled and flipped the cinnamon shaker, brown dust falling to cover her plate. She followed with the sugar shaker, but no matter how much she tried, nothing came out. She looked at him and gave an embarrassed frown.

"It's not empty." Weston looked at the shaker. "It can be tricky, though. Sometimes the powder clogs the top. Let me try?"

She handed over the shaker. Weston tapped the container on the tabletop three times then flipped it over, hitting the side. A fractional amount of powder come out, and the girl giggled.

Weston undid the top, wiped away the excess confectionary powder with a napkin and pressed the lid back on. He picked it up once more and shook hard.

The top popped off, covering his fried dough in a small mountain of white powder. A cloud of sugar flew through the air and stuck to his black shirt and hair. The girl laughed so hard that she snorted.

Weston nodded, accepting an embarrassing defeat, then started laughing too. He picked up the fried dough and held it at an angle, allowing some of his sugary mess to fall over onto her piece.

"Thank you." She was still laughing as she walked away with her fried dough plate in hand.

Weston kept his gaze down the beach, imaging that younger version of himself as his adolescent years flashed before his eyes. He shook the memories away and returned his attention to Mark. "I was only chasing after one girl."

"Whatever happened to her, anyway?" Mark grabbed a towel to continue his cleaning.

"She got away." Weston slapped the bar top with his palm and winked before turning away and heading back to his predetermined path. Achilles bounded to his three legs, following behind him without being told.

The path came to an abrupt halt at the end of the shuffleboard courts and immediately turned to acres and acres of sandy beach at the lake's edge. Weston continued his jog, both his real foot and his prosthetic one kicking up sand as he ran down the untouched beach. Achilles kept pace, his paws stirring up a dusting of sand alongside Weston's. They ran the length of the main beach area, past the snack bar and mini-golf course, then turned left before finding a dirt pathway that led into the marina. He slowed as his feet hit the wooden dock. The structure, which extended into the lake, creaked under his weight. He kicked off his shoes, taking a seat on the edge of the dock and dipping both his feet into the water, only feeling the lake's cool temperature around his right ankle. Achilles sat next to him, proud and tall, as if the multiple-mile run had taken nothing out of him.

"We did it, Achilles." Weston wrapped his arm around the dog's shoulder blades. Achilles licked the side of Weston's face, stopping the salty sweat from dripping past his ears. The dog lay down next to Wes and inched forward, trying to reach his tongue into the rippling lake.

Weston removed his prosthetic and pushed himself off the dock, submerging in the water. He resurfaced and used one hand to balance on the wood. Achilles paced the edge of the dock, deciding between jumping in after him or remaining dry.

Weston used his free had to slap the water. "Get in here, boy!" Before he'd finished the command, Achilles dove in, splashing Weston upon entry and paddling toward him. They swam around, cooling off in the cold lake. Weston pulled himself back onto the dock then helped Achilles up next to him. The dog braced himself and shook, water spraying from the ends of his fur and further soaking Weston in the process. Achilles lay down once again at the edge of the dock, his front paws dangling over the wooden edge. Weston looked out over the unoccupied lake.

"This is what we've been waiting and working for. We counted down the moments to the grand reopening and it's finally happening." Weston stroked wet fur out of the dog's face. "Tomorrow is officially camping season, boy. Memorial Day. Best day of the year, if you ask me."

Chapter Two

Lyla

Though it had been ten years, Memorial Day sat high among the days that Lyla Savoie-Kenney dreaded most. Well, second to September third. That crisp fall day had started like any other but had ended with a visit from a fully uniformed, high-ranking officer, who had turned her life upside down just by knocking on the door to inform her that her husband Jared was never coming home. November eleventh could be a tough day too. And, well, Jared's birthday, February eighth, ranked high on the list of dates to hate. Their anniversary, of course, made a case to top the list. When the person she had loved the most, the person she was supposed to spend the rest of her life with, was gone, no matter how much time had passed, there were as many foreboding dates as ones to look forward to.

Lyla found that for most of the spouses she had met who had lost their significant others, Memorial Day wasn't just one federal holiday marked on a three-hundred-and-sixty-five-day calendar. Memorial Day was every day. Each one that went by brought its own set of heartbreaking memories. It could be a day with no significance to anyone else, but to Lyla it held a memory she couldn't shake. It hung over her like a black cloud that belonged only to her. June fifteenth, for example, was not a holiday. Friends and neighbors didn't get the time off to grill and play backyard games with their friends and neighbors. For anyone else, June fifteenth was just another day. But for Lyla, it had been eleven years ago when a uniformed officer had knocked on the door of the house that she and Jared owned.

Or October thirty-first...Halloween, a holiday meant for kids to dress up as their favorite characters and collect candy from neighbors. Maybe they played a few tricks or TP'ed Old Man Henry's house. Either way, Halloween was almost always synonymous with fun. But Lyla had met Jared on Halloween at a costume party her friends had forced her to go to. Some dates hurt more than others. *Don't get me started on December twenty-fifth.*

Then again, she was the youngest widow of any of the others she had met. When the others she shared this spousal loss commonality with had learned her age, they had suddenly had nothing in common at all. They gave her a sympathetic look—the same one everyone else gave her—except tenfold because they had known what she was going through, but they hadn't gone through it at twenty-two and pregnant.

Hundreds of small red, white and blue flags covered the grounds of the Fallen Soldiers Cemetery she sat in. Jared's headstone was slightly faded now, losing its original shine to almost ten years' worth of battling the elements. Lyla leaned forward, fixing the patriotic wreath so the star-covered bow sat aligned with Jared's date of death, which was carved deep into the weathered stone.

"Miss you, Jared." She placed fingers to her lips then rested her hand against the warm marble, the sun reflecting on its surface. Their son Camden placed his hand next to hers. Camden, just shy of ten years old, grew to look like his father more and more with each passing day. The freckles across his nose, the dark hair that hung in his eyes — they belonged to his father.

Lyla put her arm around her son's shoulders as they walked down the pathway toward their car. She turned her head over her shoulder, glancing back at the headstone once more, as if Jared himself would be standing there and she'd get one last good look.

The car ride was just as silent as it usually was on trips home from the cemetery. Lyla reached forward, turning the knob on the dash to increase the volume of the radio. Anything was better than complete silence.

An up-tempo beat rang through the speakers. As Pat Benatar's voice followed, *Love is a Battlefield* became the featured song for Lyla's impromptu live concert for a one-person crowd. She sang loudly — and poorly — with dramatic flair. Camden blocked his ears but couldn't help but smile.

"Stop," he said unconvincingly, his laughter breaking up the word. He jabbed the volume button, cutting the loud music to a dead silence. Lyla dropped her jaw in surprise but hit the button again to resume her karaoke session. Camden kept his hands firmly over his ears but laughed until he gave himself an aggressive case of the hiccups. As the song came to an end, she turned the dial down only fractionally. Her efforts were successful. Camden was transformed from the sullen boy the cemetery often left him as to the cheerful, high-spirited child he was at his core.

She slowed the vehicle as the light turned yellow and rolled to a stop under the signal, now red.

"What do you want to do today?" She tapped her fingers against the shifter.

Camden shrugged. "I don't know. None of my friends are out of school yet."

The district had voted to experiment with an alternative calendar—a school year where summer started earlier and students returned to school in mid-August instead of September. Camden's school had been chosen to be a part of the pilot study, but his group of friends attended a school that hadn't as yet implemented the change.

"We *will* find something to do." The light turned green and she pulled forward, but a tune on the radio almost caused her to stop short, as though a ghost only she could see had run out in front of her car. A jingle that was both familiar and foreign played on the radio. Lyla knew the commercial, having heard it many times while growing up—but hadn't heard it since before Camden was born. A smile crossed her face.

"What?" Lyla asked. She turned up the radio and listened to the announcements.

"Begoa's Point, a family-friendly campground, will reopen its doors after close to a fifteen-year long closure. The campground has been revamped in many ways, repairs and upgrades coming to the cottages, bathhouses and many of the campground's amenities, but much remains the same. I had the opportunity to visit the grounds a week ago for a sneak peek and I had no cell phone service!" the perky radio host said. *"It was wonderful! You're instantly unplugged. The employees communicate on walkie-talkie-type radios. It's like stepping back in time, taking a trip to back when we*

concentrated less on technology and more on fresh air and family fun."

The more things change, the more they remain the same, Lyla thought as she pulled into the driveway.

"I had a chance to speak with the new owner." The host continued, *"Hear what he had to say after these messages from our sponsors."*

Lyla jabbed the ignition button and the car came to a still quiet in their driveway.

"I don't get it." Camden seemingly needed his mother to explain her sudden euphoria.

She stared through the windshield for a moment, as if it held stories in its transparent gleam that only she could see.

"Come on inside." Lyla opened her door. "I'll show you."

* * * *

Lyla led Camden up the steep, mostly unfinished stairs to the attic. Her eyes lingered on the boxes with Jared's name scribbled on them and the clothing rack where his uniforms hung in garment bags—the few things of his she couldn't fathom getting rid of yet, or ever, tucked away into their designated spot in the attic.

Looking back, it wasn't the knock on the door that had made Jared's death real. It wasn't the innumerable number of times she'd heard, *'We're sorry for your loss'* — or even the funeral itself. But after some time had passed, she'd put away the possessions that Jared had loved most. She hadn't been able to handle looking at them any longer. She'd zipped up the garment bag over the colored ribbon racks and medals that had hung on his darkest blue jacket with the red trim, and that was when it finally hit her that he would never button them again.

"Mom?" Camden's voice brought her back to the attic.

"Right, right." She shook her head as if to physically force the thoughts out. "It should be around here somewhere." She pushed boxes aside and looked inside trash bags scattered around the attic floor. "Aha!" she exclaimed as she leaned forward, picking up a large rectangular box covered in various bumper stickers, mostly ones that read 'Begoa's Point' in green-and-white text.

Lyla sat on the floor, and Camden sat across from her, his eyes wide and reflecting Lyla's excitement, as if the box they hovered over contained priceless treasure. For Lyla, it did. A lifetime's worth.

She dusted off the top and removed the cover. Inside sat multiple photo albums organized by year, stacks of what looked like small newspapers, handmade arts and crafts, more colorful award ribbons and medals than could be counted and one faded, tie-dyed T-shirt that simply read 'Camp Champ'.

Lyla smiled and cried, all at the same time. So many memories had sat just above her head all these years, but she'd never thought to look for them—not until today.

"Grandpa used to take me to Begoa's Point every single year for the entire summer. He was a teacher, as you know, so we both had the summer months to spend together. We vacationed at Begoa's Point from the time I was born until..." She thought back, swallowing a memory. "I was seventeen the last time we went." Lyla found a faded photograph, a grainy photo of her in a bathing suit and blown-up water wings on her arms. Her father kneeled behind her, sporting now-out-of-date swim trunks and a head full of hair.

"Why'd you stop going?" Camden still scanned the contents of the box.

"They closed." Lyla's smile fell into a partial frown. "Grandpa said I was getting close to aging out of the activities anyway. I disagree, though. If they'd stayed open, I would've kept returning."

Camden thumbed through the award ribbons.

"What are these?" They twirled in front of his eyes like a mobile. He ogled them as they swayed in front of his inquisitive gaze.

"Read the backs." Lyla reached forward, flipping them over. Each ribbon was marked with a white cardboard piece that contained the date it had been won and the activity it had been given for — basketball, triathlon, softball, dance-off, talent show and more.

"Hot dog eating contest?" Camden's eyes widened as he read the words on the blue first-place ribbon. "I can't believe you won an eating contest." He laughed out loud as he continued flipping through the ribbons, each one holding a new story.

"When it came to a challenge, I had no fear. I participated in every event I could. I loved softball and soccer, but mostly basketball. I was very competitive. I just loved getting into any activity."

"I wish I could have seen that." Camden shook his head and laughed again.

Lyla ran her fingers across the hem of the faded T-shirt.

"Maybe you can," she added, a figurative lightbulb brighter than the one in the attic burning above her head.

Camden leaned forward and pulled a photo book from its space in the box.

"These are so old school." His amusement heightened his voice to a pitch that cracked. He opened to a middle page and scanned the photos.

"Look at Grandpa's hair!" He stifled a giggle. "You all wore weird clothes."

"That's what was in style at the time." Lyla grabbed the album out of Camden's hands. She smiled as she scanned through the photos. *He's right. So old school.*

"Who's this?" Camden pointed to a photo of Lyla sitting at a bonfire with her head thrown back in a hearty laugh. He hovered his finger over a photo of a young boy with summer-kissed skin and hair that could've used a cut.

"That...well... His name is Weston Accardi. He's just someone who I used to know."

Chapter Three

Weston

The fire sparked bright while dark smoke billowed upward off the slightly damp logs into a clear sky. The smell—a mix of the pine trees surrounding Weston's off-the-beaten-path accommodations and the fragrance of burning wood—entered Weston's nose and settled deep in his chest. This was the smell he would always associate with home—not just in the 'roof over his head' kind of way but in the 'where he truly came from' sense. He'd been raised beside a fire just like this one on this exact campground under this same sky.

A mix of songs played through a small speaker, the shuffle feature allowing the playlist to bounce around from the early eighties to the later part of the decade and back again.

Finally, after months of work, tons of money and battling through every obstacle that had come about, in just a few hours' time, the doors to Begoa's Point would reopen at last. Old campers would return to revisit the grounds, surely comparing each and every step to the original version of the campground that they remembered. *What if I fail?* It wasn't a thought he had allowed to litter his mind — not even once — until now.

The sweat that formed at his brow and on his palms had nothing to do with the heat of the flame and everything to do with the sudden unrelenting feeling of incompetence. *This is a mistake. I'm not my father. I never could be.*

He sank back into the director's-style camping chair, leaning the chair on its legs and balanced himself with only his remaining foot. He'd ditched his prosthetic hours ago. Self-doubt settled into his chest and threatened to stop his heart. He looked at his watch — three-fifteen a.m. Achilles had long ago gone to sleep. Weston would usually have retreated to his quarters as well, but tonight it was going to be a futile effort. He couldn't sleep. Excitement and anxiety wrestled with each other, tossing him back and forth to both sides of the spectrum. The adrenaline of those emotions coursed through his veins, leaving him in a state that was going to keep him awake until the doors opened and one of two things happened — either his dreams or his nightmares would come true.

The unexpected snap of a twig brought Weston out of his head and back to the fire, and he leaned forward quickly so the legs of his chair met solid ground again. He turned to see two bright eyes reflecting the flames and a dark, lurking body emerged from the bushes. His heart rate quickened for a moment. He had come face to face with almost every creature the deep Maine woods held, but each experience had been different. Every animal had its own story and no voice to tell it. Weston was of the mindset that he owned the campground, but it was their land. He was borrowing space from the animals that had lived there long before he did. When he found himself on the same path as one of the forest inhabitants, he gave them space to ensure their story continued and so did his. His father had always said that there was more than enough earth to share.

The bushes parted as Achilles emerged from the thick brush.

"Really?" Weston let out an exaggerated sigh. "I thought you went to bed."

Achilles leaned into the remainder of Weston's amputated leg while he rested his hand at the back of the dog's head and used his thumb to rub Achilles' ears. Achilles pushed his head farther into Weston's hand and let out a deep, contented sigh.

"You scared me." Weston whispered, as if saying the words any louder would make him less of the outdoorsman he prided himself to be. He knew it wasn't the dog that was causing him heightened anxiety but rather the impending reopening of his father's legacy and the very real possibility that he could fail.

Weston picked up a clipboard, scanning through the 'before opening' to-do list for the hundredth time. Each item had multiple check marks next to it. The Is had been dotted and the Ts had been crossed. Everything had been checked then checked again.

"Something's missing." He scratched at his five o'clock shadow with one hand and tapped a knuckle against the clipboard with the other. Achilles used a front paw to knock the clipboard out of Weston's hand and into the dirt. Mark was right, and apparently Achilles agreed. No matter how many times Weston checked his work, he still wouldn't be satisfied. The best he could do was let go and trust that everything was under control. Even if it wasn't, it was too late to fix anything now. The first campers would check in within twelve hours. Weston looked at Achilles and nodded as they had a conversation no one else was privy to. He leaned over, picked up the checklist and threw the whole thing—clipboard and all—into the open flames. Achilles did his usual circular dance before darting back to the cabin and Weston followed, finally giving in to the idea of at least trying to catch some sleep.

* * * *

The sun's rays peeked through the surrounding pine trees the next morning as Weston refreshed the fire and set a wire rack over the open flame to heat a stainless-steel pot of coffee. Achilles chased some chipmunks across the path that led to the cabin and in and out of the bushes that surrounded the property. Steam floated off the brew as Weston poured the piping hot liquid into a ceramic cup. Just as he was taking his first sip, a company golf cart made its way up the path.

A young man in his early twenties hopped out of the driver's seat. The sun's rays blocked Weston's view. He held one hand up over his eyes to get a better look at the newcomer. As he stepped out of the spotlight the sun provided, Weston could make the figure out as Kevin—one of the younger assistants with the front office and welcome center groups.

Kevin's gaze lingered on Weston's fake leg longer than necessary. Some people just never could get used to the idea of a missing limb. It didn't bother Weston, though. The prosthetic and the looks it garnered had been part of him for nearly half his life.

"Good morning, Kevin." Weston said, but 'is there something I can help you with?' leaked through the greeting without him ever uttering the words.

"Oh, yes, good morning, sir." Kevin fumbled each syllable.

"'Sir' isn't necessary. We're all family here." Weston sipped from his too-hot coffee, the steam rising over the cup's edge.

"Okay, well, Mr. Accardi..." Kevin continued. Weston rolled his eyes.

"Weston," he corrected. Kevin swallowed hard and nodded.

"Weston." Kevin tried it on for size, but a lack of confidence remained in his voice. "Sheila asked me to come pick you up and bring you down to the welcome center."

Pick me up? Weston walked or ran almost everywhere. He didn't get into a car on the campground unless he had to leave it for business-related ventures, and he avoided the golf carts unless he had no choice. The whole idea of the campground's atmosphere was leisurely, at one's own pace. No rush, nowhere to be. That was why he hadn't invested any further time or money into the WiFi or cell service. He wanted to run a place where its tenants become closer to their loved ones and closer to the world around them while distancing themselves from the plugs that behaved more like leashes.

"Is it an emergency?" Weston leaned forward in his chair, keeping his voice calm and steady, but inside, he worried about the answer. He had known something would go wrong. It was like a brick in his stomach.

"Well, no." Kevin rubbed at the back of his neck.

"I'll walk then." As Weston stood, Kevin stepped forward as if he were going to assist him to an upright position. It wasn't the first time someone had instinctively offered to help him, and it wouldn't be the last. It came with the territory of having a visible ailment. People wanted to help. Kevin's intentions were noble, but they were just unnecessary.

"I've got it." Weston reached one hand forward, flat palmed, declining Kevin's offer. Achilles joined him faithfully at his side when he stood. "I'll meet you at the welcome center."

"You're sure?" Kevin analyzed Weston's leg once more. "I can drive you there."

Weston gave him a final, end-of-discussion glare, took his coffee pot off the fire and started walking the distance to the welcome center.

When he arrived, Weston stood on the steps and took in the sight. 'Unbelievable' wouldn't be a strong-enough word. Hundreds of people were lined up in their trucks and RVs as far as the eye could see, hours early for check-in. They walked along and conversed with the people who had parked around them. There were smiles plastered on every face, laughter echoing through the cloudless sky. It was pure happiness, and they hadn't even made it onto the grounds yet.

His assistant Sheila — more like his lifeline — joined him at the stairs outside the welcome center's doors.

"Hey, Sheila. Is something wrong? Kevin came and I thought—"

"No," Sheila interrupted, "nothing is wrong. Nothing at all. Everything is perfect, going exactly according to plan. But we're about to cut the ribbon and let everyone in, and I know you, Weston. You were going to sit up in that cabin of yours and hold your breath, waiting for good news to come to you." Sheila raised an eyebrow over the frame of her teal-green lenses. "But you belong down here. This is what you worked for. I didn't want you to miss it. Look how happy they are." Sheila elbowed him lightly in the ribs.

Weston smiled as he looked at each and every grinning face.

"There are a few camera crews over there waiting on statements and with prepared interview questions for you, then you can officially hang up the 'open' banner underneath the Begoa's Point sign at the entrance."

Weston walked the length of the welcome center lawn and found his way to the camera crews and anxious reporters.

"Good morning, good morning," he said to each reporter, shaking hands and waving to people just beyond his reach. They started asking him questions before returning the greeting. There were those he'd expected. Why did he reopen? Why did it take so many years? What had changed and what would be the same?

He answered each one as accurately as he could, then one reporter asked him the same question he'd been asking himself.

"Do you predict you'll be successful from the get-go, or do you anticipate a trial-and-error period?" the balding reporter asked. There always had to be someone to focus on the negative when everyone else dwelled in the positive.

"Well" — Weston stood up straight, his shoulders back — "our reservations are already maxed out and our waitlist is a mile long. So, we're hoping that's indicative of a stellar first year back." Achilles sat tall and proud next to Weston's artificial limb.

A blonde anchor with full, golden curls draped over her shoulders stepped forward. "Well, Mr. Accardi, how would you feel about answering some on-air questions from the campers waiting ever so patiently to get into the campground?"

Weston nodded and walked toward the expansive line of people, the news anchor on his left and Achilles at his heels.

The first gentleman reached his hand forward, and Weston took it, introducing himself.

"Does it look much different in there?" the man asked. "I'm afraid it's going to be unrecognizable after all these years."

"It was really important to me to keep as much of the original campground's integrity intact as possible. Some things needed updating and upgrading for safety and security purposes, but I think you'll find the grounds you loved all those years ago are very much the same. Thank you so much for coming out."

"What's with the dog?" another gentleman yelled out, three families deep in the crowd. "I was under the impression we couldn't bring pets."

"Oh, him?" Weston threw his thumb over his shoulder toward his faithful best friend. "He's not a pet. He's the owner." Achilles sat up proud and barked. The crowd laughed.

"Mr. Accardi," media members yelled, "can we get a photo here?" A woman behind a camera pointed to the Begoa's Point sign, which was still covered under a white cloth.

"I think that's a great idea." Weston walked to the sign. The line of patrons erupted, starting an impromptu countdown, and when they reached 'one', Weston ripped the cover off the sign and the noise from the excited campers—both new and returning—escalated to an immeasurable level.

He kneeled in front of the sign and Achilles stood next to him, their twin amputations on full display underneath the welcome sign — a piece still original to the grounds.

He couldn't have scripted it any better himself. Weston's dream was coming true.

Chapter Four

Lyla

The only thing worse than being stuck on hold was being stuck on a lengthy hold that featured terrible music. She paced back and forth at the kitchen island, the end of a pen in her mouth and a notepad sitting on the counter. The calendar had been removed from the wall, placed open next to the blank notebook pages.

The TV was on in the background, where a news anchor listed stats and information about the local sports teams but a tab at the left margin of the screen indicated an upcoming piece about Begoa's Point.

Camden watched intently, ready to call her attention to the living room if the segment started before her phone call ended.

"Is it on?" she whispered, covering the mouthpiece of her cell with her fingers.

"Not yet!" he exclaimed, popping up over the back of the couch.

"Oh, yes, hi!" Lyla stammered excitedly when she was finally connected with an operator. "I was wondering if I could make a reservation for a cabin."

The feeling in Lyla's stomach went from excited to flat like a blown tire on the freeway as she got a negative response. "How about a trailer then?" But her mood just deflated more. "A dirt lot? I'll pitch a tent. How about a parking space? We can sleep in the car." She injected a hint of sarcasm but remained sullen.

"But that's...next summer." She was surprised at the length of the waiting list for this year's camping season. "I'll call back for reservations for next year. Yes, I get that it's filling up fast—clearly." A brief moment later, the phone still stuck to her ear, she spoke again. "Yes, that would be great. I'll leave my information in case there is a cancellation. What are the chances of that happening?"

Her mood morphed from sadness to something else, something deeper...hopelessness. She clicked the phone off and placed it face down on the counter before heading into the living room.

"So, when do we leave?" Camden's emotions moved into the exact opposite neighborhood of hers.

"Next year, bud. There's no room this year. I'm sorry. I tried." She placed her hand on his cheek then shuffled without enthusiasm down the hallway.

"They're about to show the grand reopening on TV." His voice was small but clearly eager to remain strong. She glanced over her shoulder and rested one flat palm against the corner where the living room turned to meet the hallway.

"I'll pass this time. But thanks for hanging out with me today. It was really fun to look through all those old memories. I had a lot of laughs at Begoa's. It would've been nice to go back for the opening. Maybe next year." She winked and retreated down the hallway.

Lyla sat on the edge of her bed, one single tear following the track of her cheek bone. She knew she had let herself get too far away from who she used to be, and for a moment, a chance to reawaken parts of her past had sat just within arm's reach. Then it was gone. Over before it started. How had she missed all the announcements and press surrounding the reopening of New England's favorite vacation spot? *That place used to be the Disney World of the north. Okay, maybe not, but it felt that way to me back then.*

Had she kept herself so small, tucked away in a tiny box much like the one her ribbons and brochures were packed away in, that she was missing what was going on beyond the walls of her home? If she had opened to the world, even fractionally, she might have heard the news about Begoa's reopening sooner and might have had a chance at securing a spot. Taking a child of her own to the campground she'd grown up in was a lifelong dream of hers. Well, going with a family of her own had been the initial dream, but like most of the visions she'd had for her future, they would have to be altered.

During the year, her mind had been kept occupied with her work, teaching creative writing at the local community college. She'd followed in her father's footsteps, becoming a teacher just like he had been before retiring early and moving down south. But her last set of finals to proctor had been over week ago and now she had extra time to focus on other things. When she'd taken the job, summers off with no commitments had seemed to be the best benefit. Now she wished she'd taken the summer contract she'd been offered to teach some additional courses.

Camden sat in the living room watching the massive line of people waiting to get into Begoa's Point Family Campground on the television. Some wore T-shirts with the camp logo, stamped with years referencing a time before he was even born. Pictures filled the screen—old, grainy photos clearly from the original campground, then next to them newer, updated photos of what lay beyond the campground's new gate, side by side for comparison.

"Next on the news," a perky blonde anchor with a full head of curls said, "we will meet with the man behind the opening of this family favorite campground, a reopening that is long overdue and highly anticipated."

Camden was just about to click the TV off when the camera panned to the profile of the man set to be interviewed. He looked familiar, but not in an obvious way. Camden moved closer to the TV, close enough that his mother would yell at him if she witnessed his proximity. The man spoke, and just as he began talking about Begoa's Point and what to expect from the new facilities, a blue banner popped up across the screen with a name and a title. *Weston Accardi – Owner.*

The boy leaped off the floor as an idea popped into his mind and carried him through the hall so quickly that he tripped over his own two feet.

"No running!" Lyla yelled from her bedroom. Camden stood and dusted himself off, walked a few steps then returned to his quick pace once he was out of earshot. He bounded up the attic stairs and returned to the box. He pulled out the photo album and removed one solitary picture.

Camden went to his room, planning what he'd say as he went.

"What are you doing?" Lyla leaned on the door frame of his room a short while later. He deliberately didn't answer. When she came in to look over his shoulder, he moved the paper he was writing on out of her line of vision. "Hmph," she scoffed. But since her birthday was coming soon, he was hoping that she'd chalk it up to him working on a handmade card. She turned away then set off back down the hall.

Camden crumpled the paper, unhappy with the first draft. *It isn't enough.* It had to be perfect. He got a clean sheet of paper and started again, until finally the finished product was just what he'd wanted.

The sun beat down on the end of the driveway, making the dark pavement hot under Camden's bare feet. He thought about returning for shoes, but if he was gone too long, he would surely miss his chance to talk to Pam, the mail carrier. He looked back at the house, hoping his mother was occupied and wouldn't see him standing outside. He didn't want her wondering what he was doing other than just standing still, collecting freckles in the late May rays.

"Pam!" he cried excitedly, running forward to meet the mail truck as it pulled up to his house.

"What can I do for you, Camden?" Pam had been the mail carrier on this route since before Camden had been born. "And where are your shoes?"

"I need to get a letter to Begoa's Point. but I'm not sure how to fill out the envelope...and I...well...I can't ask my mother. It's...a surprise."

Pam looked down at Camden, the sun behind her casting a shadow of her body over where he stood, providing temporary shade on the pavement. She looked skeptical at first, as if she wouldn't help. Then she smiled.

"You have a stamp there, kiddo?"

Camden's smile grew so large that the joy of it practically lifted him clear off the hot concrete.

Chapter Five

Weston

Achilles and Weston ran their typical morning route down the main road, past the tennis courts, across the beach, into the main square and ending at the docks. Each day was almost the same, only now each morning they shared the paths with other runners, and as they ran across the beach, they received waves and hellos from early-bird beachgoers sticking an umbrella in the sand like a flag claiming new land. With close to three miles of beach to choose from, there wasn't a bad seat in the house, but the area that shared proximity with the lake, as well as the snack bar, general store and restrooms, was considered prime real estate.

The cheek-straining grin Weston wore as he exchanged hellos with campers hadn't faded since pulling the sheet off the sign and reopening the grounds earlier that week. Everything was coming together exactly as he had dreamed. *Better, even.*

Weston stopped at the marina as he always did, but now boats filled almost every slip. The owners put coolers on board and walked around the boats, inspecting them and preparing them for a day on the lake's surface. Weston waved from his spot at the entrance to the pier, and many of the boat owners and guests on the docks waved back like they were old friends. Some of them were.

An aging gentleman in a tan vest and cargo shorts approached Weston. A brimmed hat covered the bald spot on his head and fishing lures hung from his pockets. "Good morning, Mr. Accardi." He reached out a hand that was calloused from years of hard work and wrinkled from the frequent water submersion required to run the marina.

"It's just Weston." Though he knew no matter how many times he reiterated the words, the people that he called employees would have a hard time stepping away from the formal greeting, even if they had known him since he was a kid. He was grateful so many previous employees had agreed to return to the campground under his reign. "Everything going okay so far, Sal?"

"Yessiree." Sal tipped his hat. "The boat slips are at about eighty-five percent capacity—room for a few more toward the end of the summer. And our rental reservations are close to completely booked."

"Wonderful, Sal. Truly wonderful. Keep up the good work." Weston looked down the boat ramp, where Achilles had made a friend in a small girl, no more than seven or eight years old. He chased his tail, and she giggled. The sound of her laughter bouncing off the water was more valuable than any of the boats and watercraft floating on it.

"It's all coming together, boss." Sal slapped his hand on Weston's shoulder.

"I couldn't have done it without any of you—you, Mark, Sheila, Dotty. Truly, I don't think I could've got this place up and running again without the insight that all the returning employees offered."

Sal kept his hand at Weston's shoulder. "We wouldn't have missed this, Weston. Not for anything. Sure, there were other jobs, but none of those jobs were home." Sal gripped his hand along Weston's broad collarbone, giving him an encouraging squeeze before heading down the dock to help a fisherman pull his boat back into its designated place at the docks.

Weston continued on his route, stopping at the general store on the corner. The door was set in a shaded area under trees that provided ample coverage from the sun. Achilles hopped up into the mulch and curled into a ball, taking a break from the cement and heat while Weston entered the store. The bell on the door rang as he opened it.

Dotty, a large woman with brightly dyed red hair and unrealistically long false eyelashes placed over purple eyeshadow, waved to him as he entered.

"Good morning, gorgeous," she said, making her way toward Weston. She popped a kiss on his cheek that had no doubt left behind a coral-colored outline.

"Good morning, Dotty." Weston held both her wrinkled hands in his. Okay, so not everyone would have called him 'Mr. Accardi'. To Dotty, Weston would always be 'gorgeous', 'honey', 'puddin', 'sugar'—any of the sweetly embarrassing names she could get away with—but she was the only one.

"Anything I can do for you?" he asked her. She squeezed his hands and released them, turning away to head behind the cash register. Her flip-flops clicked wildly as she shuffled along.

"These are the sheets for what we need to order to restock." She handed printed sheets over the counter — hard copies, just the way Weston liked it. None of that email stuff. Weston pulled a piece of licorice from the bucket by the register and removed it from its wrapper, popping one end in his mouth.

"All this?" Weston's eyes widened into his forehead and he choked on a bite of the sticky candy. "This is great. Sales are really flying in here."

She nodded emphatically, but her large hair, likely secured by an entire can of Aqua Net, didn't budge.

"You know what I think?" Dotty batted her glued-on eyelashes.

"I have a feeling you're going to tell me whether I want to know or not." Weston winked, leaning into the counter to give Dotty all his attention. She pinched his cheeks, the same way she had when he'd come into the store so many years ago.

"I think this is your year, Weston. This is the year you find a nice young lady to share that RV with that you call a home."

"Oh, I doubt it, Dotty." He stepped toward the door. "You know I only have eyes for you."

"You stop that." Dotty waved off the comment with a manicured hand. They both chuckled as Weston backed out of the door, his focus still on the order in his hands and the licorice straw hanging out of his mouth.

Achilles sprang to action and followed Weston to the bulletin boards that displayed all the upcoming events and activities. The flyer for the upcoming staff performance of *Dirty Dancing* had turned out excellent — an eye-catching, highlighter pink page with black and purple text. Weston had caught a few rehearsals over the few weeks prior to opening. They certainly were a talented group and would be sure to put on a wonderful show.

As he scanned the activity lists, Achilles scurried around the snack bar, making fast friends with small children who were sure to drop their French fries or drip melted ice cream into his open mouth.

The brochure was separated into days of the week across the midsection of the boards. Right about now, the little kids had the option to do arts and crafts or dance class, and the older kids could choose between floor hockey, basketball or canoe races. Of course, the option to just relax on the beach, play golf or walk around the grounds with new friends was a choice too.

The younger version of himself would have been doing almost any of the above. The best friends he'd ever had were ones he'd made here. Even though they'd only reconvened for the summer months, they'd picked up where they left off, always finding their way to each other through the paths of Begoa's Point. His best memories had been made with his summer camping friends — and some of his worst too.

Unfortunately, people grew up and apart. Begoa's Point had closed. When the days of the original Begoa's Point had ended, so had the friendships they'd sworn would last forever.

Weston had wondered if he'd see any familiar faces when they reopened, but after running down the list many times, no notable names appeared on it. It was relieving and heartbreaking.

He started down the main road and Achilles followed. Though he didn't want to speak too soon, everything *was* going as planned. He couldn't have asked for a better turnout. But looking around and seeing all the faces that were familiar but didn't belong to any of those old friends made him wonder if he was reopening for the wrong reasons. Maybe he was searching for answers to questions that had expired more than fifteen years ago—answers that he would never get.

Golf carts belonging to both staff and campers zoomed past him, and he waved at each one as they passed. The grounds smelled like sunblock and stale smoke from campfires that had burned late into the night. Achilles and Weston made their way up the path that led to their site, Weston's eyes still finding the order list in his hand every few steps. The information on it didn't become any less surprising. What was surprising, though, was an unexpected visitor at his campsite.

One of the company golf carts was parked off to the side. From where Weston stood, he could see someone was occupying his chair, their feet up on the stone edge of Weston's handmade, custom fire pit. It appeared that they were taking a midday nap.

Weston smiled, crossed his arms and shook his head. He walked forward, carefully choosing his footsteps so as to take the quietest path. He stepped in line with the chair and recognized the too long, shaggy blond hair and rosy cheeks.

"Ahem." He coughed. "Kevin?"

Kevin sprang to life, kicking the chair backward and knocking over the pile of papers that had been situated on his lap.

"Mr. Accardi," he said, out of breath, leaning forward to try to collect as many of the papers as he could.

"Did you need something, Kevin? Apart from a midday siesta, that is?"

Kevin's face flushed an embarrassed purple. Weston winked and reached his hand out. Kevin turned the paperwork over to him.

"Sheila told me to come up and stay here until every one of those pages is read and signed by you. She told me to wait until you returned, because apparently, you're very hard to get a hold of...sir." Kevin dragged the toe of his sneaker in the dirt.

Weston kicked the chair to an upright position with his artificial leg and took a seat. He looked over and signed all the pages he was responsible for, then handed them back to the young employee. Kevin climbed into the golf cart and turned the key, a low vibration sounding as the motor came to life.

"How'd you end up here, Kevin?" Weston leaned against the cart.

"Umm, this golf cart, sir?" Kevin's eyes met Weston's, his lip turned up at one side.

"How did you end up...here? At Begoa's Point? For a job, I mean."

"Oh." *Poor Kevin.* At this rate of blushing, his face was never going to return to its normal, pale complexion. "Sheila is my aunt. I needed the money for college, and she offered me a summer job."

"Do you like it?" Weston asked. Kevin's eyes widened as a touch of panic set in. "There is no wrong answer, Kevin. I'm just trying to get to know you."

"I like the grounds. I like being here." Kevin rubbed his hand at the back of his neck. "I just don't know if paperwork is for me."

"I can tell," Weston said. "You remind me a bit of myself when I was younger. I'll tell you what. You look through the listings and tell me where you want to work. Do you want to work with kids? Do you want to work in the restaurant? Want to run the sports program? You tell me where you want to be, and we will get you a summer job you'll love. Sound good?"

Kevin's eyes lit like fireworks. "Sounds great, sir. I'll do that."

Weston rapped his knuckles on the top of the golf cart and stepped out of its path.

"Oh, and one more thing," Kevin said. "This came for you as well." He leaned forward, taking an envelope from the console of the cart and handed it to Weston. Weston nodded toward Kevin and walked back to his chair. He sat and turned the envelope in his hands as Kevin drove away down the dirt pathway.

Achilles sniffed the envelope all over, then licked the backs of Weston's hands. Weston tore the seal by sticking a finger in the crease and ripping the edge, then removed a white folded piece of paper from inside. The letter was written in somewhat messy but legible handwriting that was clearly that of a child.

Dear Mr. Accardi,

My name is Camden Kenney. You don't know me, but I know you — sort of.

I am writing because I need your help. My mother used to visit Begoa's Point every year. She has photos and stories and ribbons from all the years she went in the past before it closed.

My mom works hard. She says she's happy and she says she has everything she needs, but I think she needs Begoa's Point. She does so much for me. I want to do this for her.

If there is anything you can do to move us off the waiting list, I'd be thankful. My mom deserves to smile again — the way she smiled in the photo I sent with this letter.

I hope to get to meet you soon and I think she'd like to see you again.
Thank you,
Camden

Weston turned the paper over, but there was nothing on the back. He didn't know any Camdens…or any Kenneys at that. He separated the edges of the envelope, and sure enough, a photo fell into his lap.

Weston's heart stopped in his chest. His saliva caught in his throat and a cough interrupted the large breath he'd inhaled. His fingers trembled as he held the photo.

He stared at the glossy image, and the seventeen-year-old version of himself smiled back—not a forced smile, not a 'say cheese for the camera' instructed grin. It was a genuine, teeth-showing, smiling with his mouth and eyes expression. This version of Weston was sitting on a log beside a large fire, his elbows resting on his legs—back when there were two of them.

The girl to his left had a smile that reflected his own like a mirror. Her brown curls were tied up in a messy bun on top of her head and she wore a tie-dyed 'Camp Champ' T-shirt—his T-shirt. They were mid-laugh at something. Weston could almost hear her silly laugh just by seeing the photo. And the person not pictured—the person taking the photo—was his best friend, Charlie.

Weston's heart clenched. So many memories had poured out of this one, now-empty envelope.

Even though he had just finished a multi-mile run, he stood and ran down the path toward the welcome center, leaving so fast that even Achilles was likely left to wonder if he was to stay or follow.

"Sheila." Weston threw the door open to Sheila's office behind the welcome center. "Do you have a Lyla Kenney on your cancellation list?"

She scrolled through a listing on the computer, peering through her glasses.

"Oh, yes, way, way down here at the bottom." She looked at him over the lenses. "Why?"

"I need you to call her and tell her she's been removed from the waitlist." Weston swallowed then inhaled through his nose, trying to steady his bobbing chest. "Just tell her we have a spot for her."

"But, why? We have a wait—"

"Sheila." Weston took a deep, audible breath and let it out, directing the exhale toward the ceiling. "It's Lyla Savoie Kenney."

"Oh." Sheila removed her glasses, staring wide-eyed at Weston as she put two and two together. "I understand, Weston. I know you want to put your circle of friends back together. I get it. But we truly don't have any space."

Weston paused for a moment. He ran his hand across his hair and tapped his foot, deep in thought.

"Give them Site 101." His voice wavered slightly.

"Are you sure? That's—"

"I know." Weston glanced at the floor then back at her. "I'm sure."

"I'll call right away. And, Weston…?"

Weston's eyebrow raised, waiting for her follow up question.

"Do you want me to tell her you're the one inviting her? Making this happen?"

Weston bit his lip and looked to the ceiling as if an uncomplicated answer might fall from it.

"No. Just...just tell her there was a cancellation or something." He stepped out of the welcome center and sat on the steps where the sun kissed the skin on his arms and face.

Lyla Savoie Kenney. She had three names now, but he had only ever known her by one.

Savvy.

Chapter Six

Lyla

Camden ran through the backyard, using a trash can lid to shield himself from Lyla's water balloon attack.

"Drop the shield!" Her voice echoed across the yard.

"Never!" he called dramatically, tossing a green water balloon in her direction. It fell short and splashed her feet.

She positioned herself to restock on ammo, and while her back was turned, he hit her with a balloon between the shoulder blades, soaking her shirt.

"You're in trouble now, kid." She grabbed the hose, chasing him down and spraying him. He shrieked, and she caught up to him, wrapping her arms around his small frame. She shot the hose straight up so water cascaded like a fountain around them both.

Her cell phone started chiming away on the patio, singing a familiar song. In lieu of a traditional ring, she had set her ringtone as one of her favorite songs—*Wonderwall* by Oasis.

"Wait, wait, wait. Truce, truce." She raised her hands in an obvious forfeit. "Let me get that."

She dried her hands on a damp towel that she apparently hadn't moved far enough away from the battlefield, then answered her phone.

"Hello?"

Camden loaded a balloon in his palm. She gave him a 'you better not' glare and held up one finger.

"Yes, this is she." She paused as she listened to the voice on the phone.

"How did that happen?" Lyla was taken by surprise with the news on the other line. "Yes! Yes! A hundred percent. Let me get my credit card so we can pay the deposit." Lyla ran inside, not bothering to dry off as she dripped water droplets across the hardwood floors.

In the backyard, staring through the windows and watching his mother dig through her purse, Camden yelled a loud 'woo-hoo', but hoped his mother wouldn't notice. He whispered a 'thank you' to the open sky.

"Camden!" She slid across the floor and skipped out onto the patio as she yelled. "We got a spot! Begoa's Point has a space for us!"

"No way!" Camden replied as convincingly as possible. Maybe it had been his letter—or maybe it was just coincidence. Either way, the ten-year-old swallowed his secret.

The excitement faded for a moment and Lyla pulled up a chair, sat and stared at him.

"What is it?" Camden asked.

"Do you want to go?" Lyla reached for his hand. "It's the whole summer. I was so excited for myself that I didn't really think about how leaving for the summer might make you feel."

"I want to go!" he exclaimed. "I really only hang out with Chris and Corey Lenner and they are going to baseball camps this summer. I'll make friends there."

Lyla's visible excitement returned as she squeezed his hands and pulled him in close.

"I always dreamed of taking my own child to the campground. It's my favorite place in the world. I just wish your dad could be with us too." Lyla's smile remained but her eyes filled with tears.

"He will be." Camden placed his hand on his mother's cheek. "He always is."

* * * *

Lyla's father had left most of the gear they used to take to Begoa's Point in her garage when he'd moved. The tote was a large plastic box aged by years of abandonment and a layer of dust that had changed its exterior from yellow to brown. Behind the box, camping chairs in their nylon sleeves lay across the concrete floor slab, but Lyla had decided to invest in new ones. Small holes in the fabric led her to believe something had nested in her former chairs and she wasn't brave enough to evict whatever it was.

"What do we eat?" Camden flicked a flashlight on and off multiple times before throwing it into a bag.

"Fish that we catch with our bare hands." Lyla continued packing plastic flatware and other dining essentials, but looked up to see her son's horrified expression, so she put him at ease. "Anything you want, Camden. Burgers. Chicken. We can even get pizza."

"Really?" He was both excited and confused.

"We're not tent camping." She chuckled as she closed a box top over nestled pots and pans. "We're going to be in a cabin with a bathroom and full kitchen."

Camden's shoulders fell three inches as relief obviously washed over him.

"It will be fun." She tapped him on the nose as she stepped toward the next pile that needed to be organized and packed. "I promise."

Time ticked by extra slow, making the few days until their departure feel like weeks. When the morning finally arrived, Lyla almost couldn't believe it. She'd had recurring dreams about the campground reopening, and until now, they hadn't come true.

The hatch was open, and the back of the SUV had been cleaned out and readied to be packed from floor to roof. A loaded cargo box was secured to the top of the vehicle. Loud music from a playlist Lyla had created streamed through the speakers. Camden picked up a bag and tossed it into the trunk, then reached for another item.

"Wait." Lyla placed a hand against the small box he was holding. "There's an art to this. You can't just throw it in all willy-nilly. For everything to fit, it has to go a certain way, like Tetris."

Camden's face twisted. "What's Tetris?"

Lyla flat palmed her hand to her forehead. "Never mind. Can you go take one last look around and make sure we didn't miss anything?"

Camden scanned the piles of items stacked taller than he stood. "We didn't forget anything." A smile she was trying to hide crossed her face, but she managed to put on her best mom glare and throw her thumb over her shoulder. Camden took the hint and went back into the house. Lyla strategically placed each item into the truck—just the way her father had taught her.

Camden reemerged, skipping down the pathway with his hands behind his back. "You were right. We forgot something." Lyla wasn't sure how that was possible, as it seemed the whole house was packed into her SUV. She looked at Camden as he rocked back and forth on his heels. He removed his hands from behind his back and tossed her old, faded 'Camp Champ' shirt in her direction.

She held it for a moment, staring at the barely still legible colors and words. There was a time this T-shirt had been the most important thing in her world. Its hems were fraying, pulling loose at the seams, but the lifetime of memories it held were as intact and vibrant as ever.

"Let's get going." She threw the shirt over one shoulder as they walked toward their designated seats in the SUV.

Every inch of available space was stuffed with camping equipment and personal belongings neither of them could spend the summer without. Along the drive, Camden thumbed through the magazine-style brochure Begoa's Point had sent out, drawing stars next to every activity he wanted to try and circling the things he thought Lyla would enjoy. By the end of the drive, at the rate he was writing, seemingly almost every activity would have a star marked next to it.

Lyla drove the two-and-a-half-hour ride listening to a playlist she'd created entitled 'Songs That Remind Me of Begoa's Point"—the same playlist she'd listened to while she'd packed the bags and the car. Each song on it held a different story or reminded her of an event or moment from her childhood and teen years—some good, some bad.

She turned down the road that led to the campground and decreased her speed until her tires came to a stop where the paved blacktop married with the dirt and dusty roads. There was no stop sign and no red light, but she remained unmoving. Out of the corner of her vision, she could see Camden giving her a side-eyed expression, likely wondering what she was thinking. She stared out of the window and her eyes fell on the sign—hand carved wood, every inch beautiful and completely unchanged. She allowed her gaze to linger on the words etched into it for too long. Tears pressed behind her eyes, and they weren't happy tears. She swallowed them back. Very few of her memories associated with Begoa's were sad ones, but somehow that sign had brought about a deep pool of both.

She took a deep breath and pulled back onto the road, traveling down the dirt pathway toward the welcome center. The tree-lined drive opened into an area at the top of the hill where she could see the lake and main area of the campground, uninterrupted with nothing obstructing the view. The welcome center was up ahead on the right, but it was more than just a welcome center. Pulling into the parking lot to get the keys to the cabin they'd call home for the summer felt more like getting handed the keys to heaven itself. A summer vacation away from home made her feel more like she was home than she had in years.

"Wait here." Lyla jammed the car into park. "I'll be right back, just have to check in."

Lyla's white canvas sneakers met the steps of the welcome center, and though she could feel the world firmly under her shoes, she swore she was dreaming. She walked into the reception area and stood at the desk in front of a girl with a high, tight ponytail. A wad of gum blown into a bubble rested on her red-painted lips.

"Can I help you?" Her eyes never left the computer monitor.

"I'm Lyla Kenney," Lyla said, matter-of-factly — and, quite frankly, annoyed at the lack of enthusiasm coming from the first person she'd encountered upon entering. Welcome Center Barbie was really putting a damper on her parade. "There was a cancellation, and I was moved up the list. Just here to check in."

The girl behind the desk laughed. Laughed. "Sorry, ma'am. We're completely over-booked and there were no cancellations."

Lyla's mouth dropped open in surprise. These were the times she wished she was more like her father. Jack Savoie would have demanded to speak with a manager. He would have found some smart, witty remark and drenched the whole welcome center in sarcasm. Everyone in earshot would have known what he was upset about until it had been fixed properly. But Lyla hadn't inherited the forceful gene. She shied away from conflict, shrinking into a reserved, quiet stance and swallowing back tears rather than standing up for herself. She didn't know what to do. She wasn't mistaken. The phone caller had told her to come on up to the grounds. She'd even given her number for a deposit.

"Can you at least look?" Lyla finally mustered, surely not returning to the stuffed to the brim car without a fight.

"What was the name again?" the girl said with a loud snap of her gum.

"Lyla Kenney." Lyla exaggerated each syllable. As she spoke, an older woman with mint-green glasses shuffled around the counter from the back of the welcome center.

"Miss Kenney." The lady held out a hand for Lyla to take. "My word, you haven't changed a bit."

That took Lyla by surprise, though the woman looked familiar. "I, well…"

"Oh, ignore me. I remember every face that used to come through here — at least the regulars. I'm sure you don't remember me, but I bet your father would. Is he well?"

"Yes, yes. Very. Retired to Florida."

"Early retirement! Good for him." Something in the woman's voice sounded distant, like she wasn't fond of Jack, but Lyla chalked it up to jealousy, as this woman was still working while her father soaked up the sun's rays full time. "Will he be joining us?"

"I don't think so, unfortunately." Lyla's heart clenched. She would have loved to have him here for this return.

"Yes, that is unfortunate." Her sympathy lasted no more than two heartbeats before returning to her upbeat demeanor. "Anyway, I'm Sheila. I'm the one who spoke with you on the phone. I apologize. Ignore Miss Kirsten, here. She wasn't aware of the arrangement."

"That's okay. Things happen," Lyla said, though she had a sudden childish urge to stick Kirsten's gum in her long blonde hair.

"Here's your welcome packet. I think you'll find almost everything on the grounds is right where you left it. Not much has changed, really."

Lyla took the folder in her hands, complete with an extra brochure, keys, wrist bands and a resort map. She traced the map with her fingers.

"I'm certain you won't be needing that." Sheila winked. She was right. Lyla still remembered every curve of the campground's dirt roads, even after all these years—even better than the highway routes she drove daily. "Any questions?"

"Just one. What site number have we been assigned?" Lyla looked at the folder as if she may have missed it.

"101." Sheila smiled.

"101. Isn't that…that's the owners' cabin?" Her voice tailed upward into a question, though she was certain she was right.

"It was previously, yes. But not anymore." Sheila looked downward, turning her attention to a stack of papers and effectively cutting off further questions. "Off you go now, dear. Vacation awaits."

She drove slowly down the main road toward the cabin, taking in the sights as they passed. Her cheeks ached from her ever-increasing smile, which was growing further toward her ears with every quarter mile they drove—something new spiking curiosity or something old prompting a memory.

"Look at that!" Camden yelled, pointing to something in the distance, but Lyla missed it in a moment of her own marveling through the opposite window. She turned onto the circle where their assigned unit was and pulled into the first driveway on the right. The number *101* was displayed on the side of the cabin. Above the number was a square of siding, different in color against the rest of the faded cabin. Though it didn't hang there anymore, she could almost picture the small, hand-carved sign that used to be on display over the number—a large plank of wood with 'The Accardis' carved in it, colored in gold with 'Owners' Quarters' in smaller text beneath it.

Camden opened the door and hopped out of the car before she could even put it in park. He bounded up the wooden steps and peered through the window into the cabin.

She followed closely behind, taking a deep breath and preparing herself to step into the cabin, like a portal to travel back into her childhood years. She unlocked the door and slid it across the tracks. The interior was almost the same. It had been updated, which was to be expected after fifteen years of sitting vacant, but still very much the cabin she remembered it to be.

Chapter Seven

Weston

Back when they had been kids, Weston had always been able to find his friends on the grounds. No matter where they were, even without cell phones and technology to attach them, they had just had this constant, hardwired awareness of each other. They would meet at the snack bar in the morning and spend every waking moment together until the sun became the stars and sometimes, on the best nights, didn't leave each other's sides until the stars became the sun again.

But not now.

Weston hadn't seen Savvy once—not intentionally or otherwise. Lyla, he corrected himself, knowing she had probably long since ditched her Begoa's Point nickname. He hadn't seen her at any of the activities and hadn't heard her name in conversation...not even once. It was as if she hadn't existed at all, and maybe the version of her that he'd known no longer did.

But what would he do if he did see her? That part he hadn't calculated yet. He certainly couldn't just approach her. The letter Camden had written hadn't mentioned his father, but it hadn't *not* mentioned him either. Last Weston had checked, she'd been married. And that had been the last time he'd checked. He had tracked her down once, but her life had seemed perfect and that had been that. He'd stopped looking.

Weston knew deep in his heart that half the reason he needed Begoa's Point to reopen was for himself. It was a selfish mission rooted entirely in fixing what he'd broken. The other half was because he knew other people needed it too. Camden's letter had proved that. There were other people out there who needed this place, this escape, in exactly the same way he did. It just so happened that the words of affirmation had come from the son of the first girl Weston had ever loved.

Work kept Weston busy. Though most things had gone off without a hitch, someone had to keep the place running. Every few hours, someone would approach him with a question or a decision to be made. The more days that passed with him at the helm, the more he appreciated his father and how much work he had truly done to keep this place successful for so long. That feeling of admiration was followed closely by the substantial guilt, knowing that he'd played a major role in its failure.

"Mr. Accardi?" a shaking voice asked from behind him. Weston turned to find Kevin with an iPad in his hands.

"Kevin, I will fire you if you call me 'Mr. Accardi' one more time." Weston crossed his arms over his chest. "Weston is fine. Sal calls me 'boss' and even that works, if you must. Anything but 'Mr. Accardi'."

Weston kept things light, trying to achieve the ideal that even though he signed their checks, he wasn't above them, but that was only part of the reason he didn't like being called Mr. Accardi. Truthfully, his father would always be Mr. Accardi, and Weston just wasn't sure he had proved himself worthy of the same title.

Kevin gulped, his face a twisted expression that suggested he wasn't sure if Weston was joking or not.

"Did you find a job you're interested in?" Weston reached his hand out for the iPad. He hated the technology, didn't like the feel of metal in his hands, but he had already given Kevin a hard enough time for one morning.

"I think I'd really just like to be a counselor, if that's okay. I can run the sports programs or arts and crafts or wherever they need help, but I think I'd be good at that." Kevin smiled for the first time since Weston had met him. Most days, he was forcing himself to stand up straight and be impressive, like a poorly tailored suit that didn't fit. Kevin was born to wear khakis and a green counselor T-shirt. "I'm much better with kids than I am in an office or talking to authority figures. I promise." The corner of Kevin's mouth hitched into a casual smile.

"I think that's a good idea. You know where the activity window is?" Weston placed his hand on Kevin's shoulder and pointed toward the activity office. "Go there and ask for Johnny. He runs the program and assigns the counselors to each activity."

"Thanks again, Mr. — Weston."

"No, thank *you*." Weston nodded toward Kevin, handed back the iPad then watched as the now-happier young man skipped off toward the activity office.

Weston turned the corner and saw a young boy at the snack bar, standing on his tiptoes to place his order. Weston couldn't hear what he was saying. He had no identifying feature or name tag that was indicative of who he was, but instantly, in the time it took to blink once, Weston knew it was Camden Kenney. He was the exact image of his mother at that age. Weston's heart drummed hard against his chest. If Camden was near, Lyla might be too. He wiped his sweating hands on the thighs of his cargo shorts, remembering the days he'd felt this exact same way each time he'd seen Lyla after the non-summer months' time had elapsed.

Two hundred sixty-six days had passed since the last summer had ended and a new one begun. Weston hadn't talked to Lyla since Labor Day — not even once. He lived at the campground all year and his parents weren't much for technology. The main phone line existed in the welcome center down the road from their cabin turned year-round home. It shared a line with an ancient fax machine, and that was the extent of their communication with the outside world. His mother had homeschooled him from the table of the two-bedroom site they'd shared since they'd adopted him as a baby.

Even if a phone line were readily available to Weston, Lyla's father would never have allowed it. During the summer on a small campground, there wasn't much that could be done to keep the teenagers apart, but with miles of highway and her father's rules between them, their communication ceased between Labor Day and Memorial Day. Even with the distance, there wasn't a fall or winter day that passed that Weston didn't think about Lyla.

Time had passed, though, and maybe things had changed. Weston sat on a rock at the edge of the lake in an area shaded by a group of trees. He was barefoot with his hat on

*backwards and wore cargo shorts and a T-shirt that was
missing the sleeves.*

*At the close of the last season, during a long and grueling
goodbye, they'd sat on this same rock and made a promise to
meet there again. Weston kept Lyla held close to his chest, one
hand at her lower back, one hand in her hair.*

'On the first day of the season next year, I'll be right
here waiting.'

'I'll meet you here.' *She'd made the promise through her
sobs.*

*He'd kept his promise, waiting on the rocks in hopes of her
arrival without any idea if she'd show. Her father's name was
on the reservations sheet. He had checked. Weston lay back
against the rock and watched one small, sheer cloud float
across the otherwise-crystal-clear sky. Maybe she'd changed
her mind. For Weston, not much changed in the off-season
months, but for Lyla, there was a whole world beyond this
one.*

*He sat up on the rock and looked around the freshly raked
beach. No one else was here, and by the looks of it, no one else
was coming.*

*He pushed himself off the rock and put his hands in his
pockets, coming to terms with the idea that he'd held up his
end of the bargain, but she wasn't going to hold up hers.*

*He waded through the water, ripples of the lake moving
around his ankles. A movement caught his eye and he looked
up, one hand over his brow to block the sun. Her dark brown
curls shone in the brilliant light. Even with a distance
between them, he could tell she was smiling in the sideways
way that she did where only one dimple accented her cheek.
She waved from where she stood at the top of the beach, and
he waved back as she walked toward him, leaving her
footprints in the otherwise-untouched sand.*

*She kicked off her flip-flops and abandoned them behind
her as she picked up speed and ran, lunging off the sand and*

into his chest as he caught her with his arms at her waist. She almost knocked him off balance, but he steadied himself and twirled her around, her toes skimming the top of the water as they spun.

Weston and Lyla walked hand in hand, their fingers linked tightly together as if they'd never part. The sand was hot — too hot to be barefoot on — so they waded in the shallowest portion of the water where the lake met the land. The sun sparkled in the ripples they created as they ventured forward in an awkward silence, the kind of quiet that was synonymous with first crushes, flushed cheeks and overthinking what to do or say next. Weston got brave for a millisecond, his knuckles brushing against the back of Lyla's hand, but he quickly changed his mind and looked out toward the buoys that separated the shallow water from the deep drop-offs. It had been so long, so many months of silence. He had rehearsed what he would say when they were together again, but now, no words came out.

He removed his hat, ran a hand through his hair and let out a deep sigh. Hanging out with a girl was much, much different than hanging out with his friends. He wasn't usually at a loss for words, but his stomach twisted in a knot that might make him vomit instead of speak if he opened his mouth to try. He placed his hat backwards on his head once more.

"So, how have you been?" She stumbled over the words a bit. He smiled a light grin, pressing his teeth into his lip. It eased his nerves, knowing that she was feeling the same way he was.

"Not bad." He looked toward her. "Better now."

She smiled and tucked her curls behind her ear, pink flushing at her cheeks.

The silence was killing him. He wasn't good at small talk. At his core, he was a prankster, boisterous. He wasn't used to tiptoeing around, so he didn't.

He stopped and she kept walking, turning to glance over her shoulder to see why he had halted.

He leaned forward, cupping both hands in the water.

"You wouldn't." She crossed her arms over her chest.

"I'd suggest running." A mischievous grin formed at his lips. She inched backward, and he flung the water in her direction. She kicked a large amount of lake back at him and took off down the shoreline. He followed, splashing water under his heavy stomps. She veered toward the beach, and he chased her, reaching her and wrapping her in his arms. She lifted her feet, and he spun her around, carrying her back toward the lake. Her playful screech echoed over the open water.

She had come back to him the way she'd promised she would, and even with all the days and weeks and months that had passed, it was as if nothing had changed at all.

"Number one forty-seven," a voice said through a speaker at the snack bar, interrupting Weston's thoughts and bringing him back to real time. He looked to where the child had been standing, but he was gone. Weston scanned the area and found the boy at the condiment table next to a woman who wore the same dark curls she had the first time he'd seen her. Her son had ordered fried dough—*like mother, like son.* As her son flipped the shaker over and covered his plate with sugary snow, Lyla started to laugh. Weston smiled, recalling the first time he had ever talked to her and wondered if she remembered it too.

I can do it, he thought, taking a deep breath. *I can head over there, say hello and close the fifteen-year gap we've kept between us once and for all.*

Palms sweating, he took a step forward and thought about what he would say. As he got closer, she placed her left hand on her son's shoulder, but not before

Weston caught a glimpse of the sparkling ring she wore on her finger.

He had so many questions, all of which were answered in the second it took for the sun to hit the surface of her diamond and reflect a lifetime's worth of rainbows across the ground between them.

Weston took a step back, turned away and walked toward his campsite, allowing the distance that was between them to grow by just a few feet more.

Chapter Eight

Lyla

Camden skipped ten feet ahead of Lyla as she accompanied him to one of the many activities he had marked in the brochure. Part of her wanted to believe the distance was purely excitement carrying his little feet well ahead, but mostly she knew he was doing this on purpose, as he was reaching that age where being seen with mom wasn't 'cool'.

Camden ran off and joined his age group for a game of capture the flag, where he made friends as soon as he entered the gaggle of kids. She waved an unrequited goodbye. He didn't even turn around. Back in the day, that had been her. Her father used to walk her to every activity and cheer her on from the sandy sidelines until one day he didn't. Looking back, she didn't remember a specific day that the separation had taken place. *Did I ask him to stop joining me at every game and activity, or did he just know it was time to stop holding my hand?*

Having a campground of this style, with activities for every age from sunup to sundown run by qualified counselors, meant it was a vacation away from kids just as much as it was a vacation with them. *Time for myself is good*, she thought, convincing herself to enjoy some part of her day that was empty of activities.

She went up the stairs toward the snack bar and past the large bulletin board at the center of the square. She scanned each road, each circle, knowing exactly which roads and amenities were new and which were original to the property. One area of the map showed a grouping of tiny trees. To anyone else it just looked like forest with nothing beyond it worth seeing. But she knew that wasn't the case.

Hidden deep within those thickly settled bushes and trees was a clearing—a perfect circle where the trees outlined an untouched area of ground that wasn't covered in roots or rocks. The treetops formed a perfect circle as well, providing an open lens to view perfect starry nights while lying on the ground below. As kids, she and her friends had been unsure if it was manmade or a natural occurrence, but either way, they'd always imagined it had been made just for them. Maybe it had been.

Lyla went back to her cabin only to grab her sneakers for a much-needed jog. Many times, over the years, she had run the familiar route of her quiet neighborhood and imagined that she was running these pine-scented paths in this sacred place. The scenery was like nothing she had ever seen before. Even after all these years, the serene, untouched beauty of the paths, that weaved in and out of trees older than anyone left on Earth, still took her breath away.

She ran down the beach, past the playgrounds and jungle gyms at the beach's center and toward the shuffleboard courts before reaching a long stretch of trees and bushes. She didn't need to think about it. Muscle memory forced her legs forward down the shaded road and told her to turn at exactly the right spot, like an internal GPS with a favorite spots list stored for future use. Two bushes that looked like blueberry bushes but weren't—her dad had warned her not to eat the berries every day they'd spent here—marked the point she had been searching for.

She peeked over her shoulder the same way she had as a teenager, as if someone would follow her and spoil the secrets that lay beyond the trees. Eager to see her favorite view in the world just around the curve ahead, Lyla picked up speed, and her heart raced in her chest. Lyla's footsteps echoed and an excited smile grew across her lips. She slowed and took in the sights around her. She approached a tree that from afar looked like every other tree that spanned the miles, but she knew it was different. Though faded now and damaged by wildlife and overgrowth, the subtle outline of a heart and initials remained tattooed into the tree's trunk. She ran her fingers over it, thinking back on the night it had been carved — the night she'd left her mark on the campground the way it had left its mark on her. Lyla continued on. As she turned the corner, she took a deep breath and prepared herself for what was on the other side.

It wasn't what she'd expected at all.

A large RV with an expansive awning set over a handmade picnic table was parked in the clearing where she and her friends had hidden away and pretended that no world existed outside of this one.

Lyla stood still, closing her eyes and opening them again as if the motor home were a mirage she could blink away. Unfortunately, that wasn't the case. Her chest tightened in an odd, upside-down way that made her feel as if she were trespassing on someone's private property, and yet, someone was very much trespassing on her private memories. She forced herself onward, past the clearing. With any luck, the view hadn't changed. She continued on the path, up the remainder of the hill, where a large, flat rock at the top overlooked part of the campground below — exactly as it had the last time she'd traveled here.

She sat cross-legged on the cool surface of the rock and stared at the campground. From where she sat, the basketball courts were visible. She smiled, thinking back to the countless hours she'd spent on that court, trying to beat out anyone in her age group at one-on-one for a chance at a coveted 'Camp Champ' T-shirt. Though she was a good distance away, she could see a teenage version of herself dribbling an orange ball, and she swore she could hear the distinct *thud thud* it made as it slammed the blacktop echo to where she sat.

A competitive nature had been bred into her. Her dad had an 'if you're not first, you're last' attitude that he had handed down to her both through the genes they shared and the constant pressure to practice, practice, practice. Even at Begoa's Point, playing sports hosted by the campground staff, Lyla's father had cheered from the sidelines, encouraging her to play her hardest as if it were earning her an athletic scholarship and not just a first-place ribbon — or maybe, if she were lucky, the damn T-shirt.

The one-on-one basketball tournament for Lyla's age group was waning — only a handful of players remained. She was doing well through the games she had played the day prior, having knocked off a girl who was at least three inches taller than her but had no range on her jump shots and beaten a boy who had 'rolled his ankle' halfway through when he was already too far behind to catch up.

After the games, Lyla had lain out on a beach towel printed with large watermelon slices and fallen asleep there – great for an increased energy level, terrible for her complexion. The rays had kissed her bare shoulders and left a lipstick-red color across her skin.

The straps to her tank top dug into the tight, searing skin as she stretched before the finals. One game was underway. Two boys faced off. Both were tall, talented and determined to win. Sweat dripped from their hair, falling to the scalding hot blacktop where it instantly evaporated. The winner of this game would play the winner of Lyla's game, which immediately followed. She, coincidentally, was playing a boy. Three boys and Lyla, playing for the final W. She was used to it, though. In all her summers at Begoa's, that was usually how it boiled down.

One of the boys was paler than her, with a worse sunburn to boot – that should win a ribbon or T-shirt in itself – and had shaggy blond hair. His T-shirt sleeves were cut off, the holes in his shirt ripped so far down the sides that she wondered why he bothered wearing it at all. She watched for a moment, then her jaw dropped in awe as she recognized him. If she remembered correctly, his name was Charlie and the last nine months had been very good to him. He'd filled out quite a bit, losing many of the boyish features he had boasted in years past, and was developing into an easy-on-the-eyes teenager.

The other boy was no exception. She knew him too, or at least of him. Weston Accardi. He had rarely looked in her direction over the years they'd spent on these grounds. They had shared the same beach, the same grounds and the same age group for competitions most of their lives, but apart from a single moment over fried dough as small children, he ran with a different group than she did.

Since last summer's end, he had grown tall and muscular and allowed his hair to grow out slightly longer than usual. He dribbled the basketball around Charlie in a no-mercy, nothing-held-back way that left Charlie alone at the top of the key while he blew by and crashed the board, netting an easy layup.

He let out an enthusiastic yell as he landed back on his feet, while a few boys who had already been knocked out cheered from the sidelines. He shuffled his fingers through his pitch-black hair and sweat flew off around him.

After the game, they'd met under the basket and had shaken hands. "You fouled me, Weston!" Charlie had a large smile on his face. Weston nodded then lifted his shirt, revealing his abdomen and wiping his brow with the already-soaked material.

"When will you learn, Charlie? You just can't beat me." They exchanged lighthearted jabs at each other's arms.

Lyla's gaze skidded down his rib cage, finding the distinct lines of his abs. Her cheeks burst into heat as hot as her sunburn as he sauntered toward her.

"I'll tell you what," he said with a smirk that was both irritating and handsome. "If we play each other in the championship, I'll play shirtless so you can get a better view."

She rolled her eyes, but it was forced, a motion she made herself do to prevent drooling. She didn't want to be attracted to him, but she just couldn't help it.

Lyla pulled her long, dark hair into a tight ponytail and secured it with the elastic from her wrist.

A counselor in a green polo shirt came out to the free-throw line with a clipboard.

"Sav... Savo...Savvy, Lyla," he called out, and she joined him where the white lines were freshly painted on the court beneath their feet.

"It's Savoie," she corrected, "Suh-voy."

He smiled without an apology and turned his head back to the clipboard.

"Post, Jordan," he yelled out and Weston's group hooted and hollered.

The boy who stepped forward was more man than boy. There was a real chance he wasn't actually in their age group. He was hulking – more like a football player than a basketball player. Lyla started calculating a game plan almost instantly. Rebounds weren't going to be her strong point, but she could rely on speed.

At the sideline, she pulled one foot up, stretching before the semifinals began. Weston stood next to her, leaning into the fence.

"Good luck, Savvy," he said in the least sincere way she could imagine.

"It's Savoie." She kept her eyes on the court, not bothering to turn to look at him.

He stepped forward, his chest almost touching Lyla's back.

"I like Savvy," he said in a cool almost-whisper. He flicked her ponytail as he walked away. She whipped around, her dark brown curls flying in a helicopter fashion behind her, but all she could do was glare at him. Deep down, she wanted to smile, which pissed her off even more.

Weston was the competition – the only thing standing in the way of the T-shirt she so desperately wanted.

Her game against Jordan went well. It wasn't a blowout for either of them, but she kept up despite their size difference, and with the timer winding down, she was only down by one. Lyla dribbled around, twisting and turning as she concentrated on not giving up the ball. She knew she only *had half a minute left and she had to make her next shot good. If she hit it too early, Jordan would get the ball back. If she waited too long and missed, she would forfeit her chance to tie or win. She turned away from the clock, and Weston and Charlie started counting down the seconds left in the game. "Five, four, three…" they yelled, so she took a chance. She turned and threw the ball at the net. The ball arched on its way to the rim, but she missed.*

The boys, including Jordan, all started laughing. She looked around, confused as Jordan chased down the rebound and netted another basket, extending his lead. Then the buzzer sounded. They'd tricked her. The boys had started the countdown early, and she'd been so focused on the game that she hadn't realized they were just playing a nasty trick to extinguish her chances.

"But," she said to the camp counselor, "they cheated." The counselor scratched his head.

"I'm sorry, but technically the guy you were playing against didn't do anything wrong. I can't do anything about the guys on the sideline."

Lyla stormed off the court, walking past the group of boys.

"Better luck next time, Savvy," Weston stepped toward her. She shoved past him, hitting him hard in the shoulder, and stomped away.

She remembered it like it was yesterday. What everyone looked like, what their voices sounded like.

"Savvy?" someone said in a low voice. A voice that wasn't part of her daydream. Someone who was close by, in person. She didn't look over her shoulder. She didn't have to. Only one person would call her by that name.

Chapter Nine

Weston

As Weston approached the campsite, he noticed Achilles' behavior change from a stoic, cooperative manner to an excited, overzealous search. The dog kept his face low to the ground, his nose pressed into anything and everything in sight. He maneuvered slowly around the area, carefully inspecting every inch as he searched for something. Achilles bounded forward, going in circles and trying to get Weston's attention.

"What is it, boy?" Weston followed his German Shepherd's lead. The dog raced behind the RV and headed down the path, out of sight. Weston followed, turning the corner to find a person sitting at the edge of his property overlooking the campground.

Savvy.

Achilles sat in a low hunting stance, waiting to approach the newcomer and sniff them into submission, but Weston held out one open palm and Achilles stood down, taking a seat in the dirt next to him.

"Savvy?" Weston said out loud, though his voice caught in his throat, the sound coming out with far less conviction than he had intended. The muscles in her arms and shoulders tightened, freezing her body in place. She didn't turn toward him. She remained loyal to the view in front of her rather than facing the ghost behind her. He knew this could go either way. She was going to be happy to see him or she wasn't. There was no third option. Lyla Savoie wasn't the kind of person to do things halfway.

He had envisioned this moment so many times in so many different ways. It was a storyline he wrote over and over again, but always with a different ending. But those dreams, were scripted, written exactly the way he would like them to be played out. This? This was real life. This was improv. Anything could happen.

Lyla stood from her spot and faced him. She was as perfect as always. The sun beat down and created a spotlight on her. She looked him over from head to toe, lingering for a moment on the prosthetic attached to his lower half. Her expression gave no indication of what her next move would be. He wasn't sure what to expect.

She walked forward, toward him, quickly closing the space between them. He hitched his lips into a light smile in anticipation of any kind of contact—a hug, a handshake. But as she neared him, she veered left and took off down the hill without saying a word—not a single sound or syllable.

Once again, Weston was left by himself in the deep Maine woods to ponder how to retrace his steps and repair a decade and a half's worth of damage.

* * * *

Days had come and gone since he had seen her and the initial hurt of things not going as planned hadn't faded. The campground was only so big, and yet, somehow, their paths didn't seem to cross at all. Weston ran, he worked, he enjoyed some time off each day. He heated his coffee over an open flame and cooked the same few meals in circulation throughout the week. Nothing had changed. *Only, Savvy's here.* So, everything had changed.

Weston pulled out a stool at the bar, its legs screeching against the concrete pad. Mark leaned into the bar top across from him, part bartender, part therapist.

"Where's the pup?" Mark asked, looking over the bar top.

"At the site," Weston said, "probably avoiding me. Everyone else is."

"Ahh, yes." Mark tapped a finger to his chin, an aging raspiness to his voice, "the long-awaited reunion didn't go quite as planned."

Weston sat up straighter and scrunched his forehead. "How do you know that?"

"Dotty told me."

"How does she know that?"

"It's Dotty." Mark shrugged his shoulders. "She knows everything."

Weston ran his hand through his hair, pushing the overgrowth off his forehead.

"I don't know what I was expecting. She sees me, and we pick up right where we left off like nothing ever happened? I guess I thought, maybe, with all the years that have passed there would be some 'forgive and forget' factor. She hasn't forgotten and she definitely hasn't forgiven. She made that clear without saying anything at all."

Weston continued to babble, speaking too many words per minute as Mark absorbed the information across the bar.

"I wonder if she had known it was me, if she knew I was the one who had reopened the campground, if she would have come at all." Weston rested his face in his hand, elbow on the bar. "I don't think she would have."

"Why do you think that?" Mark asked using his therapist voice.

"I broke her heart. I know that. But it was so long ago."

Mark looked across the bar with an emotion Weston couldn't read, but he leaned toward something along the lines of disagreement.

"Just say it." Weston gave Mark the floor for his final diagnosis of the session.

"Timewise, sure, it was a long time ago. But, Weston, for her, it's right now. It's new. You knew she was coming, but she didn't have time to prepare for you walking back into her life. You had time to adjust to the idea of sharing these grounds with her. For her, all those wounds were just reopened." Mark turned to stack some cups on the bar top while Weston took in what he'd said.

* * * *

All Weston's daily duties had been completed, just in time to enjoy some of the final hours of the day responsibility-free. *'The best part of the day,'* his dad used to say in regards to the hours in the late afternoon and early evening when the sun wasn't quite as hot and the family would soak up some after-work, last-minute rays before gathering for dinner and a fire.

Weston walked toward his RV, passing the dirt road circles of trailers and campsites that were closest to the main square. He paused for a moment, standing directly across the street from Site 101 — the only site on the campground he hadn't been in since buying the property. He just couldn't — not yet.

Children ran and played at the center of the circle, climbing on rocks and hiding behind trees, running from each and letting their imaginations run wild. That used to be him. His parents had always occupied that site. One summer when he was young, a family had rented Site 102. A boy about his age had stepped out onto the porch with two RC cars.

'Want to race?' he'd asked, and Weston had nodded. That was it. No big to-do, no questions asked. They had become inseparable.

'I'm Charlie, by the way,' he'd said as his toy car slammed into a large log at the center of the circle, and they'd laughed.

In that circle, in those summers, they were warriors and firefighters and superheroes. They'd put on carnivals and circuses. They'd stormed enemy territory and fought epic battles. Charlie and Weston had ridden imaginary horses and fought nonexistent mutant robots. They'd always saved the galaxy. Eventually, they'd sat on that log, aged out of pretend and imaginary friends and morphed into teens whose days revolved around girls and sports. They'd grown up on that dirt road near the center of the campground.

A boy ran across the road and into the circle, chasing a rogue soccer ball. For a moment, it could have been him. His mind playing tricks on him, showing him a vision of his former self. But it wasn't him.

It was Camden Kenney.

Camden picked up the ball and waved a hello to Weston. Weston was about to walk away, leave the boy to play in the circle and dream the day away how he used to, but Camden yelled after him.

"You're Weston, right?" he called.

"Last I checked." Weston used his hand to block the rays of the waning sun from his eyes.

"I'm Camden. I wrote to you this summer."

Weston walked toward Camden, figuring yelling across the street wasn't going to get him anywhere. Yelling wasn't exactly subtle, and he didn't know where Lyla was.

"I know. I remember." Weston stretched out a hand, and Camden took it. "I hope you're enjoying yourself."

"Very much, sir. Thank you for helping us out. I... I didn't tell my mom I wrote the letter." Camden dropped his hand from Weston's.

"It can be our secret. In fact—" Weston reached into his pocket and pulled out his wallet. He removed the folded letter and accompanying picture, returning them the boy. "For safe keeping." Weston winked and smiled. The boy looked exactly like his mother, down to the freckles across his nose and hair the same shade of brown, but it was his expressions that replicated hers—a duplicate of her smile, the single dimple that dipped into one cheek.

"You're missing a leg." Camden looked at the hem of Weston's shorts.

"What?" Weston yelled, his voice echoing through the circle so loudly other campers poked their heads out and looked at the commotion. He reached down and grabbed at the metal prosthetic. Weston looked up with a broad grin, and Camden burst into laughter that shook his whole body.

Weston looked around. "Where is your mother?"

"She went to the general store to buy fire starters." Camden laughed. "You want to know a secret?"

Weston nodded, and Camden wiggled a finger in a 'come closer' motion. Weston kneeled, artificial leg forward, weight on his good leg. "We haven't had a campfire since we got here. Mom isn't any good at it."

Weston and Camden giggled.

"Back in the day, when we were kids, Savvy wouldn't even roast marshmallows. She's always been a little shy around flames."

"Savvy?" Camden asked, his face scrunched up.

"Your mother. Just an old nickname."

Camden glanced at the fire pit and back to Weston. Weston looked around, surveying the area. He didn't know how to ask the question burning in his head, but he didn't have a final answer either.

"And your dad?" Weston swallowed hard to force saliva down his suddenly parched throat.

"He died a long time ago." Camden stared at his shoes. Weston didn't know what to say to that, so he changed the subject.

"I can teach you how to build a fire. The flame part, though? Well, that's up to your mom. But I can teach you how to stack the logs right and you can surprise her so it's ready to go when she gets back."

Camden nodded a yes so fast it made Weston dizzy. He held up his hand, and Camden slapped it in a high five that echoed across the circle.

Weston headed to the back of the cabin where they used to stack the firewood. Lo and behold, the wood rack was in exactly the same spot. Weston surveyed the outside of the house. It looked the same but updated. An unused cabin was subject to a lot of wear and tear over the years, but Weston had requested that this cabin remain as intact and true to its original integrity as possible. None of the construction teams had understood. They'd had free rein with the other units, but the owner's instructions had been clear. Cabin 101 was to stay exactly as it was except for upgrades that made it safe and livable.

"What is it?" Camden squinted, trying to see what Weston was looking at.

"Just looking at the cabin." Weston leaned forward and grabbed two small logs Camden could carry. "I used to live here."

"Just for the summer?" Camden put his arms straight out and Weston placed the wood on his forearms. Weston grabbed a few bigger pieces and they headed to the fire pit.

"Nope, all year round."

"You lived here all the time?" Camden's eyes widened. "That would be like vacation all year!"

Weston let out a quick, short laugh. "Not exactly. It's cold here in the winter, and everyone leaves. It got pretty lonely. Still does."

Camden frowned. "I guess."

"Let's go, champ. This wood isn't going to carry itself."

Weston showed Camden how to stack wood for a perfect fire, leaving space between each log in a tepee style. "Oxygen is important," Weston said. "So, when you light the fire, the flame will start in here." Weston pointed to the open center of the log structure. "If you pack the logs too tightly, they won't breathe, and the fire won't stay lit."

"Got it." Camden gave Weston a thumbs up.

"I'll go find you some small pieces for kindling to start the fire." Weston trekked behind the cabin once again. As he leaned forward to pick up the scattered wood on the ground, a voice that wasn't Camden's echoed through the site.

"What do you think you are doing?" Lyla asked, a ruffle of bags from the general store accompanying her question. Her tone wasn't angry or mad. It was confused, if anything.

Camden didn't answer, and Weston couldn't just hide out behind the cabin forever. He hesitated but stepped forward into view. Lyla's eyes widened. If the bags she was holding hadn't been looped over her arm, she would've dropped them.

"I was...in the neighborhood." Weston half-smiled. "Just showing the kid how to build a proper fire."

She didn't speak. Her gaze met the perfect tepee then found his again.

"I could have done that," she snapped, but her voice lacked the assurance it needed to be believable.

"Not from what I hear." Weston laughed. Camden elbowed him in the hip.

"Camden, can you take this inside please?" Lyla handed a bag to Camden, and he retreated as he was told.

Lyla turned away and crossed her arms over her chest. She paced in a small circle, kicking rocks and dirt up under her canvas sneakers.

"I didn't expect you to be here." Her voice was small.

"Like I said, I was walking by and —"

"No," Lyla interrupted. "Here, here...at Begoa's Point." Lyla lifted her arms and motioned them around the wooded area. "Dotty told me you bought the place."

Weston nodded, his mouth dry. He didn't know what to say. What would be enough? What wouldn't be enough?

"What else did she tell you?" he asked. Dotty was lovely, but she was also the campground gossip. He knew that if he told her that he'd had Savvy moved from the waitlist, Dotty would be the first to tell her about it.

"She didn't have to." Lyla turned toward Weston and took a step closer to him. "The convenient timing of being removed from the waitlist? This particular cabin?" Lyla looked at the door of the cabin then back to Weston. "It wasn't hard to put two and two together once I knew you were the owner."

They stood close, the closest they had been in more than fifteen years, and all the words Weston had rehearsed, all the things he'd thought he would say in this moment, were lost.

"Anyway." Her voice was quiet and difficult to read.

He braced himself for any version of 'please leave us alone', or 'it would be best if we just keep our distance.'

"Thank you." Weston's eyes popped open wide at the words he'd least expected, and she continued, "I never thought I'd be on these grounds again. It means a lot to Camden." She paused — an awkward silence thick in the space between them. "It means a lot to me too."

That's a spark of hope. The kindling and one single flame that would be enough to ignite the fire — as long as it was given time and space.

He nodded, and she moved away, taking a seat on the picnic table, where her canvas sneakers rested on the attached bench.

"You look exactly the same, West." She smiled for the first time since their reunion. Weston melted at the sound of the name only she called him. The day he'd shortened her name, she'd shortened his. They spoke a language only the other understood. "Well, most of you anyway." She pointed to his feet and they smiled twin, unsure smiles. "How's the leg?"

"Gone," he added, and they chuckled. She stifled the laugh with her hand over her mouth. The jokes and laughter cut, just fractionally, into the murky tension between them.

"Anyway, I have to get in and get something cooked for Camden and maybe get this fire going. He's been asking since we got here."

Weston nodded and stepped backward, ready to leave his parents' site — the ground he'd grown up on — and retreat to his new home on the wooded path. Lyla hopped off the picnic table and put her feet on solid ground.

"Savvy?" Weston said. She turned to him, her eyebrows raised. "Can we get together and catch up, maybe? Dinner or coffee or something?"

Lyla looked through the screen door, contemplating an answer that was clearly longer than just yes or no.

"I can't." Her voice was an almost-whisper.

"Why?" Weston's mouth had worked faster than his brain. He hadn't meant to say that out loud. She didn't answer. She just moved to inside the door, out of view. "I just… I have questions. I'd like to catch up, I guess."

Lyla shook her head in a slow but definitive no and left him standing there by himself as she retreated into the cabin.

He turned on his heel, heading back toward the main road.

"I'll tell you what," he heard her call, turning too quickly to see where it was coming from. He looked up to see her on the back porch of the cabin, leaning over the railing. "I'll race you for it."

He twisted his face in curious confusion.

"How do you mean?" he yelled, his voice carrying to the treetops.

"Tomorrow morning. We can run the usual path. If you beat me to the Begoa's Point sign at the end of the road, I'll consider chatting with you."

"Seems a little unfair, don't you think?" He knocked on the constructed frame where his prosthetic connected to the remainder of his thigh.

"Please, West. Give me a break. You run by here every single morning."

"So, you noticed?" He laughed and her cheeks reddened.

"The marina at seven a.m.," she yelled, he nodded. "And, West? Bring the dog."

Chapter Ten

Lyla

The picnic table shifted as Lyla leaned forward to lace up her running sneakers. She stood and stretched one leg then the other. The screen door creaked open. Camden stood on the other side with tired eyes and a yawn bigger than he was.

"It's early, kiddo." Lyla placed both feet on the ground. "Go back to bed."

"Okay. Have fun on your date." Camden turned away from the door.

"It is not a date." Lyla corrected him. He turned to her, pushed the door open and stepped outside in shorts and bare feet. "Come here." Lyla patted the picnic table bench and took a seat herself.

Lyla stared at him. Everyone said he looked like her, that he was the spitting image of his mother, but in her eyes, he would always be more his father. He looked so much like Jared, but it was more than that. He was smart like Jared and sweet like him. He was generous and outgoing and funny. He made friends everywhere he went, and that was something he definitely didn't get from her. In each of his expressions and his over-the-top personality? Well, Jared came through in all of it. Lyla knew it was time to have a discussion with her son, but she was never sure how.

"This is the part where you ask me if I'm okay with you dating, right?" Camden looked up at her with an expression that only had curiosity in it — no accusation, no sadness, just a genuine curiosity.

"It's not a date." She emphasized every word. "But what if it was?"

"I think it should be." Camden sat up straight and spoke his words matter-of-factly.

"Oh, yeah? Why's that?"

Camden turned to her, straddling the picnic table bench. "Well, you're lonely. And Weston is lonely. You could be lonely together."

Lyla's chest seized with mixed emotion — sadness that her son was clearly impacted by the black cloud she thought followed only her, but happiness, too, that her son was wise beyond his years.

"And how do you know West is lonely?" She raised one eyebrow.

"He said so." Camden shrugged and stood from the table. "Can I go back to bed now?"

Lyla nodded and laughed, kissing him on the forehead before shooing him into the cabin. She should have expected that her son would accept change with an open mind and logical thinking. It was exactly what his father would have done.

Lyla walked down the path toward the marina. As she neared the docks and the water, her palms began to sweat and her heart rate increased—and she hadn't even started running yet. The symptoms were a mix of being nervous about seeing Weston for the first planned time since finding out he was here and stepping foot into the marina again for the first time since her last stay at Begoa's Point. Her final night there was never supposed to be her final night. They'd still had a few weeks left, but she walked into the marina and, in many ways, she'd never left it.

Charlie was the oldest. He turned eighteen first while the rest of them lingered at seventeen for a few more months. It was a late, clear night under a cloudless sky with as many fireflies as there were stars. The group was left to their own devices and wandered around the campground with no real plan or destination. 'Boredom equals trouble,' her father would say. He would be right.

The group hopped the locked gates to the marina and made their way down the docks, not causing any real trouble but certainly not avoiding it either. The dock shifted and rocked under their collective weight, the creaking of the wood and hinges that held it together echoing across the rippling lake.

She stood at the dock's edge. Weston ran up behind her, knocking her forward as if he were going to push her in then catching her just in time, pulling her body close to his own.

"Nice night for a swim." He pressed his nose into her hair as he wrapped her in his arms, hugging her from behind.

"No way." She leaned her head onto his chest.

"Come on, Savvy. Do something daring." His words were like velvet. Something about the way he said it made the thought sound appealing. Tempting, even.

She looked around the docks and took in the sights of the marina.

"I've got a better idea." She took Weston's hand and led him up the dock.

"Hey, you okay?"

She jumped at the sound of the voice, her feet leaving the wooden planks beneath her. She turned to find Weston and his dog on the dock.

"Yeah." She breathed in short, quick inhalations. "You just scared me."

"You ready to go?" He threw a thumb over his shoulder, and she nodded. *Yes*, she thought, more ready to leave the marina than she could've explained. She hadn't expected it to haunt her the way it had.

"What's his name?" she asked as they reached their imaginary starting line on the beach.

"Achilles." The dog's ears perked up at the sound.

"Clever." Lyla laughed and stopped where they stood, using her heel to draw a line in the sand. The dog popped one paw up, holding it in the air with his head cocked until she took it. "Nice to meet you, Achilles." The dog sat up straight, as proud as ever.

"So, what's the grand prize when I beat you?" Weston warmed up, his fingers cracking as he pushed them away from his body in a stretch.

"What do you want?" Lyla said. "Or rather, what are you willing to lose?"

"I want answers. I have questions and I want answers. It's been a lot of years."

"Fair. You beat me to the sign, and I'll tell you anything you want to know."

"And if you win?" Weston said, an eyebrow arched.

"I tell you nothing."

Weston stared at her for a moment, seemingly about to counteroffer, but she had other plans.

"Go!" she yelled, taking off down the beach. Her echoing laughter and his shouting after her caused them both to run at slower speeds than they were capable of.

It wasn't a stolen race by any means. One would pull ahead, the other would pace then the second-place person would take a decent lead. They switched places back and forth with no indication of a runaway victory for either of them. Achilles stopped every once in a while to sniff something on the beach or investigate a sound, but caught up without difficulty each time.

They rounded the final corner where the sign was located, the finish line in sight. Lyla was ahead by a few strides, but just as she thought she could taste victory, Weston ran alongside her, neck and neck, until he stopped in his tracks, allowing Lyla to take the lead and the win.

She placed her hands on her knees and leaned forward, taking a few deep, steadying breaths.

"What'd you do that for?" she scolded.

"I don't want to know things about you on a bet, Savvy. So, you win. You don't have to tell me anything." Weston turned away, walking in slow, tiny circles as he obviously was trying to calm his inhalations.

They stood a dozen feet apart, with the sign between them.

"What do you want to know?" She threw her hands in the air in an obvious forfeit. "I'm changing the rules. You get one question. Call it a consolation prize. Everyone gets a ribbon."

Weston stood still, facing her, a hand on his chin scratching at his five o'clock shadow. Achilles took off to explore in the woods.

"You only get one, West. Don't be wasting it on my favorite color or anything."

"Yellow," he whispered, but the way her lips came together and her eyes widened said she'd heard the response and the answer remained true.

"Okay. Earlier I asked you if we could spend some time together. You changed your mind, obviously, but you first said, *'I can't'*. Now, maybe I'm reading too much into this, but I feel like there is a difference between 'no' and 'I can't'. And you didn't say no."

Weston crossed his arms over his chest and rocked back and forth, the loose gravel sticking to the soles of his shoes.

"Is there a question in there?" Lyla asked, her sarcasm in full bloom. Weston pursed his lips, and his eyes bored into hers. He didn't have to specify what he was saying. She already knew.

"I said I can't because…I really didn't think I'd be able to just sit and talk to you like everything was fine. I didn't think I could look at you and pretend…" Her eyes filled with puddles she blinked away in her best attempt at holding them back.

She went on. "I can't just stand here and pretend that you didn't destroy me. That this place didn't destroy me. As much as I love it… As much as I wanted to come back… This place broke my heart. *You* broke my heart."

"I know." Weston stepped toward her, likely believing he needed to do something to calm her. She held out both palms, stopping him from coming any closer.

"You don't," she whispered. "You *don't* know." She shook her head and pointed both her hands to the ground. "This is the spot I was standing on when I knew I'd never hear from you again."

For Lyla, only seventeen at the time, the worst pain had set in when she'd realized that from then on, she'd be longing for his laugh instead of listening to it — that she hadn't known that their last day would be their last day, or that their years of outlandish memories and inside jokes had crossed a finish line she hadn't realized was coming.

Every summer had ended the same way, with their group of friends hugging over laughs and tears, giving some indication that they'd be back next year. *'See you later. Until next time. It's only eight months.'*

But not that summer. For the first time in her life, there had been no promise of what was to come. The person she'd felt most connected to hadn't been reachable, seemingly didn't want to be and had left no sign that he would be changing his mind.

"I think we can agree that that summer when we were seventeen was the best and worst summer of our lives." Weston nodded as she spoke. His face contorted into an expression that suggested he didn't want to revisit the details. "We were all ripped apart from each other that summer — after building what should have been lifelong friendships, knowing every single year that we left, that we would be coming back and picking up where we left off. But you know my dad, West."

Lyla's father had been supportive of his daughter and wanted what was best for her, but he had also been strict, setting unbreakable laws that his daughter was to abide by at all times.

"He said I wasn't to see you anymore. That I got stupid the minute I got around you. That I wasn't myself and boys were just going to ruin my life before it got started."

It was harsh, but it was true, and all her Begoa's Point friends knew it.

"But I loved you, West, more that summer than any other. For years, we talked all summer then went our separate ways for the school year. I was okay with that because I knew that when Memorial Day rolled around, I would belong to you and you would belong to me. So even though our love was limited to three months of a twelve-month year, those months were the ones that mattered."

Weston swallowed. His Adam's apple bobbed in his throat as she talked.

"I didn't want to have a love reserved for warm weather and one location anymore. Not after everything we had been through. So, I broke all the rules. I called off season. I called the campground and there was no answer. I wrote to you and the letter was returned."

"Savvy," Weston said, craving the opportunity to jump in and explain before she had the chance to finish her piece, but she kept on.

"I needed you, West!" Her voice echoed through the leaves, causing birds to retreat from their treetop homes and fly into the crystal blue sky. "I needed you and I know… I know you needed me too. So, I did something that to this day I still haven't figured out why. My dad was right. When it comes to you, I make decisions I wouldn't usually make." She paused and took a deep breath. Weston's face took on a sympathetic, sad expression.

"Months later, in the beginning of winter, I stole his car in the middle of the night and I drove all the way here. The entire way I was thinking about you — about the way we left things, about all the poor decisions we'd made and how we were just kids and we didn't know any better. I was going to tell you that I loved you and promise you that no matter the wreckage or the consequences or what my father said, that we could make it work."

The tears spilled down Lyla's cheeks, all her efforts to hide them failing. "I pulled up to the gates and everything was gone. The sign was covered up. The property was boarded up. Begoa's Point was gone. *You* were gone."

"I didn't know, Savvy." Weston stepped toward her. She allowed the closeness now, and he clutched her forearms. He ran his thumbs across her skin. "I had no idea you came all the way here. I didn't know you'd called or written or anything."

"Why didn't you try to track me down, West?" Her voice changed from sad to mad in the time it took to blink away tears. "There has to be a reason. You left me with nothing—no explanation, no indication that you were okay, not even a goodbye. You know that's worse? Not ever being given a reason. I was just left to wonder how everything that was so right went so wrong."

"Savvy, there are...so many things I wish I could tell you, but I can't." Weston cast his gaze downward, his lips pressed into a tight line. "There are reasons. I just can't explain them."

Lyla slid her forearms through Weston's grasp and held his hands for a moment, staring deep into his eyes before speaking.

"Those aren't reasons then, West. They're excuses." She dropped his hands and headed back down the path, leaving Weston standing in the same spot she had been in when her world had fallen apart all those years ago.

Chapter Eleven

Weston

Weston tapped a finger of one hand against the tabletop during a meeting with the campground accounting team. His head spun. One hour into the meeting, which was close to ending, and he hadn't absorbed a word of it.

"Mr. Accardi?" Gordy Garrett, head of finances, asked. "Does that sound acceptable to you?"

Weston looked at Sheila, who nodded a slight yes. Thank heavens for her. Her note-keeping, delegation of tasks and all-around assistance kept this place running more than he did.

"Yes, sure," he added, as convincingly as possible. Weston seemed out of place in his khaki shorts and forest green T-shirt, while the accountants were dressed in button downs and slacks. He had told them time and time again that they could dress comfortably, but they wouldn't hear it.

"Everything okay?" Sheila asked, sliding a cup of coffee across the table once they were alone. Weston took a sip. The difference in taste between a cup of coffee brewed in a metal machine and the coffee he made over an open flame was noticeable. He preferred the over-the-fire technique, but this would do for now.

"I don't know." He sank into his chair. "I spend most days trying to figure out why I did this in the first place."

"What? Reopen?" She was surprised. "Because you love this place. Everyone does."

"That's what I used to think." A yawn escaped from his lips. "Now I'm not so sure."

"This sudden change of heart wouldn't have anything to do with Miss Savoie's return, would it?" Sheila chewed the end of a pen, and Weston stood from his chair.

"It's Kenney now." Weston stood and headed out of the door, finally understanding that just because he'd returned and Begoa's had reopened didn't mean everything remained the same.

* * * *

Weston sat on the edge of the dock, foot in the water and Achilles at his side. Sal pulled up to the dock in a teal-blue paddle boat. He reached out one hand and held the dock. Weston rested his artificial foot on the front of the small boat to anchor it in place.

"You've been out here for hours." Sal looked at Weston from under his floppy-brimmed hat with a fishing lure stuck through it.

"Just doing some thinking." Weston made circles with his foot in the lake that caused it to stir and ripple.

Weston gazed out over the open water to one small cove in particular. He closed his eyes and took a deep breath.

"You're too hard on yourself," Sal said. "You were just kids." Weston shut his eyes tight.

"I have a better idea," Lyla had said, stepping out of his hug and pulling his hand down the dock. The group followed.

"Isn't it past your curfew, Lyla?" Charlie prodded. He wasn't being nice about it. "You're usually long gone by now, missing out on all the real fun." He wrapped his arm around Christy, a girl who was newer to their group of friends.

"Shut it, Charlie," she said. Lyla was so fierce that night, a new adventurous side coming through that Weston had never seen before. No one had.

"What's this great idea?" Weston asked, pulling Lyla in close and kissing her on her sunburned forehead.

She held both hands out in a drastic fashion like one of the girls on The Price is Right *showing off the prize car.*

Only it wasn't a car. It was a boat. Weston's parents' boat.

She hopped aboard and sat in the Captain's chair, pretending to spin the wheel.

"You want to sit on the boat and pretend to drive it?" Charlie asked. He was still of the mindset that making fun of others impressed girls.

"I guess." Lyla blushed a deeper red than from the day in the sun.

"What if we didn't pretend?" Weston morphed into a mischievous smile. "The keys are in Sal's office." Weston was off and running before anyone could agree or decline. He returned with a set of small keys.

He could tell Lyla was just putting on a brave face – that she didn't really want any part of the plan, but she didn't want to be left out either.

"It's just a little bit of fun. How much trouble could we possibly get in?" Weston asked before hopping from the dock to the boat. Charlie and Christy didn't hesitate to follow him on board.

"I'm exactly the right amount of hard on myself," Weston said to Sal, finally opening his eyes again and pulling his gaze off the water and the distant memories it held.

* * * *

The crowds gathered along the sand, the night of the carnival on the beach. It had been such a hit when he was young, so he'd wanted to bring it back. This was a trial run. Being the first year and not having quite as much of a budget as he would have liked, the plan was to see how this carnival went prior to committing to it as a more frequent celebration. An outside company had brought in their games, vendors, equipment and the like. With any luck, it would go well enough to make it a monthly or more event for the campground.

"Good turn-out." Sheila scrolled over an iPad screen. "These are the kinds of things we need to bring in some extra money so we can proceed with the expansion project for the other half of the resort."

"Is it always business with you?" Weston asked. He knew being the owner came with a lot of responsibility, but the incessant decision-making and weighty subjects only made him wish he were a kid again, more so than this place already did.

"Is it ever work with you?" she retorted. Weston smiled as he pulled his baseball cap off his head, adjusted his hair and placed it back over his sweating brow.

"You're so different than your father was." She shook her head. "He was all business, all the time — head in the books and the numbers, always stressed every single day that this place would close due to not being profitable and that he'd have to lay all these people off."

"That's very encouraging." Weston clapped his hands together. "The place did close, but it wasn't anything he did wrong." The memories of his father mixed with his conversation with Lyla and formed a thick ball at the top of his throat. He swallowed hard in a futile attempt at dislodging it.

"It was a compliment," Sheila said. "Your father was great. Don't get me wrong. But he was so busy figuring out how to make the place better that he never took a minute to enjoy how great it already was."

Weston smiled and frowned all in the same muscle twitch. He had memories of Begoa's — so many of them — but not nearly enough of them included his father. They'd always had family dinners, and on Sundays, they'd spend their days on their boat. Those were standing appointments, but apart from that, Weston could hardly pull a memory that had his father in it. Beach days, mini golf, tournaments, ribbon and T-shirt activities... He couldn't remember a time when his dad had volunteered to step away from the books and be part of the fun.

Lyla's father, on the other hand? Well, Weston had more memories of him than he cared to. Lyla's father had been involved, almost to a fault. To Weston's father, this place was a job, a business, but to Lyla's father, it was a family vacation and he'd held on to spending those waning childhood moments with her for as long as he could. Each year, she'd strayed a little farther until she let go of his hand completely and held Weston's instead. Her father had hated every moment of it and he'd made it known.

Charlie and Weston, over the years, had developed quite a reputation for being the bad boys of Begoa's Point. Not all of it had been true and most was grossly exaggerated, but everyone loved a good scandal involving the owner's boy. It was a big campground — but not *that* big. Secrets didn't stay secrets long and Begoa's Point had its very own set of fables and tales to be shared over campfires, each story gaining new, added details as they traveled from site to site.

He'd made it clear from day one that Weston was the type of boy Lyla should stay away from, because a reputation was never fixable once it was broken.

"We have a meeting scheduled next month with investors to talk about your ideas for the expansion and how their backing would come into play—"

"Mr. Accardi..." A man Weston had never seen before interrupted. "I'm sorry to bother you, but we had an electrical issue and shorted out some of the tents and machines. Too much power to one area, I think. Do you have a moment to take a look and help reassign some vendor spaces?"

"We can pick up on this later, Sheila." Weston nodded and went forward, following behind the gentleman overseeing the carnival setup. "And Sheila?" he called as he walked backward down the beach.

She perked up over the edge of the tablet screen. "Put it away. Go enjoy yourself."

Weston quickly took care of the issues at hand then headed down the sandy beach, taking in the sights and sounds of people laughing, cursing the air when they lost the game they were playing or cheering victoriously when they won a prize.

"Step right up!" a gentleman behind a booth hollered. Weston looked toward the tent with rows of moving basketball nets posted at the back of the booth. A mess of brown curls and tan-lined shoulders peeking out from a tank top stood in front of the worker, waiting to toss the basketballs for a chance at a prize. "What's your name?" He never fell out of character.

"Lyla," she said, and the guy hopped up on the table at the front of the tent, leaning off the pole that held his booth up. "The lovely Lyla wants to play basketball, ladies and gents! Who will challenge her?" He pointed to random customers in the crowd. "You there! You look like a basketball player." The man shook his head no. "Anyone? Anyone?"

"I'll play," Weston said, walking toward the booth. The worker tossed a ball at him as he approached. Weston caught it in one hand and held it against his chest. Lyla rolled her eyes.

"All right, all right," the attendant called, "we've got ourselves a game!"

"Watch this one carefully," Lyla told the booth worker. "He cheats."

The worker's eyes widened, the obvious tension between them filling the tent with a dense uncertainty.

"And...go!" the attendant yelled as the basketball hoops began to shift on their posts, coming closer, moving away and getting higher and lower as they tossed arching throws toward them. The attendant counted down five...four...three. Weston didn't miss it when Lyla found the clock habitually, checking that the final countdown truly was the final countdown.

"And the winner!" the man sang, handing Lyla a small teddy bear stuffed animal. She immediately turned and handed it to a small toddler near her.

Weston was about to turn away to go in the opposite direction to her, the way his head was warning him to go to give her space and time, but to his surprise, she requested otherwise.

"Take a walk with me?" she asked, and he agreed.

They strolled along the beach. With so many others enjoying the evening activities, the area was entirely vacant apart from them.

"I wanted to apologize for the other day. I just... I've been sitting on that, holding it all in for so many years. I wondered what I would say to you if I ever had the chance, and that...? Well, that wasn't how I expected it all to happen."

"I don't blame you." Weston kept his gaze toward the sand as he spoke. "I deserved it. You're right. I didn't give you any reasons why."

Lyla took a seat on a swing at the playground, swaying gently. Weston leaned into the climbing structure next to the swing set.

"It wasn't just you I was mad at. I was mad at me too. That summer—the best and worst summer—it should have gone so much better. If I could do anything over, it would be that year. If it was going to be our last time here, Begoa's deserved better. I think that's why I wanted to return so bad—to get a do-over, even if it is more than a decade later." Lyla continued to swing back and forth, looking out over the glassy lake before it swallowed the last of the golden sun.

"Why do you think I reopened it?" Weston shrugged. "I was looking for the same type of do-over. And you're right. Begoa's deserved better. I'm doing what I can to give it that chance."

"You're doing an amazing job." Her voice fell, slightly smaller. She scanned the lake, beach and carnival. Her cheeks brightened as she found something new to focus on — Camden.

He ran down the path closest to the carnival with a group of boys, their heads thrown back in laughter and sweat weighing down their hair.

"You are too," Weston whispered, and there was a moment of silence between them. Weston cleared his throat and took a chance at starting a real conversation based in the present, learning about this version of her rather than dwelling on the past. He couldn't return to the past, neither of them could, so they might as well move forward. "Tell me about you. What are you doing now? What's your life like?"

"I teach." She leaned her head into the rope holding the swing up. "I met my husband, Jared, while I was in college. We went to school together for a few semesters, but he went into the military. It was his calling, what he wanted. He loved it. He married the military first, but eventually, he married me too." She smiled as she spoke of him, her voice a mix of longing and awe. "Everyone said we were too young, but the military got to choose where he lived, and if I wanted to go with him, we had to be married. And I wanted to go with him — I was sure. It worked out for us. He gave me a beautiful life. We saw gorgeous places, but most importantly he gave me a beautiful son."

Lyla continued to swing but it moved only inches forward and back, hovering in small circles. He didn't dare interrupt her.

"He was only a few weeks into his mission when they told me he wasn't coming home. And I found I was pregnant a few weeks after that." Lyla dragged her fingertips under her eyes, turning them up toward the sky and blinking away the remaining tears.

Weston nodded as she concluded her story. There were no words worth saying. 'I'm sorry' was futile. But his respect for her, the awe he felt when it came to her, grew in leaps and bounds. She had raised Camden by herself, and from what he could tell, she was doing a tremendous job.

"Most people don't get it, you know? How much energy it takes to mourn and grieve and try to hold yourself together all the time. But I know you understand how I feel. You may be the only one I know who does."

Weston arched his eyebrow, and a curiosity set into his eyes. He took the swing next to Lyla and let it rock him back and forth.

"I know it's not exactly the same. But losing Charlie couldn't have been easy. We all know you two were the real Begoa's Point love story." She elbowed Weston lightly, his swing shifting into a side-to-side motion. "I'm sure you miss him."

"Every day." Weston's Adam's apple trembled against his vocal cords. "Especially now. I would've loved for him to be here to see this."

They swung side by side quietly for a while, saying nothing at all. Then again, there was nothing left to say. Words wouldn't cut it. Sentences weren't going to bring Jared and Charlie back. But it wasn't her words or her silence that finally gave Weston any indication that everything could be okay again. It was when she dropped her hand beside the swing and linked her fingers into his.

Chapter Twelve

Lyla

Lyla pounded the cement. Weston, for the first time since they'd started these daily runs, had fallen a bit behind. Achilles kept pace with Lyla, looking back at his trailing owner. She picked up the pace to a sprint, using a final burst of energy to catapult toward the Begoa's Point sign. She hit her palm against the carved wood as she passed it, and Weston did the same when he reached it a few seconds later.

"You can stop letting me win any time now." Lyla giggled, leaning against the welcome sign and stretching out her legs.

"Trust me." Weston breathed heavily, his chest rising and falling. "I'm not."

"There's a road race at the end of the week," Lyla said. "Are you going to run it?"

Weston shook his head.

"It's for a T-shirt," Lyla tried to tempt him in a sing-song tone. Oh, the coveted 'Camp Champ' T-shirts. Lyla had fought tooth and nail every year, every summer, to get one but she'd always fallen short, earning an impressive ribbon collection but never the specially designed shirt given to winners of specific events.

"First of all, the T-shirts lose their excitement when you're the one who designs and purchases them. Second, and more importantly, you have a 'Camp Champ' shirt, if I remember correctly." Weston grinned, stepping off the road and leaning against a nearby tree. "I mean, you stole it. But you have one all the same."

"I didn't steal it!" she disputed, her voice echoing through the empty road. "It was rightfully mine! But you and Charlie and the rest of your friends tricked me."

"You shouldn't have fallen for that." Weston doubled over, as if the joke had happened in that moment and not half their lifetime ago.

"I still can't believe you did that." She shook her head but eventually, she laughed too. "I never understood it."

"I wanted to win." Weston shrugged his shoulders. "I wouldn't have beat you."

Lyla's mouth dropped open. She hadn't expected that answer. "I'm not sure about that."

"I am. You were a great basketball player. I was, what? Fourteen at the time? I was too proud at that age to lose to a girl."

"You're not proud anymore?" A genuine curiosity cloaked the sentiment.

"No. I make it a point not to be. That pride lost me more than I ever gained from it."

Lyla nodded. She could see that change in him, but in many ways, they were getting to know each other anew. The two people who stood across from each other knew almost everything about each other and, at the same time, were complete strangers, familiar with who the other used to be but learning more about who they were now. He'd used to walk the line of confident, charismatic...fearless. Now he was obviously more cautious, thinking before he spoke and weighing the consequences before committing to an action.

"Want to come back to my site for a cup of coffee?" Weston shoved his hands into the pockets of his gym shorts.

"Only if you still make it over the campfire."

"It's the only way," he said, and she skipped forward, clapping her hands.

* * * *

Of all the things she missed about Begoa's, the coffee Weston brewed was at the top of the list. She hadn't even liked coffee at the time unless it had been made by him. Now, normal coffee still didn't hold a candle to the way she'd learned to love it as a teenager.

"I still can't believe you got an RV up to the clearing," Lyla shook her head as they approached his site.

"I knew I didn't want to be on the main property. And I didn't want to stay in 101. I didn't ever plan on letting anyone stay in that cabin." Achilles ran ahead as they walked, stopping to lap up water from a metal bowl.

Lyla's heart clenched. He was a stubborn person. When he made his mind up, he usually didn't change it. At least that was how it used to be. Some things never changed. For him to put her in that cabin when he'd decided it was to be unused meant he must have really wanted her there and really wanted to see her, even after all this time.

"Can I ask you something?" Lyla's voice lost some of its volume. "I don't mean to keep revisiting the subject. But I'm confused, I guess."

"Is there a question in there?" Weston asked, quoting Lyla's exact statement the last time roles had been reversed.

"I get it. Your family always lived in a different time than the rest of us. Technology wasn't your thing. You relied on the camp landlines and never had computers on the property. Everything was done by hand. So I guess in many ways I understand why you didn't reach out and why there was always this huge disconnect between us. But why now? Why didn't you ever reach out or find me any time between then and now?"

Weston stayed quiet. At first, he twisted his face into an unreadable expression like he knew something, but then shifted to something different. *Remorse, maybe?*

"Maybe I should just go."

It seemed they were just going around and around in an incessant circle, running a mile forward and then ten miles back. She asked the same questions, and they stayed unanswered. So why keep running?

She was ready to head down the path she had traveled so many times, where she'd pass the masquerading blueberry bushes — the tricky ones that looked safe but weren't.

"I did."

That was all he said, but the intensity of the words anchored her to the spot, rendering her unable to float away from him. She turned slowly, her eyes finding his and in them, the truth. He'd looked for her. She swallowed hard. Lyla had believed that he had never tried to find her, but she had also never considered the alternative. She didn't have anything to say. She'd never once given him the benefit of the doubt.

"I tried at first, after that summer. I mean, some time had passed. But when I reached out, every time I tried, your dad intercepted it. He told me to stop — and eventually I did." Weston's voice carried across the clearing. Her heart fell into her stomach. She knew her dad wasn't Weston's biggest fan, but that?

He'd known how heartbroken she'd been when Begoa's had closed. He'd known how long it had taken her to recover — physically and mentally — from that final summer and that any kind of contact from Weston might have changed things. Her father was a strict man and in that, had taken a lot of things from her and extinguished a lot of opportunities, but this...? This was almost unforgivable.

She and her dad got along okay, though their relationship was complicated and a bit strained. Even with his move south, they talked frequently, mostly for Camden's sake. When she looked back at her Begoa's memories, so many of them cast him in a leading role. She told him everything — always. He, apparently, didn't tell her quite as much.

"Then, a few years after that, I found you on the Internet. Found your profile."

Lyla's eyes widened, more so because the idea of Weston Accardi sitting at a screen of any type was far more surprising than the revelation that he'd tried to reach out in the first place.

"But," he continued, "you were happy. Your profile picture was a wedding photo. The last photo you had posted was of a baby boy. That was as far as I looked. It wasn't my place to go any further or read any more into it. You weren't Savvy anymore. You were Lyla Savoie Kenney, and I wasn't about to intrude on that."

Lyla's eyes filled with tears. All the information was too heavy to hold—her father interfering with her connections to people she had been dying to hear from, Weston thinking about her as much as she'd thought about him. And worst of all was the internal turbulence that had set in. She was happy with how her life had turned out. Jared was truly the best thing to have happened to her. He had been an honorable man and had given her the best gift of her life—Camden. Wondering what might have been and how different her life may have turned out if Weston had reached her all those years ago created a guilt that ate into her chest, decaying her like rust on old metal.

"It all worked out, Savvy." Weston took steps toward her. He placed his palm on her cheek, wiping away a tear she hadn't realized she'd cried. "Everything truly does happen for a reason."

She nodded in agreement, his calloused hands scratching against the skin of her cheek.

"Come on." He took her hand in his. "I promised you coffee."

They approached the campfire, and he pulled a chair out, gesturing for her to take it. Lyla obliged, taking a seat near the flame but moving the chair back a bit. She had always been a bit afraid of fire. She wasn't really sure why and could never really pinpoint a reason. As a kid she had always shied away from anything unpredictable. She'd liked things ordered and sure. She hadn't been one to take many chances...until she'd met Weston.

She scanned the site, taking in Weston's living space, trying to find clues to who he was now. Her gaze fell upon a small, black, zippered case in the shape of a tiny guitar.

"You still have that?" She pointed to the ukulele.

"I do." He grinned.

"I remember the summer you got it. I asked you to play my favorite song and you said you would learn it." Lyla raised her eyebrow toward him, wondering if he remembered as much as she did. "You never did. You said it was 'too new'." She laughed, another tiny memory of Weston resurfacing. "Do you still listen to eighties music exclusively?"

Weston smiled a charming half-smile, the corner of his mouth picking up at one corner. "Of course." Weston placed the aluminum coffee carafe on the flame and grabbed the ukulele, unzipping the case. "But there's an exception to every rule." He winked, sat in the chair next to her and strummed chords to *Wonderwall*.

Lyla broke into a smile, her eyes filling with tears, different from the ones she'd previously cried.

"That's my song," she said, and he kept playing. "I can't believe you remember that."

He stared at her, pulling his fingers away from the strings, leaving the final note he'd played to fade into the open air.

"I remember everything when it comes to you."

"Play it again," she whispered — and he did.

They sipped coffee, and Weston played the songs he knew. They reminisced over their younger days, giggling until their stomachs hurt at some memories and crying over others.

"I should get going." Lyla checked her watch. "Camden wants to do the parent-child canoe race down near the marina."

"I'll be there too. Sal is doing a boating safety course with the teen groups today, so I'll be in the area."

Lyla gripped tighter around the mug, a cool breeze reaching her skin and sending a chill down her spine. "Teen Boating Safety. Is that new?"

Weston nodded over his sip of coffee.

"It's important," he said once he finally got the sip down. "I have a few things I have to take care of today after that—meetings, work, etcetera. But I was thinking maybe we could do dinner tonight?"

Lyla tipped her cup back, enjoyed a hot sip of joe then placed the cup down. "I was thinking about fixing something special for Camden. He's been off making friends and can't get enough of the activities, but I want to see him."

"I agree," Weston said. "I was thinking I'd grill steaks for the four of us."

"The *four* of us?" Lyla asked. Weston nodded toward Achilles, who didn't miss the mention of steaks. "That sounds great. Camden loves steaks, and heaven knows I'm not cooking them for him."

"Okay. Sounds good. I'll come to you?"

Lyla agreed. "And, West?" she added, his eyes meeting hers. "Do you think if I head down to the welcome center, Sheila would let me check my emails on her computer?"

"Everything okay?" He placed his cup on the ground beside his artificial foot.

"Why wouldn't it be?" Lyla collected herself and stretched as she stood.

"Just seemed sudden. Besides, you were always so fond of the disconnect and lack of technology."

"Yeah, everything is fine." She forced a smile and kept her words upbeat. "Just something I have to take care of."

"I don't think she will mind." Weston stood and stepped forward. Both he and Lyla rocked back and forth, looking anywhere but at each other while trying to select the most fitting exit from a list of thousands of awkward parting rituals.

"Well…until later, then."

She waved a goodbye and took off down the path.

Chapter Thirteen

Weston

Weston kept a slow and steady pace as he walked down the docks and on to the sandy beach. Lyla sat on the sand in a bathing suit and shorts with her long, tan legs stretched out in front of her. She leaned her face back, inviting the sun to kiss her skin. He picked up the pace, just the sight of her instantly improving his already-good mood. He sat directly beside her in the sun-warmed sand.

"This is different." Lyla placed her hand on Weston's prosthetic.

"This one is rated for water. I usually switch to this one on days I spend a lot of time at the marina. I prefer the other one though."

"The running blade? Why?" Lyla's eyes scanned the length of his legs.

"Just feels more natural to me, which is uncommon. The company that made it doesn't recommend wearing a blade outside of running because of the altered gait and the effect it can have on some people's balance and their back and hips, but I feel like it's lighter and more agile."

"I guess I never really thought about all the different types of prosthetics."

"Most people don't." It wasn't meant to be harsh. The majority of people just didn't have a reason to educate themselves on the subject. The conversation came to a halt. Weston could see a thousand more questions circulating behind Lyla's eyes, but she didn't ask them. He changed the subject.

"Is he ready?" Weston looked around for Camden.

She slid her sunglasses into her hair and turned to him.

"I think so. He's been talking about this canoe race for a week." Lyla reached her hand so her fingers rested against Weston's.

"Are you ready?" Weston squeezed her hand tight. "I know how you feel about boats and the lake." But before she could answer, another voice joined them.

"Mom! Mom!" A small voice carried over to them. Weston didn't miss it when Lyla pulled her hand away from his, hiding their physical touch from her young son. "We're about to start!"

Camden reached out both his hands, and Lyla grasped them. He tugged hard, pulling her into a standing position. They started down the beach, leaving Weston behind with his own thoughts.

"Hey," Camden yelled. Weston looked up, cupping his hand over the rim of his ballcap to further block the sun. "Are you coming?"

Lyla turned to look at Weston then at her son, a smile that showed her perfectly white teeth shone on her cheeks. Weston stood and picked up the pace as he moved toward them, slowing as he reached them. They walked toward the inlet where all the canoes were lined up, ready to race.

As they approached the area, Lyla headed toward the counselor responsible for signing in each team. She took a clipboard and started filling out the attached form. Camden looked around, his enthusiasm evaporating in the hot sun.

"What's up, Camden?" Weston asked, taking note of the other teams.

"It's all father-son teams." The words were small, barely audible. His head fell so his chin hit his chest. Lyla looked up over the clipboard as the two of them talked a few feet away.

"Yeah, it looks that way. But that's okay, bud. Your mom is going to be with you."

"She'll be the only girl." Camden dug his toes into the sand.

"She's used to it." Weston smiled. "Growing up, your mom always played against the boys here. It never bothered her that she was the only girl. She tried anyway, and you know what? She was pretty darn good."

Camden's eyes lit up again, his enthusiasm restored. He went toward Lyla, who mouthed a 'thank you' over the clipboard.

Camden and Lyla climbed into the canoe and waited for the counselor to blow the whistle, indicating the start of the race. As soon as the high-pitched noise rang through the air, they started paddling like their lives depended on it. It was a T-shirt prize activity, after all. If they won this race, they competed in another round. If they were victorious there, they'd participate in a finals lap. If they won that one, Camden and Lyla would be the proud new owners of two of the elusive 'Camp Champ' T-shirts. Water splashed up behind them, the onlookers yelled and cheered — none louder than Weston, though.

They safely made it around the buoy to turn back toward the finish line. The other team struggled to make their turn and Lyla and Camden gained a large lead. The campers clapped as Lyla and Camden pulled in. The counselor took Lyla's hand, assisting her out of the boat. Camden jumped out, splashing into the shallow water and running toward Weston, throwing large droplets of water all around as he ran.

"We did it! One down, two to go!" he called out, his voice echoing through the air.

"Nice work." Weston held a hand up high and Camden jumped to reach it. They sat back to watch the next race.

The counselor in charge called Camden and Lyla's names before their second race. They climbed into their canoe and shot out at the whistle. This race was closer, the other team a bit more skilled than the first. They dipped their paddles into the water and splashed water up around them as they paddled. The two canoes picked up speed, the parent teammate of each boat picking up the pace, more competitive than either of the kids. It was clear neither wanted to lose.

The nose of the two boats came in so close, so exact, that Weston couldn't tell from the beach who had won. He held his breath in unison with the gaggle of campers that had formed a crowd to watch. The counselor raised his hand and pointed to Lyla and Camden. Weston let out a loud cheer and jumped off the sand, fist in the air. "There ya go, Cam!" he yelled with his hands cupped around his mouth to enhance his volume. Camden threw his arms around his mother.

Weston jogged across the beach and joined them at the edge of the cove. "One more, bud!"

Lyla looked Camden over. "You're getting really red, Camden. We really should've applied more sunblock to your face."

"I have an idea," Weston said, removing his ball cap and popping it on Camden's head. "Lucky cap. That should buy you enough time to get through the last race."

Camden's face lit up like he'd been given a cash prize, and Lyla's walls appeared to corrode just a bit more. The guarded expression she tried so hard to maintain while Weston was around faded a little each day.

Lyla and Camden got back into their canoe, and he remained their one-man cheering section on the sand at the starting line.

Camden turned around in the boat, pointed to the hat on his head and gave Weston a thumbs up. Weston returned the motion.

The whistle blew and Lyla and Camden paddled onward. Camden was fighting so hard for every stroke that his paddle barely ever touched the water's surface. Lyla's paddle dipped deep into the rippling current, propelling the boat forward. It was a close race. The turn around the buoy would have a huge impact on who would win. Whoever could make the cleaner turn would more than likely be the winner. Lyla and Camden had the canoe flying, and Lyla stuck the oar straight down to slow their speed only fractionally as she directed Camden into the turn. As the canoe started to take the proper direction, a gust of wind skated over the lake, taking Weston's hat clear off Camden's head. The cap landed on the water's surface near the buoy. Camden reached for it instinctively and Lyla automatically reached for him.

Weston had been on the water his entire life, long enough to know how this was going to play out before it happened. Lyla and Camden shifted their weight into the turn they were taking, changing the center of gravity, effectively capsizing their vessel.

Both bodies hit the water with a splash, the canoe floating upside down on the surface of the water. Weston ran into the water up to his knees. The other team headed toward the finish line.

Lyla and Camden popped up in the water, bobbing over to the overturned boat. A campground lifeguard made her way over on a paddle board and helped them flip the boat back to its correct form.

Weston expected Camden to be upset that they lost, but instead, he made eye contact with Weston, a mischievous smile crossing the young boy's lips, then he splashed his mother. She turned to him, surprised, even though they were already soaked, and splashed him back. Weston watched as the mother and child pair let out screaming laughter at the center of the racing area, messing around and making memories.

They swam a few feet forward and walked the rest of the way once their feet gained shallow enough ground.

"So much for lucky," Camden said, tossing the sopping hat toward Weston.

"Guess it's only lucky for me," Weston said with a teasing expression. Camden kicked water toward Weston, soaking his shirt and face.

"Camden," Lyla tried to scold him, but the attempt was futile. She wasn't mad. It was clear she thought it was hysterical.

"You both better run," Weston said, pulling his shirt off and using it to dry his face. Lyla and Camden took off in the opposite direction, Weston in pursuit of Camden. He reached him and picked him up, acting as if he were going to throw him out deeper into the lake water. Camden laughed, then Weston put him down.

"You thinking what I'm thinking?" Weston said, Camden nodding.

"Boys versus girl!" Camden yelled, and they chased Lyla down, dragging her out into the water once again.

They all forgot entirely that the elusive T-shirts had slipped through their fingers once again. The celebration for second place was much, much better.

Weston called a truce and they walked to the beach, sopping wet. "I have to get to the marina for the class." Weston said, stepping the opposite direction of Lyla and Camden.

"Will we see you after for dinner?" Lyla asked. Weston smiled his agreement and took off for the marina.

* * * *

Sal sat leaned back in an office chair, his feet up on the marina's check-in desk.

"Afternoon, Sal," Weston said, entering Sal's workspace.

"Afternoon, boss." Sal tipped his hat and removed his feet from the desktop. He leaned back, pulling an extra Begoa's T-shirt from the shelf behind him and tossing it to Weston.

"How are we looking this morning?" Weston pulled the shirt over his head and leaned over the desk, trying to sneak a peek at the computer monitor. Sal slid a folder from underneath a large desk calendar and handed it to Weston. "Printed, just the way you like it."

Weston opened the folder and flipped through the pages. "The Teen Boating Safety course is almost entirely full?" He scratched at the scruff growing along his jawline. "We might have to open a second class if it keeps going at this rate."

Sal stood. "Looks like the first group is here now." Sal and Weston headed to the docks to intercept the group and give them their first instruction.

"You sure you want to be here for this?" Sal asked, clapping his hand against Weston's shoulders. Weston nodded, though the motion was more unsure than definitive.

A group of young kids, all different ages, walked down the pathway to the marina. Sal had them all sit along the edge of the dock as he stood on an anchored boat and walked through the basics. The front of the boat was the bow, the back was the stern. He talked about boat types, from paddle boats to canoes to jet skis to sailboats and speedboats. He instructed them how to find the right fit for a life vest and fasten it properly.

"You're out there on an open lake or body of water, there isn't much traffic and you can see for miles," Sal said, continuing his lecture. "I know it seems so unlikely, but boating accidents do happen. Let's talk about the most common causes."

Weston rocked back and forth, shifting uncomfortably on the dock while standing in the sun's harsh rays. A bead of sweat released from his hair and ran down his forehead.

"Does anyone have a guess what the number one cause of boat accidents is?"

"Weather or big waves," one kid called out. He leaned backward into the dock, almost lying down while the others sat at attention. His sleeves were cut off his shirt. Blond hair peeked out from under a backward cap and sunburn covered his pale skin. He was carefree, borderline rebellious and, truth be told, he reminded Weston of Charlie.

"Of course, there's the waves and weather, but believe it or not, these factors don't play into as many accidents as you would think. Any other guesses?" Sal sat on the bow of the boat now, facing the teens.

"BUI?" a girl called out, and the others giggled.

"Ahh, boating under the influence — or operating under the influence." Sal lifted a hand, quieting the giggling group. "That causes more accidents than waves, weather or dangerous conditions do. But it's still not number one. Any last guesses?"

No one answered. They all looked at each other, shoulders shrugged.

"Weston?" Sal's voice carrying over the water. "Thoughts?"

"Under-experienced operators and excessive speeds." The group turned to look at Weston as he answered. There was a pause in the conversation, a silent exchange between Sal and Weston before Sal carried on further into the discussion.

"Exactly, Weston. Inexperience and speed accounts for..." Sal carried on, but Weston's mind was elsewhere, miles away. Years into the past, even.

"It's just a little bit of fun. How much trouble could we possibly get in?" Weston asked before hopping from the dock

to the boat. Charlie and Christy didn't hesitate to follow him onboard.

"A lot, actually," Lyla said, standing from her spot on the boat and returning to the dock.

"Get in the boat, Lyla," Charlie said. "It's just a short ride around the lake. To the cove and back. You only live once."

Lyla wrapped her arms around herself, obviously trying to calm the goosebumps she had from the cool moonlight air and her nerves. Charlie leaned forward, pulling the knots loose that held the boat in place at the dock.

"West, please don't," Lyla begged. Charlie started the boat and pushed off the dock. They floated away in a quiet departure. "Please!"

"Okay, okay," Weston said, jumping the length of the space between them and landing on the dock. He wrapped his arms around her and pressed his lips against her forehead. "We don't have to go. It's not a big deal."

"You don't know what you're missing." Charlie called, as the boat turned in the tide and floated until it faced the opposite direction. Charlie forced the boat into gear and took off toward the cove, the moon the only light on the otherwise pitch-dark lake.

"Any questions?" Sal asked. A few hands raised. Sal selected each teen and they asked questions about no-wake zones and how to decide between sailboats and power boats. Sal answered each one, his many years of water experience shining through in every answer.

Sal pointed to the boy with the backward cap and he sat up straight for the first time since the lesson had begun.

"Is it true someone died here?" the boy asked.

Sal shot his gaze upward, his mouth pressed into a hard line. He didn't speak. A harsh silence set in over the area.

Weston couldn't avoid the questions forever, but he hadn't expected this question, in this moment, in this spot.

"Yes," Weston answered. The entire group turned and looked at him in unison. Their eyes widened and their mouths dropped open. "Next question."

Chapter Fourteen

Lyla

The computer went into sleep mode, a black screen taking over where the Begoa's Point screensaver had lit the monitor. She sat at the computer, letting it drift in and out of its sleep and wake cycles, as if she didn't know how to use it.

She really just didn't know what to do.

She brought the screen to life again, clicking on the Internet icon and signing into her email account. The arrow hovered over the 'to' box and she typed a few letters, the suggestions box pulling up her father's email.

Dad, she wrote, then typed and deleted, choosing words and removing them repeatedly. Type. Delete. Repeat.

She had thought about what she would say, drafting it out in her head, but she took a step back and thought better about her intentions. If she yelled, if she attacked him, he would never respond. So, she tried a different method.

Miss you... Did you hear Begoa's reopened? How wonderful is that?

I know it's last minute, but Camden and I got a site all the way through August. It wasn't well planned, but what else is retirement for if not for impromptu vacations?

I hope you'll consider coming to spend some time with Camden and me. He would love to see you.

We spent so many beautiful years here. I do hope you'll consider giving it a visit.

Lyla

She hit send and sat back in the chair, wondering if she would get a response and what it would say.

Not more than three minutes later, her inbox had a bold number one next to it, and the computer chirped a bell-like notification sound.

There are so many wonderful places to spend your time and money. Begoa's Point is a thing of the past.

Her heart shattered. She hadn't expected anything promising, but the childhood memories she'd had when they were a functioning family had started and ended at Begoa's. Surely there had to be a part he'd missed.

She had home videos of herself sitting on her father's lap at the campfire. She'd seared her marshmallow into a charred, sticky mess and cried. He had wiped her tears and given her his perfectly roasted, golden brown marshmallow and her tears had dried. That was what good fathers did. They sacrificed the big things *and* the little things for their child. That was the thing. He had been a good father — right up until the time Lyla had started making decisions for herself. When she'd found a voice, when she'd started choosing paths differently than he would have chosen, their relationship had smoldered out like a candle at the end of its wick for a few years. Her teen years had proved difficult, and though they had gotten along in her adult years, she remembered well the days when their opinions had differed so greatly.

That and his complete dismissal of the idea of returning to Begoa's Point only reinforced everything Weston had said. Her father was willing to go endless lengths to keep her away from the place she loved the most in the world, no matter how much pain it caused her.

Lyla stopped at the general store on the way home from Sheila's office to pick up a few things to have with dinner and the makings for s'mores for dessert, since with Weston around they'd finally have a proper campfire that lasted longer than twenty minutes. She just couldn't get the hang of it.

"Lyla!" a familiar, spirited voice called. She turned to find Dotty, the general store cashier, hustling toward her. Dotty loved working the register, where she could chat too long with every customer and trade licorice straws for the latest gossip, but she also did all the other jobs for the store too — management, scheduling, inventory and book balancing. She was a regular jack of all trades. "Lookin' as lovely as ever, my dear!"

Dotty wrapped Lyla in her arms, squeezing her tight and shaking her from side to side. Dotty's perfume floated off her body and invaded Lyla's nose and lungs, making her cough. The entire general store smelled like

Dotty. The scent was immortal. In fact, everyone always knew where Dotty had been, because her robust floral perfume always lingered. It was her own personal 'Dotty Was Here' signature, left at every location.

"It's just so nice to see you around here again."

"Hi, Dotty." Lyla wiggled free. "I know. This is the third time I've seen you this week after, what? Gosh, fifteen years or so?"

"Oh, that can't be, deary," Dotty said, leaning forward to look in the mirror on the jewelry counter. "I'm only thirty, after all." She let out a high-pitched, screeching laugh and shuffled back to her post at the register.

"How's Weston? Other than handsome and rugged and chiseled and — well, you know!"

Lyla blushed and walked around the counter, grabbing the things she needed as she talked to Dotty.

"He's doing well." Lyla tactfully avoided agreeing with everything Dotty had said. It was all true and hard not to notice, but she had trouble admitting how much attraction was still there. "He's done a great job with this place. Just the same as before." Lyla placed the items on the counter and pulled out her wallet.

"Oh, sweetie, it's better." Dotty was right. The place, if possible, was even better than before.

"Can I tell you a secret?" she asked, though she was going to tell Lyla what was on her mind whether Lyla wanted to hear it or not. She wouldn't be Dotty if she didn't. "He wasn't happy. A few months back, he didn't smile. He didn't laugh. He was an echo of who he used to be. Even with the plans for the grounds to reopen coming together, it was like something was always missing. He's happy now. He smiles. And don't think the timing of it has been lost on us. We're old but we're not senile. You've got that boy smilin' again."

Lyla warmed at Dotty's words. The notion that she was changing him the way he was changing her was a sweet revelation. But something inside Lyla was preventing her from letting him in again.

"He's a great man, Dotty. Different than he used to be but so, so much the same. But—"

"Oh, sweets, there's a but?" Dotty squealed. "I don't believe it."

"I just... All those years ago, he hurt me. I thought I had meant more to him. But if I meant anything at all, how could he just break my heart like that while he moved on without a second thought of it?" Dotty looked at Lyla in a way she never had before. It was difficult to put a finger on it, to identify the emotion. *Disappointment, maybe?*

"Oh, heavens, dear." Dottie finally scanned and bagged the items Lyla was purchasing. "There wasn't anyone more broken than Weston Accardi. It was true then and it's true now."

Dotty handed Lyla the bag and directed her attention to a new customer entering the store.

"And, Lyla?" she called. Lyla turned in the doorway to face Dotty once more. "He never moved on."

Chapter Fifteen

Weston

Weston carried the steaks on ice in a small cooler as he walked toward Lyla's campsite, Achilles following at his heels. Camden sat at the picnic table, flipping through the Begoa's Point activity book.

"You are your mother's child." Weston placed the cooler on the table. "She couldn't get enough of the competition here."

Camden smiled and put the brochure aside. "It's so cool that you knew her as a kid. Were you two always friends at Begoa's?"

"No." Weston answered too quickly, with a short laugh that came out more like a scoff. "Definitely not. She wasn't my biggest fan at first." Weston thought back to the first summer Lyla had finally given him the time of day.

The sun hadn't peeked through the clouds in days. It was the rainiest summer on record and the kids were getting restless following the indoor activity schedule instead of the usual outdoor competitions. The forecast called for morning rain, but it was a clear afternoon, so the activities coordinator made the call to hold the three-on-three basketball game in its usual spot.

As fate would have it, Weston, Charlie and Lyla were placed on a team. As always, the other team was composed of three boys, leaving Lyla as the only girl. It was clear that they all had a buildup of energy, a result of being cooped up for the whole week prior. The boys played a bit too aggressively for a pick-up basketball game, but Lyla didn't complain. She just adjusted her game to match theirs.

Lyla was flying over the court, twisting and turning to dribble around guys twice her size. Charlie and Weston passed her the ball frequently, even when they had an open lane. She was having the game of her Begoa's Point career and they let her. Lyla put up another basket, the point that effectively put the nail in the coffin for the other team. As they reset for the next play, Lyla high-fived Weston and Charlie — a first for them, as they usually exchanged eye rolls and light vocal jesting.

They set up at the top of the free-throw key and a light rain started to fall. Thunder sounded through the sky not too long after the rainfall.

"All right, all right," the counselor said, "next basket wins."

"How's that fair?" Weston refuted. "We're up by nine."

"Why don't you go cry to your dad about it?" a boy from the other team teased. Weston clenched his teeth. "I mean, talk about unfair. The owner's son gets to compete in these events? And don't think we haven't noticed the calls always seem to go your way."

Weston moved toward the other team with his hands in white-knuckled fists. Then a hand was on his wrist, and a sudden calm coursed through his veins. He turned to find Lyla with her fingers wrapped around his lower arm. All she did was shake her head in a soft but steadfast 'no', and he listened.

"Let's just play." Weston took the ball from the counselor.

"Pretty bold of you to be wearing that 'Camp Champ' T-shirt, Weston," the boy continued to press. "Was it just handed to you? Everything else is."

Weston dribbled the ball, knowing the best revenge would be sinking the final shot and ending the game.

Lyla clapped her hands together, asking for the ball, but suddenly Weston changed the game from three-on-three to one-on-one — just him and the loud-mouthed kid from the other team. Lyla stood with her hands on her hips and rolled her eyes as Weston went in for the final lay-up. He took one step then the other, and his feet came off the ground. The other boy stepped forward hard and fast, lifting his elbow, which connected with Weston's jaw with a nauseating crack.

Weston fell backward, sprawled out on the blacktop with blood streaming from his nose. The clouds opened up and the rain fell hard, puddles forming on the court where Weston lay. Lyla and Charlie ran to him and helped him as the counselor took the other boy away from Weston and to the picnic table benches beside the court.

"I'm going to give his dad a head's up." Charlie jogged down the beach.

"I'll get ice," Lyla added, heading toward the restaurant closest to the courts. She ran back only moments later with ice in one hand, paper towels in the other and took a seat next to him. "Here." She placed the bag gently on his face and used a wet cloth to clean the area around his nose and mouth. Weston reached to place his hand on hers.

"Why are you doing this?" he asked.

"The truth?" Her voice raised a bit at the end. Weston tried and failed to nod into the ice bag. He thought – hoped – that maybe, just maybe, she'd admit she had noticed him all these years too, that she was just as nervous to converse with him as he had been to talk to her. That wasn't the case.

"I just don't want you to get blood on that shirt that is rightfully mine."

She let go of the ice pack, he took over and she went back to the court, ignoring the rain that streamed over her.

"I'll tell you what." Weston abandoned the ice pack and joined her at center court. Lyla turned to look at him, awaiting his proposal. He grabbed the hem of the T-shirt and pulled it over his head. "I'll play you for it."

"You're feeling up to that?"

He nodded. He had wasted so many years being too nervous to talk to her – sharing the campground but never any one-on-one time – so he didn't plan to let any more moments pass by. He touched one finger to his nose then the other, then shifted both arms straight out, stepping on the white painted lines like a tight-rope walker. Weston turned over his shoulder and looked toward her. "See? I'm fine."

"Okay." Lyla said, going to the small tent near the courts. She set the timer. "I'm in."

They played a ten-minute half-court match, keeping pace with each other. He didn't take it easy on her, and she didn't want him to. The rain got angrier, pouring in sheets over the basketball court. Weston dribbled to the left, and as Lyla went to move with him, she slid on the wet surface. Weston shot his hand forward, grabbing her bicep and steadying her before her slip became a full fall. She swallowed hard, his face inches from her own, then she reached forward and stole the ball. She dribbled but he stayed close, blocking any obvious route to the net. The game was tied.

"Twelve…eleven…" he said with a hint of a smile.

"Very funny." *She picked up the ball.* *"I'm not falling for that again."* *Her eyes danced over to the clock, realizing he was being honest this time. She stood at center court, too far to shoot, and she had already picked up her dribble.*

"Five." *He stepped toward her, the rain and the ball the only two things between them.* *"Four, three, two."* *He inched closer. She dropped the ball at her feet, letting it roll away.*

"One." *He leaned in, placing his lips on hers – and she kissed him back.*

"Where is your mom anyway?" Weston unpacked the cooler.

"General store." Camden reached forward to scratch Achilles' ears.

"She should be right along then. Want to help me season these?"

As always, it didn't take much to get Camden excited about something. To him, the little things really were the big things. He was gracious and thankful, always appreciative.

"How'd you learn all this stuff?" Camden asked, watching Weston prepare the meat. "The best way to build a campfire and how to cook on the grill and all the other things you're good at?"

Weston handed Camden a shaker full of spices, and Camden did exactly as he had seen Weston do.

"I watched my dad, mostly." Camden's eyes and mouth turn downward as soon as he said the words. Weston wasn't sure what the right words were in that second, but he took a chance. "He died a few years back, though."

Camden's eyes returned to their usual brightness. It wasn't that hearing of Weston's dad's death was anything to smile about, but Weston could see it in the boy's eyes. It was something else they had in common. *Someone else who might understand, even fractionally, how hard it is to wade the confusing waters of grief.*

"I was adopted," Weston spoke as he showed Camden how to do the next seasoning. "My parents were older when they adopted me...already in their fifties. But they never had kids and they were at this campground providing these wonderful amenities to all these families. So they decided they had room in their lives and in their cabin to give a kid a great life — and they did."

"And your mother?" Camden asked.

"Oh, she lives in a retirement community in Texas. She loves it there. She's very happy."

Camden and Weston stood at the table, preparing the meat and starting the grill. Weston allowed Camden to take the lead anywhere it was safe to do so. Camden followed directions and eagerly accepted each task.

"How's it going?" Lyla entered the campsite with bags in hand. Camden ran to her and took the bags without being asked.

"He's a good kid." Weston scraped the grill with a metal brush and closed the top once more. "Hungry?"

Lyla nodded and sat down at the picnic table. There was quiet for a moment, though it was clear they each still had a million questions but probably weren't sure where to start.

"So" — Weston adjusted the temperature on the grill — "what made you decide on teaching?"

"Charlie, believe it or not."

Weston shifted his full attention to her.

"That last summer, we were talking about our plans for the next year, and I was up in the air about what I wanted to do. He said I'd make a brilliant teacher. It stuck. How about you? Did you go to college at all?"

"No." He shook his head. "They couldn't teach me what I needed to learn at the time."

"What was that?"

"Mostly how to walk again." Weston fell into a hard silence, the world around them pausing for a moment. Lyla faded into the stillness for a few seconds.

"Right, sorry about that." She changed the subject. "After that? You never got married? Thought about having kids? Anything?"

Weston took a seat next to her.

"No. Even if I had found someone I could see spending the rest of my life with, I never really wanted kids."

Weston could tell by the pained expression on Lyla's face that that answer was not the right one. In his head it hadn't sounded as bad as it had once he'd said it. *Add it to the lengthy list of things I wish I could take back.* She didn't say anything as she pushed herself away from the picnic table.

Lyla headed inside the cabin to take care of the sides while Weston and Camden grilled the steaks. Achilles lay by the grill, hoping they'd drop something he could have for a snack.

"Was he missing a paw when you got him?" Camden looked at Achilles' back leg.

"Yes." Weston peeked under the grill top then closed it again. "I heard about him and I knew he was the dog for me."

"And your leg?"

Weston was sure Camden had been dying to ask that question since day one.

"That's a story for another day," Weston said. "Why don't you go ahead and set the table for your mom?"

Camden laid out plates and silverware for three settings, followed by the salt and pepper, napkins, cups and condiments. "What's next?" he asked. Weston looked around.

"You want to be in charge of the fire tonight?"

Camden nodded and ran to the back of the cabin, obtaining a few pieces to start the tepee.

"Remember...lots of space for air."

"Smells delicious." Lyla rejoined them outside, carrying a salad and a tray of baked potatoes.

Dinner came together well, the salad and potatoes a perfect complement to the expertly cooked steaks and corn on the cob off the grill.

"Thank you." Camden spoke through bites of food. "I thought I'd go the whole summer without grilled food."

Weston and Lyla laughed. Achilles sat beside them attentively, waiting for his owner to pick off some scraps to feed him under the table, even though he'd polished off an entire steak in record time.

As the sun faded and left the sky a brightly speckled black, Lyla relaxed in a chair while Weston and Camden cleared the table.

"What can I do?" Lyla leaned forward to offer.

"Nothing at all." Weston wondered when the last time had been that Lyla had gotten to sit and relax while someone took care of her. His guess? It'd probably been years.

Weston helped Camden light a fire under the tepee they had created. A thick blanket lay on the dirt driveway where Camden had an array of chocolate, peanut butter cups, graham crackers and marshmallows. He laid on his stomach, facing the fire, holding a marshmallow over the flame. Lyla moved to sit on the back corner of the blanket, away from the heat.

Her hair fell from the loose bun it was tied in, and a large, faded Begoa's Point sweatshirt hung over her shoulders. The light from the dancing fire flickered in her eyes, and Weston knew in that moment, a simple, insignificant second, that he'd never stopped loving her.

The fireflies floated around, lighting the area with twinkling lights, as if the stars had fallen from the sky and joined them in their sacred space. Before too long, Camden fell asleep on the blanket with his head on his mother's lap.

"I'll have to wake him. I can't carry him inside like I used to." Lyla shifted slowly, Camden adjusting his position but not waking.

"I can do it." Weston stood from his camping chair and walked toward the blanket. He kneeled, artificial leg forward, and rolled Camden into his arms, fireman-carry style. He stood and turned to the cabin. "Where am I taking him?"

"The room to the... Your old room." Lyla pointed to the right side of the cabin, her voice softening.

Weston carried Camden into the cabin and laid him on the bed. He remembered the days when all the sun, activities and fun had drained him into an unconsciousness that allowed a sleep like no other.

He closed the door and looked around the cabin. This was the place he'd grown up. This was the place where the dream he was living in today had all started. He ran his fingers down the corner where the wall was marked with his height measurements from the beginning of every summer.

He hovered his hand over the light switch, taking in one long last look before flicking off the lights.

"He's a heavy sleeper," Weston said as he walked back toward the campfire.

"He's just heavy." Lyla giggled. "Not in a bad way. He's just not a kid anymore. It goes by fast. One minute you're carrying them around in one arm and the next you can't carry them to their bed anymore."

Weston pulled a small, portable speaker from the outer pocket of the cooler and an iPod from his pocket.

"An iPod?" Lyla gasped dramatically and placed a hand to her chest for emphasis. "I don't know whether to be surprised or impressed."

"I can't just very well carry around hundreds of vinyl records or cassettes or CDs now, can I?" He grinned and started the music.

"You could opt to listen to some music that, ya know, existed sometime after the year we were born."

He selected a song and the soft beat echoed from the speakers.

Just Another Day by John Secada crooned through the speaker. Lyla cocked her head to one side.

"I take it back." She pulled her knees in and wrapped her arms around herself. "This is from the nineties. Totally more modern than the rest of the stuff you listen to."

"I can't say I've ever been accused of being modern before." Weston's mouth hitched into a sarcastic smile.

"I promise it is unlikely to ever happen again. You know no one uses iPods anymore, right?" Lyla laughed. It was clear she was amusing herself with the grief she was giving him, and he allowed it. It made him happy to see her laugh, even if it was at his expense.

Weston went to the back of the cabin to collect more wood. He placed the pieces at the side of the fire pit.

Whitney Houston's *I Want To Dance With Somebody* played next, and before the words even began Lyla was on her feet in a dance Weston hadn't expected.

She stopped for a moment, her cheeks flushing.

"I have no idea what just came over me." She chuckled at herself, then more followed until she was in a fit of giggles where breath seemingly didn't come easy and tears threatened to spill from her eyes. "You know, I haven't been the best version of myself for a while. And just being here under this sky on these grounds, I feel like some of those frayed threads are spinning themselves back to where they used to be, pulling me together little by little."

"I totally get it." Weston walked toward her. "Like you just can't be unhappy here, no matter how much you try."

"I just feel like a kid again." She bit her lip and, without a care in the world, no matter who was watching, broke into her wild dance once more.

"Dance with me, West," she yelled over the music, and he did. He had to. He was like a moth to the flame when it came to her. He moved alongside Savvy and the dancing fire.

As Whitney's voice turned to George Michael's and George's sound morphed into Bryan Adams', Weston placed his hands at Lyla's waist, and she moved in close to him, wrapping her arms at the back of his neck. They swayed from side to side, and he leaned his forehead into hers. She looked up at him with eyes like portals into her innermost thoughts.

Weston thought back to the day on the basketball court where they'd shared their first kiss, and his mind continued to travel. He had kissed her at almost every spot on these grounds during that summer of their seventeenth year. The marina, the basketball courts, the beach and the clearing, but mostly right here at this cabin. As he considered the possibility of placing his lips on hers, of reigniting a fire that had burned out long ago, she stepped back a bit.

"We're losing our flame," she whispered, and, for a moment, Weston wondered how she was reading his every thought. He glanced to the fire pit, where the remaining embers were begging for replenishment.

"I've got it." Lyla leaned forward and grabbed a few logs from the pile, plunging them into the waning flames.

"You never would have done that all those years ago." Weston watched as Lyla effortlessly rebuilt their fire as if flames were never anything to shy away from at all.

She stood up, watching as the fire absorbed the newly placed logs. "I'm not that girl anymore, West. Sometimes you just have to face your fears. I'm not afraid anymore."

"Of the fire?" Weston moved in close to her, wrapping an arm around her lower back.

"Of anything." She turned into him and placed her lips against his. The world spun around them, and the heat from the flames seemed warmer than it had only seconds prior. The stars shone a bit brighter and lightning bugs flickered around them like a silent fireworks show, perhaps intended only for them.

Chapter Sixteen

Lyla

News of Lyla and Weston's newly rekindled relationship didn't take long to travel through Begoa's Point's staff and even campers who had heard their story. Surely, Dotty was telling each person who checked out at the general store how they had experienced an epic love that spanned over multiple summers and now had found their way back to each other.

She and Camden spent time throwing the ball with Achilles and jumping off the docks, swimming around the lake while Weston attended his daytime meetings and tended to things that needed his attention.

As they walked down the beach, sand sticking to their wet feet and legs, Sheila approached her.

"Miss... Mrs... Umm...Lyla?" She stumbled over what would be the appropriate name to address her.

"Lyla is fine," she said, Camden running ahead, chasing after Achilles. Sheila looked out of place with her too-formal attire on the beach. While every other staff member wore green polos or T-shirts and khaki shorts, Sheila would always be seen in a skirted business suit.

"You had a phone message at the welcome center."

Lyla's eyebrows lifted, giving her surprised eyes room to expand. "Me? You're sure?"

"Yes." She handed over a slip of paper with a handwritten message on it. "Come by anytime if you want to use the phone."

"Thank you so much, Sheila." Sheila walked away, and Lyla turned the paper over in her hands. Confusion clouded her thoughts as she read the handwritten digits. She knew the number right away. It belonged to her dad.

Camden and Achilles rejoined her and they all walked down the beach toward the picnic area where they'd planned to meet Weston for a barbecue hosted by the campground.

The area smelled of charcoal, barbecue sauce, smoked meats and an array of other scents that made it impossible for anyone to walk by without stopping for lunch on the beach.

Lyla ordered a half-rack of ribs and a small chicken breast. Camden opted for a burger and fries. They split sides of macaroni and cheese and mashed potatoes. The potatoes were always among Lyla's favorite part of the whole trip. It was a food she'd craved over the years, her favorite, second only to Weston's open-flame coffee.

Camden and Lyla sat at a picnic table, shade on his side, sun on hers, just the way they liked it. A DJ was set up at the perimeter of the picnic area, leading campers through group line dances. The campers danced and laughed on the beach while the music played. People at the picnic tables clapped and sang along as they ate.

The DJ pulled out a limbo stick, and Camden ran off, his mouth still full of food.

Achilles looked up at Lyla and put one paw up on the edge of the table. Lyla pulled a small piece of chicken from the breast on her plate and fed it to the dog.

"Shhh, don't tell your dad." She laughed and turned her attention to the beach where Camden was leaned all the way backward, trying to limbo under a very low pole. He fell and a cloud of sand rose around him. The onlookers 'awwwed' in unison, but he hopped back to his feet, running to the lake to rinse off.

"Hey there, beautiful, is this seat taken?" Weston said as he approached the table. She moved over, making room, and he swung a leg over the bench, kissing her forehead as he took his place.

"How'd the meeting go?" she asked. "What's the next big plan for Begoa's Point?"

"You want to see?"

Her eyes lit up as she nodded an enthusiastic yes.

Weston reached into his side pocket, pulled out rolled up papers and smoothed them on the table in front of her.

"This" — he pointed to the main area of land where most of the Begoa's Point's accommodations and amenities were located — "is obviously where we already own and operate. "But here" — Weston moved his finger to a blank area covered only by tiny drawn trees on the map — "is what we are trying to acquire."

"For?" Lyla followed the trail his finger made.

Weston moved the map to the back of the packet, revealing a new page with a bulleted list.

"Indoor sports complex, dog park, pools, splash pad," Lyla read out loud. "This is what you want to put in that space? Which one?" she asked, looking away from the list and back to him.

"All of them." There was a sureness to his voice that suggested he could see the vision that she couldn't.

"Why?" She was less impressed than it was clear he'd thought she'd be.

"I want this place to have something for everyone. People leave comments throughout their stay here, and I read every single one of them. These are the kinds of things people are asking for."

"Too much of a good thing can be bad, though, you know?" She took on the role of devil's advocate. "It's going so well exactly the way it is. Why change now?"

"Everything has to grow, Savvy. We have to keep up with what everyone else is doing. If we don't, campers will find somewhere else to go that can keep up with this modern lifestyle."

"What's next? WiFi?" Lyla flipped the page over.

Weston swallowed audibly and looked away.

"You're kidding me." Her smile turned to a deep frown.

"We just have to stay competitive." He placed a hand on her sun warmed shoulder.

"You sound like your father." She pushed her plate forward. "This place is exactly perfect how it's running now. People appreciate not being tethered to their devices and getting a break from the speed of the real world."

"They don't, Savvy. Trust me. We do, but most of these people don't have jobs that let them have an entire summer off the way you do. Most people only come for weekends or a few weeks at a time. Some just Saturday to Saturday. More people could stick around if they could do their work from here. In our current state, that's not an option."

"Okay, so, what's the problem?" She wanted to know more but she still disagreed.

"Finances mostly." Weston scratched his head. "I don't have the capital to move forward with any of this on my own, so Sheila has planned meetings coming up with backers and investors who have shown interest in coming aboard and expanding Begoa's Point."

Lyla's expression changed from a frown to a flat grimace.

"What?" Weston moved a loose curl from her face.

"I just want this place to still be yours when all this is said and done."

Weston smiled and dropped his hand to her thigh. "It will be."

The business side of Weston was both disappointing and completely captivating. Though she didn't agree with his plans, in a way, she loved to watch him work — to see his dedication come through in the words he said and see how wholeheartedly he defended his ideas and ideals.

"It's your world," Lyla said. "We just rent here."

He laced his fingers into hers, and she leaned her head onto his shoulder.

"Did Sheila find you?" he asked. "There was a message for you at the welcome center."

"Yes. It was my dad. I had emailed him and invited him to come, but —"

"You *what*?" Weston's voice hardened to a growl. He shifted from her, pulling away from where her head rested at his shoulder.

"I asked him to come here—you know, like we used to. Look... I know you and my father didn't see eye-to-eye, but I didn't think that would be a problem. Everything is so different now."

"No, Savvy." Weston stood from the bench and backed away from the table. "Almost everything is different now—but not that. You shouldn't have done that."

"He's not even coming, West," she pleaded. "He said no. So why does it matter?"

"It just does." Weston shook his head and turned on his heel, leaving the picnic table and taking his dog and all his secrets with him.

* * * *

Lyla and Camden spent the afternoon eating ice cream and fried dough at the snack bar and trying on new Begoa's Point gear at the general store. Lyla found a long-sleeved shirt that she had to have, and Camden found a baseball cap just like Weston's.

"Hey, Mom?" Camden asked as she tried on a new zip-up sweatshirt and looked in the mirror. "Can we do this one day?" He handed her the price list for speedboat rentals. Her throat dried and her palms sweat against the edge of the papers.

"Maybe someday." She couldn't keep her son off the water forever. It wasn't fair for her to hold him back because of her own memories of that fateful night during her and Weston's seventeenth summer, but the idea of renting a boat with her son—the most important person in her entire life? Well, she wasn't quite that healed yet.

Camden returned the flyer to its holder and looked through some more garb. "Where has Weston been?"

"Wish I knew," Lyla whispered. She settled on the long-sleeved T-shirt for herself and a T-shirt and hat for Camden.

As the sun went down and the weather cooled to a tolerable temperature, Camden took off to an evening movie on the beach with his new friends, and Lyla laced up her sneakers for a twilight jog.

She placed her headphones in her ears and took off down the main road. She jogged through the main square and onto the beach, kicking up sand behind her as her feet carried her forward. She slipped off her socks and sneakers and held them in her fingers, wading through the shallowest portion of the lake's edge. The water rippled around her ankles as she walked toward the end of her chosen path.

Leaving the water, she trekked through the sand and ended up at the basketball court. She took a seat at center court, lying backward so her shoulder blades and head met the blacktop. The sky was in the gray area now, not the bright blue that hovered above the campers as they enjoyed their beach day but not the dark black that backdropped the night's campfires either. It was just a hazy type of outro that ended the day and invited the night to take its place.

The rain soaked through her T-shirt and shorts, saturating her hair, weighing her curls down in a straight mess around her shoulders. He moved his hand to the nape of her neck, holding her closer to him, as if that were possible.

She placed her hands at his back, the rain rushing down his bare shoulders and dripping down his torso.

She had thought about her first kiss so many times – how it would be, who it would be with – but none of the scenarios she'd imagined compared to this. This was the real thing, the thing the storybooks told about and movies portrayed. But it wasn't a book and it wasn't a movie. It was her fairytale coming to life at her favorite place on Earth.

Even the rain couldn't ruin this moment. It was perfect in every way.

"Lyla Joyce Savoie." She heard an angry voice say, cutting short the happily ever after. Her father stood at the edge of the basketball court, an umbrella protecting him from the downpour and leaving his reddened, irate expression clear to see.

Lyla stepped away from Weston, realizing how that moment must've looked to her father. She started to stammer an apology, but he didn't want to hear it.

"You're going to the site with me. Now." Her dad left no room for ifs or buts in the command. Lyla obeyed, walking slowly off the court, turning one last time to take a look at the boy who gave her life an exciting twist, and even though her dad's grip on her arm was borderline intolerable, even though he probably wouldn't speak to her for a week, she smiled at Weston, and he winked in response.

The next day she walked outside to find her father drinking coffee on the deck.

"You said you were going to the basketball game then returning for dinner," her father said. "When you didn't return, I came to look for you. Can't say I'm too pleased about what I found."

Lyla shoved her hands in the pockets of her jean shorts and rocked onto the balls of her feet, focused on the spacing between the deck boards so she didn't have to see the

disappointment in his eyes — mostly because she wasn't
sorry. Not even close.

"Do you know what people say about that boy and his
friend?" Her father leaned forward and wagged a finger at
her. "It's not good. They're trouble, those boys, and they're
going to take you down with them."

"You don't know them," she said, talking back to her
father for the first time in all her years.

"Neither do you. But you won't get a chance to. I won't
allow it."

Tears pressed at her eyes and anger burned in her throat.
He couldn't keep them apart and he wouldn't. But just then
something else caught her attention, something that spoke to
her louder than her father did. Weston's 'Camp Champ' shirt
hung on the clothing line.

"I figured I'd find you here." Weston took a seat next
to her at center court, lying down so his head was by
hers and their feet pointed in opposite directions.

"I didn't know you were looking." She turned to lie
on her side and propped herself up on her elbow.

"I'm sorry about earlier. I think I've changed, for the
better, quite a bit. But, I don't know... Hearing you talk
about your dad coming here just sent me right back to
my old ways and short temper. He hates me, Savvy.
And all this...me and you...Begoa's Point reopening...
It's all new. I just don't want any negativity getting in
the way of everything I've worked so hard for —
everything *we've* worked so hard for."

"I know." Her eyes were soft and sympathetic. "I
wanted to tell you why, but you walked away. I invited
him after you told me that he was the one who got in
the way of me seeing you again. When he rejected the
offer like Begoa's Point never meant anything to him at

all, it solidified the fact that he had a great deal to do with keeping us apart."

"So…you couldn't just take my word for it?" A hurt set in behind Weston's eyes. "You didn't trust me?"

"West." Lyla leaned forward and placed her hand on his chest. "I didn't know what to believe then. I spent all these years thinking you never came for me because that's what it looked like. When you returned to my life with all this new information, I was overwhelmed. One day with you didn't change my mind about all the years that had passed. But these few weeks with you? They've changed everything. I know now that you told me the truth. You always did."

Weston turned on his side, his position matching hers.

"Look at us." She ran her hand lightly down his bicep. "He's not even here and he's ruining us. Can we please just put all this behind us? Put his interference behind us?"

Weston nodded and leaned forward, his lips touching hers, sealing the definitive yes with a kiss.

"I need to get back." She rolled up to a seated position. "The movie is about to end, and Camden will be at the site."

"I'll go with you." Weston stood, taking her hands and pulling her into a standing position. Weston started walking along the sand as Lyla slid her sneakers on and ran forward, jumping onto Weston. He stumbled for a second but regained his balance and grabbed underneath her thighs. Their childlike laughter echoed in the air as he carried her down the beach, two people leaving only one set of footprints that led exactly down the same path.

Lyla slid down Weston's back and placed her feet on solid ground as they crossed the main road toward her cabin. She stole his baseball cap from his head and put it on. He shook his head and took her hand in his, continuing along the dirt road toward the site.

As they turned the corner, West stopped in his tracks like something was preventing him from moving forward.

"Lyla." It was a familiar voice. Lyla snapped her head toward the porch. "Mr. Accardi," her father added, standing from his chair.

Weston didn't say a word.

Chapter Seventeen

Weston

Mr. Savoie had ruined Weston's life in more ways than one all those years ago. He had thought about it every day since. Yet here Jack was, on his property, ready to throw his incessant judgement around like confetti.

Weston walked back to Site 101 the next morning, irritation fueling his speed. He stepped up onto the deck where Mr. Savoie was sipping a steaming cup of coffee.

"She's not here." He placed the cup on the picnic table. "She took a walk with Camden to the store to pick up a few things."

"Good." Weston's eyes narrowed into a glare. "Then I don't have to pretend to be cordial."

"I wouldn't expect anything less." Mr. Savoie looked at Weston over the rim of his glasses. "It's not like you to put your best foot forward." The insult wasn't lost on Weston. He dug his fingers into the handrail of the steps outside.

"Your accommodations will be ready by this afternoon." Weston reached deep into himself to find and pull out anything that resembled a respectful owner's voice.

"I planned to stay here with Lyla and Camden."

"That's not going to happen," Weston snapped.

"I was under the impression there was a waitlist, but suddenly, there's availability?"

Every word Mr. Savoie spoke pushed Weston further toward his breaking point. *You are not the person you used to be*, Weston reminded himself.

"There is. A lengthy one. But, sir, I would build a cabin from the ground up with nothing but my bare hands before I let you stay one more night in my father's house. And before you try to insult me again, yes, I am putting my foot down on this one."

Mr. Savoie grinned, his mouth twisting into a confident smirk.

* * * *

Lyla sat on the beach in a chair watching as Camden played at the water's edge. Her bronze skin glistened in the rays. Weston approached her, two root beer floats in his hands.

He placed one against the back of her neck. She scrunched her shoulders and leaned forward, goosebumps covering her flawless skin. She turned to look up at him, and he stood over her, casting a shadow where there once was light.

"Well, hello to you too." She rested her back against the chair again. Weston handed the drink over. "Thank you. You're an angel." She took a sip as Weston plopped down into the empty chair beside her.

"I'm not so sure everyone would agree with that. Quite possibly the opposite, in fact."

"I'm just as surprised as you are." She put one hand on his knee — or, where his true knee would be if it still existed. "Honest... I didn't know he was coming."

"Did he say why he came?" Weston sulked into the chair, letting the sun warm his face.

"I guess he just had a change of heart. He was against it at first, but he thought about it and wanted to come to build some of the memories he had with me with his grandson. He said he didn't want to miss out on spending a summer with his grandchild or his daughter."

"A heads-up would've been nice." Weston slurped his float, crushing the cup under his fingers in a pressure he didn't realize he was applying.

"Well, that's why he called here. He called to say he was flying in. I didn't call back, so it's my fault, I guess."

"So even after everything, you're just going to hang out with him and put on a happy face?" Weston put little, if any, effort into hiding his disdain.

"He's my dad, West. What am I supposed to do? I plan on talking to him and telling him how I feel about what he did, but I'm hoping we can just fix that road and move on."

As if on cue, Lyla's father approached with a beach chair in hand, heading their direction.

"Anyway, I have to go. I have a meeting with Sheila to discuss the proposal for the upcoming meeting with the investors."

"Super convenient timing, West." Lyla hissed. Weston kissed her on the forehead and took off down the beach.

* * * *

"Good afternoon, Sheila." Weston waltzed into her office and took a seat in a chair across from her desk.

"How's everything going, Weston?" She perched onto the desk.

"You tell me. How is everything coming along with potential investors?"

Sheila's face contorted into an expression that made Weston's stomach drop. It wasn't a promising look.

"There are some...concerns." She tip-toed around whatever issues were at hand.

He leaned forward, rubbing his finger and thumb at his chin. He waited for an answer, but she didn't offer one.

"Are you going to tell me what these concerns are, or am I supposed to start guessing?" Weston smiled as he spoke, trying to keep the atmosphere light. It was clear Sheila didn't want to be the bearer of bad news.

"This is serious, Weston." She tapped a pen on her clipboard, but she smiled too, succumbing to his playful nature.

"I know. I know. Just tell me. What's going on?"

Weston thought about every decision he'd ever made, all the way to his preteen years. The list was miles long, more bad than good, but which poor decision had he made in his past that was coming back to haunt him now? Which story attached to his name did the potential investors see as a threat to the success of this business venture?

The most obvious black mark, of course, was any of Weston's greatest hits featuring Charlie. From the moment they'd met to the moment that would haunt him for the rest of his life—the moment he'd died—they'd constantly been finding some way to cause trouble. Weston had hoped, with the long lapse in between closing the grounds and reopening them, that people would forget or at least understand that he wasn't the same kid he was then. Unfortunately, it seemed that it was true what they said—*a reputation is forever*.

"You see, Weston." Sheila laced her fingers together on the desk in front of her. "There has been a lot of concern about your marital status."

Weston raised an eyebrow. He wasn't expecting that—nor did he understand what it had to do with anything.

"The investors seem to think it will be hard for you to truly oversee a family campground when you don't come off as a family man at all." Sheila's eyes softened. "Every time they see you on the news for interviews or in the newspapers, it's just you. Anytime you're seen on the grounds—up until recently, of course—you were alone. You live in the most reclusive area of the grounds. You just don't give of the appearance of a 'family first' guy, which wouldn't be a problem if you were exclusively hosting bachelor parties. But you're not. You are the person in charge of keeping this place as the go-to campground for families across New England and farther. Yet, you don't have one of your own."

Weston turned his head one way then the other, a distinct crack sounding from his stiff neck.

"That's not really a problem I can come up with a quick solution for." He shrugged and rested back in the chair.

"We have a tour and a lunch here at the restaurant coming up with the group of investors we have our sights set on. I think you should invite Lyla and Camden—"

"Absolutely not." Weston stood from his chair as he dismissed the idea. "No way."

Sheila stood from her desk and walked to the front of it, leaning against the oak wood top. "What do you propose, then?"

"Just focus on showing them how happy families are here and how much they're enjoying everything we offer. Show them that we've been nothing but successful so far and my personal life hasn't impacted this place in a negative way." Weston placed both his hands on the back of his neck, let out a frustrated exhale and paced the floor in front of Sheila's office windows.

"This time. Your personal life hasn't impacted this place *this time*. But, Weston, people haven't forgotten your past. They haven't forgotten your involvement—"

"They need to get past that, and so do you." Weston shot the words like a bullet leaving the barrel, aimed perfectly at its intended target. *Maybe I should have changed my damn name when I purchased the property.*

"Okay." Sheila crossed her arms over her chest. "But I think you should at least consider asking Lyla and Camden to join us for lunch. I'm not asking you to propose to the woman at the investor lunch, Weston. It's just an appearance thing. Show them you have support in your corner. A united front with a beautiful woman and an adorable kid might just be the extra factor they're looking for."

Weston leaned against the wall nearest the door and nodded, understanding what she was saying but against her plan to include Lyla and Camden in anything to do with any business transaction, especially since Lyla was so against the expansion project in the first place.

* * * *

Mark Jenson stood in his usual place behind the lakeside bar, serving drinks to patrons who occupied the stools. Weston sat at one end of the square bar top by himself, listening to the live music being played during the day's happy hour festivities.

"Trouble in paradise?" Mark dipped a cup into the ice box to fill it then topped it off with water, Weston's drink of choice.

"It has been a complicated few days." Weston drank half the glass then placed it on the bar top harder than he'd meant to. Droplets of liquid splashed onto the wooden ledge.

"You might live at a vacation destination, Weston, but it's not always going to be a vacation…not for you." Mark tossed the white rag over his shoulder and leaned into the bar. "But you'll overcome the challenges as they present themselves. You always do."

"I'm not so sure about that." Weston slouched forward, his usual perfect posture bending under the pressures that seemed to be piling up.

"You forget that I was at the first meeting you called to present the idea of reopening this place."

Weston lifted his head.

"You said you had plans to reopen and half the room gasped in horror and the other half laughed."

"Every single person in that room snickered and sneered or discounted me before they even heard me out—everyone but one." Weston held up his index finger as he spoke, then pointed it at Mark.

"And look at us. We were right. This place is doing a world of good for everyone here. Those people who thought it couldn't be done? Their opinion never mattered before, and it certainly doesn't now. The only people who matter to me are the ones enjoying this gift that you have given them. You should be proud of that."

Weston nodded and sipped from his glass. Mark turned to tend to another group at the opposite end of the bar, and the screeching sound of stool legs versus cement pad sounded through the hut as someone took the seat next to Weston.

"Weston," he said as he offered a slight wave to get Mark's attention, even though he was clearly occupied with another group.

"Mr. Savoie." Weston suddenly wished he enjoyed anything stronger than water.

They sat in silence and stared ahead.

"Jack," Mark said as he approached their silent standoff. Mark's surprised expression floated to Weston's. "What can I get for you?"

Weston pushed his stool out as Mr. Savoie ordered, attempting to take the opportunity to depart.

"Sit down," Mr. Savoie said. Weston shifted his jaw with annoyance but he did as he was told.

"I didn't know you were the one who got this place up and running again, Weston."

Weston shifted his gaze to Mr. Savoie.

"I wouldn't have come if I'd known it was going to cause this many issues. That's the truth." Mr. Savoie looked at Weston, speaking to him in a tone fit for a conversation between two adults for the first time in all the years they had known each other. "My daughter asked me to come, and at first I was against it. This place? It just holds so many memories, both good and bad. It's where Lyla and I became the close, tight-knit, happy family we were then. It was a solution to so many of our problems, but it was also the cause of too many of them."

"And that's *my* fault?" Weston turned in the stool, facing Mr. Savoie to finally say the words he'd been wanting to get off his chest for so many years. "We were just kids, Mr. Savoie. You look at me and talk to me like I am the very worst kind of person. I know I hurt your daughter. I do. But you hurt her worse. You look down on me like we're so different. We're not that different."

"You're right, Weston." Jack lifted his drink and swirled its contents in the glass. "We are both to blame. I see that now. But the way my daughter is behaving — distant and retreating every time I try to speak to her — tells me that she knows I played a hand in that hurt you speak of. I'd imagine you had something to do with that?"

Weston turned his eyes away and wiped his brow with the back of his hand. "I told her I came looking for her and that I tried to contact her, but you wouldn't allow it," he admitted, staring into his now-empty glass.

"Nothing else?" Jack asked, his eyes returning to their straight-ahead gaze.

"No, sir. I didn't tell her the rest." Weston stepped off his stool again, prepared to make his exit. "But you should."

Chapter Eighteen

Lyla

Camden sat on the floor of the newer-style cabin Weston had assigned her father to and played a board game with some of the friends he had made. Jack had a chair reclined and a newspaper pressed to his face. The rigid atmosphere in the room was lost on Camden, who was under the impression that all was well and good, but Lyla and her dad had a hard time finding common ground to talk about. Lyla kept her nose shoved in the middle of a book, opened to a random page but apparently with no clue of what was going on in its text.

Camden jumped up from his spot on the floor. "Winner!" he yelled with his arms in the air.

"This is boring," one boy added. "Let's go get ice cream."

"Can we go, Mom?" Camden pulled the book away from Lyla's face. "Please?" Camden's lip folded over into a perfected pout — the kind he knew she couldn't say no to.

"One scoop." She held up a finger synonymous with her statement. "You haven't had dinner yet."

Camden ran to collect his hat and shoes as Lyla stepped out onto the porch, pulled a towel from the clothing line and folded it. She grabbed another and did the same, all the while wondering if she would talk first or if her father would finally give in and start a conversation, preferably with the words she was waiting for — a confession of his role in interfering with her past.

Lyla watched her father through a window as he scanned the newspaper. Her heart ached. He was so close but so far away. She was mad, but only carrying around half an argument. He might not even know why she'd been acting the way she had, but she hadn't mustered up the sliver of her that was confrontational to talk about the problem.

She missed her father, the way they used to be. She was sure he missed her too, only he wasn't good at showing it. She knew how he was. He couldn't be wrong. But she believed, deep down, he'd really thought he was doing what was best for her at the time. Lyla leaned into the railing. She looked at her father, remembering all the best things about him. Maybe she hadn't given him the benefit of the doubt before because she'd been thinking like a kid, but she was a parent now too. She could see it from his side in a different way than she had. It didn't make it okay, but it made it fractionally more understandable.

Camden ran through the door. His friends followed closely behind as they jumped down the stairs and ran off toward the snack bar, the screen slamming after them.

Lyla couldn't stand the divide between her and her father any longer. As she paced the deck, deciding what she would say through their involuntary alone time, he made the decision for her—the way he always did. He came out onto the deck, closing the door behind him. There was nowhere for her to go now.

"I'm going to hit a bucket of balls at the driving range." He replaced his bifocals with sunglasses. "You'll come with me."

It wasn't a question. The statement left no room for debate. It was the same way he used to act, always trying to control her—always tightrope-walking the line between being a caring father and an overbearing one. Just when she thought there might be a chance of him turning over a new leaf, he crushed it under his foot.

"I'd rather not." Lyla returned her attention to the towels on the line.

"We used to go to the driving range together all the time when you were a young girl." His voice softened. She couldn't resist wondering if the sudden calm in his words was sincere, a genuine attempt at revisiting who they used to be—or if it was manipulation disguised as reminiscing.

"I'm not a kid anymore, Dad."

He walked down the brand-new steps of the deck of his cabin. Without words, he hopped into the driver's side of the golf cart and started it up, its small engine rumbling to life. He remained in the driveway for a moment, not peeling out the way she thought he would.

"Why did you even invite me here?" His voice carried over the golf cart's purr and to her ears.

She shrugged.

"I didn't think you'd actually come," she answered, the honesty in her words hammering away at the tough exterior her father hid behind. He looked downward, staring at his hands in his lap. She walked down the steps of the deck and climbed into the passenger seat of the golf cart. He clicked the key, cutting off the engine and leaving a dead silence in its place. Lyla wished he hadn't. The quiet only amplified their awkward pauses. They hadn't always been like this. There was a time, before she was married, before she had a kid of her own, well prior to Begoa's closing or when she got tangled up in what her father called the 'wrong crowd'... There was a time they'd laughed together.

Her favorite night of the activity calendar had arrived. The campground held a dance on the beach with a DJ and bright lights where all the kids in her age group would go and dance the night away under a natural disco ball of endless stars.

About six hours remained before it was time to head to the dance. Her dad had her at the driving range, a once-per-week tradition for the two of them. They always made time between his eighteen-hole reservations and her incessant activities to spend this time together.

"Feet a little farther apart there, Ly." She rolled her eyes. "Not that far apart," he corrected. And she stomped her feet closer together. "Bend your knees!" He raised his voice as if he were coaching her at the sidelines of the Masters rather than a driving range. "Your hands, Lyla..."

She'd had enough. She flipped the club onto the green and stamped away from the lane they'd rented.

"Lyla!" Her dad followed her toward the door of the club house. "What is going on with you, young lady?"

"Nothing is ever good enough for you." Tears dripped from her long lashes. "No matter what I do, you just correct me."

"You're being dramatic." He narrowed his eyes, and his voice quieted. "I just know you can do better."

"Stop!" she yelled, her short fuse and misunderstood hormones mixing in an explosive combination. "Just stop. I'm never going to be a golfer, so why are we wasting our time?"

The words visibly hurt him. He apparently swallowed his sadness and took a step back. Neither of them knew that would be the last time they hit a bucket of balls together.

Lyla's day was saved when her friends finally arrived to get ready for the dance. On the campground, usual attire was limited to T-shirt and bathing suits. There was nothing fancy — not even for dinner at the restaurant with the water view. But the dance was different. They applied glitter to their eyelids and gloss to their lips. She and her campground girlfriends giggled as they crowded around a small mirror in an AC-less cabin, sweating off their makeup before anyone could see it.

They left the cabin with a goodbye, not pausing for the parental inspection they had felt they had long grown out of.

"Wait," her father demanded. She rolled her eyes — an action she had perfected over that summer. "Get a sweater."

"It's not supposed to be cold," she argued, her cheeks likely flushing as red as the thin-strapped tank top she was wearing that her father clearly disapproved of.

"Cover up or don't go. Those are the options." His face was stern. Lyla mumbled something under her breath and stomped away, grabbing a zip-up sweatshirt and throwing it over her shoulders.

"*I think I'll walk you there,*" *her dad added. It was the needle that popped the balloon of fun she and her friends were floating on. Their giggling turned to a cold silence as they walked the road to the dance. Lyla knew she was still in trouble from the kiss she and Weston had shared. She shouldn't complain about the sweater and the supervision. She was lucky to even be going to the dance at all.*

As the other girls ran forward, reaching the spot in front of the DJ and immediately breaking off, running toward the boys they'd each had their eye on for the summer, her dad kept a grip on her arm.

"*You just dance with your girlfriends. You don't need to be dancing with the boys here…any of them.*"

Over his shoulder, Lyla saw Weston approaching by the snack bar. His shaggy hair was pulled back under a backward cap. He leaned into the corner of the building and used his hand to imitate her father's lecture, his face contorting to a mocking expression.

She giggled, but as her father stopped his lecture to check out what had her attention, Weston stepped behind the wall like he had never been there at all.

"*Have fun,*" *her father said as he walked away. As soon as he was out of her sight, she slid her zip-up sweater off her shoulders.*

"*Come dance with me, Savvy.*" *Weston said as he slinked out from behind the snack-bar wall once Jack Savoie was out of sight.*

"*Didn't you just hear my dad?*" *she asked, embarrassed about saying that out loud as soon as the thought traveled from her brain to her mouth.*

"*I did.*" *Weston was confident, intrepid – all the things she craved to be more of. He took her hand in his and led her to the beach. "Do something daring, Savvy.*"

Her head was on a swivel, turned to see if her father was really absent or if he was waiting to find another reason to scold her.

"Hey," Weston said, "if you're going to keep looking over your shoulder, look over this one." He placed his finger on her jaw and turned her head toward him. He raised his lip at the corner, exposing a rogue grin she wanted to see more of.

"You knew how hard that summer was for me. I genuinely felt like my life was over. And I know you thought I was just being dramatic and that I didn't understand, but I was in the worst kind of pain. You could have told me he tried to call, you know. It might have made things a little easier." Lyla picked at a thread on her shorts. Even in the summers where she'd tiptoed the line between innocent and rebellious, she'd never questioned her father. Sure, he was hard on her, but she always thought that was just because he cared too much. That was how he showed his love for her, by keeping her protected under his thumb.

"It wouldn't have, Lyla. Nothing about anything that was happening at the time was easy—not to you, not to me. I tried to protect you. I tried to keep you close and keep you out of trouble."

"Do you ever think that was part of the problem?" she asked, her eyes finding his for the first time in a long while. Lyla looked at her father, so similar in appearance to who he used to be, but so different too. "I was timid as a kid. I didn't like fire because you taught me it burned. But you didn't teach me about the beauty of it or how to enjoy it. I didn't want to stray too far because you constantly reminded me about how much bad was in the world. But you never let me far enough away to discover how wonderful it could be.

Weston? He was like the fire, and this place was my world. I knew you saw the bad in him, the parts where I might end up hurt. But I saw everything else. The adventure. The possibility. The fearlessness. And I fell in love with being curious. In the end, I know you were right. Curiosity harmed a lot more people than it helped. But it might not have happened if you'd let me make my own mistakes rather than take charge of every aspect of my life."

"Don't pin that blame on me, Lyla. If you had respected my wishes, if you had stayed away from that group, you never would have been in that marina in the first place." His breaths shortened into quick huffs that caused his chest to rise and fall under his polo shirt.

"Hindsight is twenty-twenty. There are a lot of things I would've changed. And you were right about many of them. But being told not to be with Weston? That was half the attraction."

Her father swallowed hard and looked away from her, surely pushing back any further thoughts that would be unwelcome.

"But we can't go back, can we?" She placed her hand on his and squeezed tight. "We do have a chance to start over, though. All of us."

Her father nodded and looked around the circle Weston had assigned them—a newer addition to the campground. "He has done a superb job here, hasn't he?"

"He really has." Lyla's heart thawed. With the thoughts she had been carrying around all this time finally aired, her chest felt less heavy. "Hey, Dad?"

Jack's eyes met hers.

"How about we go hit that bucket of balls at the driving range?"

Chapter Nineteen

Weston

The air around Weston's site was crisp and clean, the way only a light, early morning rain could make it smell after washing away all the previous night's charcoal and ash aromas. He walked to the back of the RV, started the outdoor shower and removed his prosthetic as the water warmed. Once he stepped in, he allowed the steady stream of water to rush over him for a few moments, washed his hair and body then cut off the water supply. With a towel, he dried his right leg and the thigh and stump of his left leg before hopping into a pair of his usual khaki shorts and reattaching and adjusting the components of his artificial limb. It was a morning exactly like the rest, for the most part.

He turned the corner to see a beautiful brunette occupying his favorite chair, sipping a cup of coffee. He leaned into the RV wearing only his shorts and used the towel to shake the remaining water droplets from his hair.

"Well, that was for me." Weston laughed and moved toward the fire to start a new brew.

"Should have made extra." Lyla took another sip.

"I didn't know I was having company this morning."

"Are you complaining? Because I can go." Lyla adjusted her footing as if to stand to leave.

"Don't you dare." The command was quiet and playful.

Her eyes twinkled, and she pressed her teeth into her bottom lip.

"It used to be backward. You used to always tell me to being daring. Now you're telling me the opposite?"

He walked toward her, stopping at her chair to place both his hands on her collar bones, rubbing at the tense spots between her neck and shoulders.

"I don't know if you've noticed or not, but my daring side turned out to be my stupid side."

She nodded and handed over the coffee, sharing the cup until the next batch was ready.

"How're things going with your dad?" he asked.

"Surprisingly well, actually." Without looking, he could tell there was a glimmer of happiness in her eyes, but he was thankful she couldn't see his face. He wasn't quite as thrilled that Jack Savoie was still there.

"He wants you to come to dinner tonight," she added. Weston almost choked on the hot sip of coffee he had taken.

"I don't know about that." He handed the cup back and turned around to face her.

"Come on, Weston. Do something daring."

* * * *

Weston changed from his usual khaki shorts to a dark gray pair he had purchased for his days on the golf course, which were currently few and far between.

He couldn't explain the impending feeling of doom that sat so heavy on his shoulders that it left him unbalanced. Something was going to go wrong. He just knew it. At his core, he was a guy who relied on his instincts, and here he was ignoring them. He chalked it up to nerves—like the ones so often associated with meeting the family for the first time. Only, it wasn't the first time—far from it—and none of his times around Lyla's dad had gone exceptionally well. There would always be this chasm between him and Mr. Savoie, and Lyla only knew about the top layer of it. But this was her father. If he had a chance to have one more conversation with his own father, he surely would take it.

It was a big pill to swallow, but perhaps Weston could try to leave the past in the past and let this turbulence between them be water under the bridge. *I can try, but will Jack?*

He stepped out of the RV and let out a quick, short whistle. Achilles hopped up from his usual shaded spot and trotted alongside Weston. They made their way down the main road. Dinner at the campground was one of Weston's favorite times to witness. The entire area smelled of a mix of burgers and hot dogs, barbecue, fish and smoked meats. The aromas were mouthwatering, but it was the atmosphere he loved most. Families gathered on the decks of the cabins or sat around picnic tables outside of their RVs. The beach and main square of the grounds were empty and completely still as their usual occupants returned to their sites for some family time where hands, hearts and mouths were full.

He admired it, but he also envied it. What he wouldn't do to have his mother and father together again at a picnic table. There was nothing he wouldn't give for one more chance to sit across from Charlie at the snack bar. He wouldn't hold back. He would say all the things he'd never said, finally ask all the questions he wanted to ask.

Charlie stuffed his mouth full of yet another hot dog. The boy never stopped eating. His body had changed quite a bit from the prior year, muscle popping out in places that used to be skin and bone. His appetite had increased to keep with the changes.

"It's not like you to care," he said through a mouthful of bun. "So, her dad doesn't like you. Newsflash, Weston…most of the dads here don't like you."

Weston spun a quarter on the snack bar tabletop then stopped it in its tracks.

"It's different now." He tapped the coin on the wooden surface.

"How so?" Charlie unwrapped a snow cone from its wrapper.

"Every year Lyla and I come here we flirt, we chat, we invest ourselves in this little summer fling that has an expiration date. When she leaves the campground, she takes that love with her. But she always brings it back. We pick up where we left off. But what if this year was different? What if this was the year we tried to make it work all year long?" Weston spun the quarter again, and Charlie grabbed it from his fingers, tossing it behind him clear across the snack bar.

"So, do it." Charlie sucked all the blue out of one side of his snow cone, leaving the clear ice crystals behind in the useless, decaying paper cone.

"Her dad is never going to let me talk to her outside of here. You know, since he doesn't even let me talk to her here." Weston stood up and walked to retrieve his quarter, throwing it lightly at the back of his best friend's head. Charlie rubbed the spot with the palm of his hand.

"Look, man. You've already won her heart. If her father is the only thing preventing you from getting what you want, it's not her you need to focus on. It's him. You need to win him over too."

Weston thought about the words for a moment, spinning the quarter in his fingers.

"How am I supposed to do that?" he finally asked, realizing that Charlie might be on to something.

"Well, for starters, stop being you."

Charlie said it as a joke, but he was right. If Weston wanted a real chance to convert his and Lyla's summer fling to a yearlong love, he'd have to change his ways. He had no other choice.

The memory was so well timed, so perfectly inserted into his current dilemma that it was as if Charlie had appeared in front of him in person.

"Thank you, Charlie," Weston said out loud to no one but a memory.

Weston walked into the driveway of the site he had assigned to Lyla's father. It was a newer lot he hadn't planned to rent, a concept piece he intended to use when trying to woo investors, but sometimes sacrifices had to be made. 101 was not an option. His father would have rolled over in his grave if he knew Weston had Jack Savoie staying in the house he'd built from the ground up.

Maybe that was why Weston had such a hard time letting go of the grudge. When he'd decided to reopen this place, on top of his own resentment that he harbored toward Jack, he'd inherited his father's as well.

He took a deep breath and decided to start anew.

Jack Savoie had started a battle years ago when he'd made moves to ensure Lyla and Weston would never speak again.

He'd lost.

"Hello, Mr. Savoie." Weston switched on his very best customer service voice. It was the best attempt he had in him. Jack didn't respond vocally. Instead, he offered just a simple head nod, not even gracing Weston with so much as some eye contact. Weston walked by Lyla's father, shaking his head and letting out a frustrated exhale once he was out of earshot.

"Hey!" Lyla said upon seeing him, glancing up from the potatoes she was cutting. "You came after all."

"Yes, and it was a grand old time. I have to be going now." Weston looked back over his shoulder at Jack then to Lyla again.

"Be nice," she whispered, returning her attention to the cutting board at her fingertips. "I know he was never very nice to you, but it was a long time ago. Can't you just let it go? He has."

'He has.' The words cut into him with the sharpness of the knife she was using. Jack had very few redeeming qualities, but the way he'd manipulated his daughter hovered at the top of the list of reasons Weston couldn't get past their differences.

Weston, even as a teenager, could see that Lyla was often mistaking her father's kindness as just that—kindness—when in reality, it was deception at its finest.

To Weston, Jack was as transparent as a clean window, but when Lyla looked through the same pane, it was clouded. She couldn't see to the other side. This was her father, and no matter how many instances proved time and time again that he wasn't as noble as he appeared, she chalked it up to him being protective or looking out for her and she forgave him every time. She always would, and Jack knew it.

Even now, in a place where Weston owned the property and Jack was a guest, Jack had Lyla convinced that he had changed his mind about Weston, that the past was in the past—and yet when Lyla wasn't around, Jack couldn't even muster up an audible hello.

"West!" Camden ran out from another room and jumped into Weston's arms, almost in a full tackle. "Did you bring Achilles? I want my Grandpa Jack to meet him!"

"Of course. Can't go anywhere without him. He's the boss." Weston winked at Camden, who slapped Weston's hand in a high five on the way out of the door.

"He's so excited to have his grandfather here." She poured the cut potato cubes into a pot for boiling. "I feel kind of bad that I haven't been in touch with him as much. I know we have had our issues, but I really think my father has let up on the reins a bit. Retirement has been good for him. Maybe it's time I start letting him be more involved with Camden. A boy needs his grandfather..."

Lyla's eyes softened, full of admiration as she watched her son's excitement about his grandfather's presence unfold. The sentiment didn't sit as well with Weston.

She rambled on, more words flowing in this moment than she had spoken cumulatively since arriving at the campground. Her voice was soft and light, with not even a fraction of hesitation or second-guessing. As she talked about her father, her eyes glittered, and she spoke through a broad grin. In those seconds Weston realized that he was either going to stay angry with Jack or be happy with Lyla, but he couldn't have it both ways, and he had already been without Lyla long enough.

She was happy. In the end, that was all that mattered. Weston bit his tongue and swallowed back his thoughts, not willing to be the reason Lyla's smile diminished — not today or ever again.

* * * *

At the picnic table, Lyla and Weston sat across from Jack. Camden sat at the edge of the table, where Achilles stayed close by.

"Can we get that dog away from the dinner table?" Jack slammed his drink too hard onto the checkered tablecloth.

"He's not just a dog, Grandpa. He's the boss." Camden smiled largely, proud of himself for recycling Weston's words. Weston made eye contact with Camden and shook his head, drawing his fingers against his throat as discreetly as possible. Lyla used her napkin to hide her giggle.

Weston let out a quick, sharp whistle and Achilles looked up at him, ears straight to the sky. Weston said nothing and yet his dog sulked away from the table and lay down in disappointment a few yards away.

"He's a very smart dog. I'll give him that." Jack spoke in a strained way that made small talk even smaller, glancing over the dog and stopping at the area of his missing extremity. "Did you rescue him?"

"He rescued me," Weston said without missing a beat. "I was going through a bit of a rough patch. I had just lost my dad. I was trying to figure out what I wanted to do with my life. A friend of mine who runs a rescue had called and said he knew of a stray dog who was recovering from a hind leg amputation and needed a home. When I asked where they'd found him, he said *'up by the campground – your dad's old place'*. Everything fell into place after that. I'd love to take credit for the idea, but I think it was Achilles' idea before it was mine."

"I didn't know that." Lyla looked over at Achilles with a large smile.

"I do hope it goes well," Jack said, and for a second the thought could have been sincere – but he couldn't leave well enough alone. "At least it can't get any worse than last time."

Weston dropped his fork and a new kind of annoyance formed in his throat. Lyla put her hand on his thigh, and his gaze shifted to hers. She bit her bottom lip and looked up at him from under long lashes. She said nothing yet begged him to swallow the less-than-kind words she knew he wanted to say.

"I really should be going soon." The high road truly was a much more strenuous path. "One of my counselors, Kevin, organized this after-dark camp-wide scavenger hunt for the preteens, and I told him I'd help out."

"That sounds awesome." Camden mumbled through a mouthful of food. "Can I play?"

"Preteens." Lyla repeated. "You're only ten."

"Yeah, but I know a guy." Camden threw his thumb over his shoulder and pointed to Weston, who tried to stifle a laugh.

Maybe that was it. Maybe the bridge to Jack didn't connect to Lyla. Perhaps, the way to show Jack how far he had truly come was to prove it by protecting Camden in a way he'd failed to protect Lyla all those years ago.

"Can I?" Camden asked with puppy-dog eyes in full effect.

"I don't see why not," Weston said, wiping his hands on a napkin.

"That really should be up to his mother," Jack interjected. Lyla's expression was torn. It was clear she was somewhat worried about her son participating in an activity geared toward kids a few years older than him, but there was also a hint of annoyance in her eyes, a look that said she could make a decision for herself without Jack's constant direction.

"Okay, you can play," Lyla said. Camden let out a loud "yessssssss!" before she could finish. "Let me grab my sweatshirt."

Camden's exaggerated yes turned to a horrified no without hesitation. "Mommm," he whined, "none of the other kids' parents are going to be there."

She thought for a moment. Weston couldn't help but wonder if she was looking back on her own activities at Begoa's Point where she'd rarely lacked parental supervision.

"You listen to every word Weston says and be careful."

Camden stood on the bench of the picnic table and jumped off, running wildly toward the circle.

"I'll bring him back in a bit." Weston leaned forward and kissed her forehead. "Mr. Savoie." Weston paused for a moment, choosing between a snarky exit line that guaranteed he had the last word and a proper goodbye, but not controlling his temper would only prove Jack right. "Always a pleasure," he added before heading down the stairs and following Camden down the dirt road.

"How's everything going, Kevin?" Weston asked as they arrived at the meeting spot on the beach. Young teens crowded the area, sitting on the rock wall and the fence to the mini golf course.

"Great. I think we're ready to go."

"Okay, here are the rules. Take a sheet from my helper here." Weston handed the checklists to Camden, whose face lit up like a firework. "Split up in groups of four. The team who has the most items checked off at the end wins. All the clues can be found on the main roads of the grounds. Stay off people's sites, don't go in the woods and the marina is off limits. Got it?"

The groups broke off, running ahead to the location of the first clue.

"Ummm, sir?" a young girl asked. A group of two girls and one boy stood in front of Weston. "We only have three in our group."

Camden tugged at Weston's shirt, a suggestive grin on his freckled face.

"Go for it, kid. And be careful." Camden ran off with his newly assigned group.

"Achilles," Weston whispered. The dog's ears perked up, his head tilted to one side. Weston nodded toward Camden, and Achilles took off after the boy, staying close at his heels.

Weston found himself constantly checking his watch. It wasn't five minutes in before the self-doubt hit him like a tsunami wave. *Is Camden wearing bug spray? I don't even know the kids he's with. Do they know their way around here? Maybe I should've given him a walkie-talkie.*

The idea that Achilles was with him was comforting, but as more time passed, a few groups walked around the main part of the grounds with the list in their hands, but there was no sign of Camden's group. Weston walked by the general store where Dotty stood outside smoking a cigarette. She snuffed it out on the rock wall behind her. Dotty always tried to hide her tobacco habit, but everyone knew.

"Dotty, have you seen Camden?" Weston kept his eyes on the area of the beach where the event started.

"Lyla's boy?" Her voice grew into a dramatic exasperation. "No, no he hasn't been in here. I can radio you if I see him, though. Everything okay?"

Weston nodded and returned to the scavenger hunt starting point. Turning to Dotty was probably not the best choice. In Dotty's hands, his generic question was sure to turn into a missing child rumor that would reach Lyla long before the scavenger hunt was over.

He had half a mind to start running the grounds, following the same route he ran each morning, but he wasn't willing to let the scavenger hunt starting point out of his eyesight. That was where Camden would look first when he returned. *If* he returned.

With time dwindling down on the event and Kevin waiting at the starting line to collect the sheets and calculate points from the teams as they raced back in, Weston's nerves became more twisted. He had seen many of the other teams collecting points and checking things off their lists at the nearby spots. *Where in the world is Camden?*

Kevin sounded a horn and yelled, "Five minutes to go!" into a megaphone. Kids started running toward the starting line, yelling and laughing, holding their papers up, allowing them to flap in the wind like a flag as they ran. Kevin jumped up and down, cheering them on. As the first campers ran in, trying to be the first to get their sheets turned in, a movement across the beach caught Weston's eye. He choked on the worry he tried to swallow. Every possible bad situation ran across his mind. Every time he tried to blink them away, they only got worse.

He watched as Achilles ran down the beach toward him. Alone.

Just as Weston started thinking about the next steps, panicking on what to do at that point, the shadows of three preteens and one slightly smaller boy turned the corner and started running down the beach behind the dog.

"Kevin," Weston said through a relieved exhale, "how long has it been since you gave the five-minute warning?"

"Uhh" — Kevin looked at his stopwatch — "forty-eight seconds."

Forty-eight seconds. It amazed him how time stood still when thinking the worst, and how in a few moments where things had seemed to being going from bad to worse, the seconds seemed to age like years.

"Where have you been?" Weston's words came out harsher than he meant them.

"We started at the bottom and worked our way up," the strawberry-blonde girl interjected excitedly. "The bottom clues were farther away but they were worth more, so we started at the bottom of the list to get more points faster."

"That's..." Weston rubbed his hand at the nape of his neck, embarrassed at his lack of composure. "That's actually really smart."

"It was the kid's idea," the older boy said, throwing his arm around Camden.

Camden smiled widely and stepped toward Weston as the other three turned their sheets in. He bent to one knee, getting on Camden's eye level.

"You okay, West?" Camden asked. "You seem stressed."

"Yeah, I just... I didn't see you around... I just started to worry."

Camden rolled his eyes and laughed. "You sound like my mom."

"Trust me, bud. That's a compliment." Weston took a deep breath, and his heart resumed a normal, even beat.

"You worry too much."

"You might be right." Weston nodded. "I don't think you're done yet. Go get your next set of instructions." Camden took off toward Kevin. Weston stood and followed.

"Okay. The three teams that had the highest scores get to stay for one last clue. Only one can win! The teams who will be searching for the last clue are..." Kevin tucked the pages under his arm and drum-rolled on his thighs. He really was the perfect fit for counselor-led activities for the kids. He handed two teams their pages back and loud, victorious screeches filled the air. Weston looked over at Camden to see his fingers were crossed so tight that his arms were shaking. When Kevin handed their paper back to Camden, the boy jumped with a fist in the air, leaving the ground with excitement. His teammates high-fived him, then Weston did too.

"Okay," Kevin said to the remaining groups, "this is the last clue. Take this paper and see if you can figure it out. There is a box of four 'Camp Champ' T-shirts hidden for whoever finds it first using these clues. Got it?"

The kids nodded and bounced around, ready to get underway.

"Three... Two... One..." Kevin said, "and go!"

The kids took off down the beach, all in different directions. Each group had their own idea of what the last clue suggested. Kevin walked around, peeking in on each team periodically to see what they'd come up with. Weston took a seat on the rock wall by the mini golf course, and Achilles lay at his feet. He stared out over the lake as the moonlight's reflection danced upon it, and for the first time all night, he relaxed.

No work to be done. No parents to impress. No decade-old secrets weighing him down. Nowhere to be. Nothing to worry about. For one moment he allowed himself to be proud—proud of what he'd accomplished with the campground, proud of the man he had become, proud of how far he had come with Lyla and Camden.

He took a breath and held it as a panicked Kevin ran back toward him. "Mr. Accardi... Uh... Sir... Umm boss..." He stammered, still unsure how to greet Weston.

"Spit it out, Kevin. What do you need?"

"It's the boy, Weston. The one you brought with you. I need you to come quick."

Chapter Twenty

Lyla

Cleaning up from dinner with her father was oddly comforting to Lyla. Many things had changed over the years and they weren't as close as they had once been, but it seemed everything was falling into place. They were rediscovering the family they used to be. That was what Begoa's Point was for, after all. In this place, people found their way back to themselves and each other.

'Incomplete' was a word Lyla had used frequently over the years to describe herself. There was always something missing. The more she analyzed that missing piece, the further she realized that the vacancy was more than just one piece limited to Jared. It was a whole section — and one that included her father.

Weston had given her a gift he'd never intended to when he'd reopened the grounds. It was a second chance at love — but not just in the romantic sense. The love of family was becoming as abundant as the stars in the sky on Begoa's clearest nights — seemingly never-ending, only getting brighter in a way that made her wonder how it had ever been cloud-covered in the first place.

Her plan of inviting her father here had backfired in the best way. She'd been angry when she'd sent that email, but it had opened a door she'd once thought was forever locked. Begoa's Point had reopened its doors and in turn, Lyla had unlocked her heart.

Lyla poured two cups of hot chocolate and walked outside, handing one cup to her dad.

"I missed this." She looked up at the stars. She sat on a blanket next to him, near to the fire, and counted the stars, the way they had closed almost every summer night they'd stayed at Begoa's Point every year of her childhood.

"Me too, Ly. Me too." Her dad patted his palm against her hand. For the first time in too long, she didn't pull back.

"I never thought I'd see this place again." A tear ran down her cheek where it tracked her ear and dripped onto the blanket. She was stuck in a broad smile. The ground underneath her brought on an array of emotions and memories that were difficult to sort and file into categories. Some were happy, some were devastating and some were so resolutely interweaved with good and bad that there was no chance at defining the memory as one or the other.

"Me neither," her father said, but his tone was jaded, low. She was so lost in her own dive into memory lane that she almost missed it.

"What happened to us?" She sat up straighter, wiping a tear that started as happy but took a sad turn as it avalanched down the terrain of her face. "When I was a kid, we were the family everyone was jealous of. I was always your little girl, even when I didn't want to be." She took a deep, trembling breath and pulled at her knuckles to keep her hands busy. Lyla turned and looked at her father, her eyes trying to find answers in his. "You were my best friend, Dad. So, what happened to us?"

"You grew up." He leaned backward beside her, but his voice sounded miles away. "You did most of your growing up here on these grounds. At home, during the school year, you mostly stayed the same. Went to school on time, came home before your curfew. You never got in trouble. Hung out with girls your age and ones that had the same interests as you. I never, ever had to worry about where you were or who you were becoming."

Lyla swallowed audibly as her father spoke. She already knew what he was going to say but she had to hear him say it. That was what would make it real.

"I used to love this place too," he continued. "I looked forward to it. I thought it didn't get any better than this. You fell in love with the summer and the campground and the people you met here, and each year you left a little bit less...you."

"I disagree." She cut him off, arguing the same way she had as a teen. "Begoa's was always the place I felt I fit in most. The place I felt the most whole, the most complete, was right here under this sky."

"It's the same sky, Lyla. It's the same sky at home. It never changed, but you certainly did." He wiped his brow with his hand. "I always thought that as a father, I was genetically hardwired to always know what was best for you. That's why I focused on the negative.

That's why I always highlighted the danger of every situation. You were my only child. Your mother left when you were born. I raised you by myself. You were the only thing I had, Ly. I thought the only way to keep you safe was to stress all the ways things could go wrong. Then you started to hang out with Weston and Charlie and that crowd —"

"Will you ever let him off the ropes?" Lyla cried, the volume of her voice raising but fading out into an echo to the sky.

"If you would listen —" he began, but Lyla couldn't let him talk.

"I don't need to listen. I've heard this story a million times. It's a classic, Dad. A tale you revisit every so often about how you gave me the perfect life, and I let it all go up in flames. The one where you set me up for success, and I failed. I know it well." Lyla scurried to her feet and stomped away from him, as if to cut him off completely, but she turned around, her curls whipping through the air and landing over her rising and falling shoulders before confronting her father again. "Let's skip the story and jump right into the end — the part where you say you were right and I was wrong."

He looked up at her, his lips pressed into a harsh line. She turned away, not expecting a sympathetic reply. Kind words didn't break through the locked lips of her father often. He hardly ever caved, very rarely admitted his faults. But the campground had the power to change people, even Jack Savoie. "You weren't wrong, Ly."

The words paralyzed her in her spot, her heart as frozen as every other muscle in her body. She had to have heard incorrectly. She turned slowly, the dirt and rocks of the campsite crunching under her tennis shoe.

"You weren't wrong." He pulled himself to his feet. "I was."

Tears streamed down her face. Since she'd found out about her father's role in her and Weston's ending, she had thought about what she'd say, and what he would say in return. She'd wondered if he'd lie or cover his tracks. In all those moments, she had never envisioned him waving the white flag first.

"I always thought that I would be the only person who would know what was best for you. That no one else would ever come into the picture who had your very best interest at heart. Then Weston came along. And though I think he went about it the wrong way, and the two of you seemed to only ever find trouble and misguided adventures, I think he meant well. It took me a long time to see it—well after Jared, even."

Lyla drew her fingertips under her eyes to clear the tears. The words from her father were difficult to process. "Why didn't you ever tell me that before?" she asked, sniffles breaking up the words.

"It didn't matter. You had Jared and Camden. The campground had closed. That part of your life was over. By the time I realized that...maybe I was just a little bit too hard on you, it was all in the past."

Lyla paced back and forth, the earth crunching beneath her feet. It was the only sound, for a moment. Neither of them were talking. All the other campers sharing the circle around the site had already called it a night.

"So...you...like Weston?" She raised both hands then dropped them against her thighs with an audible clap.

"Oh, heavens no."

Lyla laughed. Though she knew the timing was inappropriate, the comment warranted a chuckle.

"I didn't say I liked him. I said I can see that he cared about you. I understand where I could have backed off a little and let you live your life. Maybe that terrible last summer here wouldn't have been so terrible if I hadn't pushed you away. Maybe our Begoa's Point story could have had a better, happier ending if I'd given you room to grow."

Lyla moved forward, wrapping her arms around her father and crying into his chest, soaking his shirt. She wanted to tell him it wasn't his fault—that the night that had ended their Begoa's Point runs had been her fault, not his. She couldn't, though. The tears kept falling—fifteen years' worth of tears that she'd kept buried deep down, just waiting to spill over. She couldn't fight him anymore. She didn't have the energy. No matter who shouldered the final blame, she didn't want to keep debating whose fault this fallout was. They didn't need to keep revisiting their painful path. They could just build a brilliant future.

She could see it now. Restarting their Begoa's tradition where they came to the grounds every summer, but this time, she wasn't a kid anymore but rather was making memories with a child of her own. He would see his grandchild grow, make the kind of memories with him that she held on to so tightly from her own years of growing up on this dirt.

"So"—she stepped away and looked at the million sparkling stars above—"what happens now?"

"With us? Or with you and Weston?"

"It's all kind of the same thing, isn't it?" she asked. There was still a clear divide between Jack and Weston.

Everyone could feel it. Even Camden seemed to shy away from certain subjects when they were both around. "You and Weston are still carrying around some kind of grudge, and it seems neither of you are willing to take the steps in the right direction."

Jack ran his hand through his salt-and-pepper hair. "I'm still not convinced Weston is the best option for you, Lyla. I'm not sure he's the best fit for you or Camden. But I'm willing to give him a second chance. So, one of two things is going to happen. He's going to prove me right or he's going to prove me wrong."

Lyla smiled. She had seen the changes in Weston and knew he was turning into the kind of man who her father could be proud of. He was running this campground, chasing his dreams and making hers come true in the process. Camden adored Weston. She knew he could step up and show her father that getting to know the new Weston Accardi was worth his time. He could prove Jack wrong.

The sound of tires over dirt road disrupted their silence. The headlights of a golf cart hurtled toward them, screeching to a stop just inches away from them. A young man in a green polo with shaggy hair and worried eyes breathed short, panting breaths from the driver's seat.

"Are you Lyla?" he asked. She nodded, but in the deepest part of her chest she already knew why he was here. She looked at the golf cart and instantly the scenario morphed. The golf cart wasn't a golf cart anymore. It was a blacked-out SUV. The campsite wasn't a campsite—it was her quaint suburban home with the pristine landscaping and farmer's porch with the swing. The boy in front of her wasn't a young man in a Begoa's Point polo, he was a commanding officer in full uniform with a grim expression planted on his face.

The situations were so different but so close. She knew in her chest that good news wasn't going to be the next thing out of the messenger's mouth. She had been here before.

"What is it? Is it Camden?" She was in the passenger seat of the golf cart before he could answer. She already knew. A mother just did.

Chapter Twenty-One

Weston

Weston had heard Camden's wails and cries long before he could actually see him. He ran down the beach as fast as his legs would carry him, following the horrible sound. He approached Camden, and for that brief second where Camden's eyes found Weston's familiar face, he quieted, his eyes flooding with relief more than tears. Camden's arm was bent at an impossible angle, enough to make Weston's stomach churn, even though he had seen worse. This was Lyla's child. The boy was his responsibility.

"My mom is coming?" Camden swallowed back pain and tears.

"Yeah, bud. I sent Kevin for her."

Camden took a deep breath through a clenched jaw, the kind of wince where the air hissed as it passed through his teeth.

Blue and red lights filled the sky, a siren wailing away.

"Why do we need an ambulance?" Camden asked as the bus drove up the beach. His eyes took up half his small face as they widened in fear. His breath quickened to an unmaintainable rate. He was beginning to hyperventilate, likely as a mix of pain and fear rushed through him.

"Just a formality, Cam. Deep breaths. Looks like a break. Happens all the time." Weston rambled on, trying to convince Camden that everything would be okay, but more so for his own benefit.

Another counselor sent all the other kids off, sending them to their sites and rendering the scavenger hunt over. Weston watched as the lights turned from blue to red to purple and back again, lighting the sky like fireworks on the Fourth of July.

The boom-hiss combo of the fireworks above the beach could be heard for miles. The bursts glittered in the sky and reflected on the glassy surface of the lake. Campers were covered in red, white and blue but mostly pride. 'This Land Is Our Land' was on the banner across the main square, flying high above the heads of the onlookers of the golf cart parade. Weston knew the sentiment was about the country, but he couldn't help but look around at the campers on the beach and feel it resonated with the campground too. The families that were here, the friendships that formed, this land, the property of Begoa's? This land was their land.

Weston sat on the beach behind Lyla. She sat leaning against his chest, looking down where everyone else was looking up.

"I hate them," she said. That was Lyla. She was scared of everything.

"Why?" Weston asked. "They're so cool."

"They're so dangerous," she replied, but it didn't sound like her voice that came through. It was more her father's.

"They're beautiful. Explosions of light in the sky. Like stars we are responsible for."

"I like the way they look," she admitted sheepishly. "I don't like the way they sound. They're pretty. I like the light in the sky and the way that just for a second, it brightens the otherwise dark world. I just wish they were silent."

She looked over her shoulder, and Weston smiled his signature mischievous grin. As the next firework took off, he pressed his hands over her ears and she smiled, turning toward the in-sky show.

The crowd erupted in an explosion of their own applause as the fireworks finale came to a close.

"Come with me," Weston whispered in her ear, keeping her in a close hug from behind.

"Where?" she whispered, sinking into him.

"On an adventure."

"I have to get to my site in less than an hour. I'm not even supposed to be with you. If I don't make curfew, one of us is dead. My guess would be you." They both laughed and stood from the sand, shaking it off and leaving it where they found it. "Seriously." She held up a finger. "One hour."

"Better run fast then," he said, taking off in a sprint.

"I don't even know where we're going."

He stopped and turned to her, smiling. "Sure you do."

They ran down the main road under a dark sky only lit by a map of stars that neither of them knew how to read. Their laughter and footsteps alternated and echoed, Lyla beating Weston to the faux blueberry bushes and going right, taking the path they were sure was a secret to everyone except them.

They slowed their pace to a walk, and he took her hand in his, leading her to the clearing. She looked at him with a curious expression and he sat in the middle, lying down on the ground. She lay opposite him, staring at the same sky that in this spot seemed more light purple than midnight black.

"What are we doing?" she asked. He held up one finger, directing her to wait just a moment.

As she stared into the sky, it brightened for a moment. The flash lit the whole area, there and gone again faster than the time it took to blink.

"It's heat lightning..." She giggled. "It's beautiful...and silent."

"Wish granted, Savvy." Weston watched her stare at the sky, noting the dimple above her lip when she smiled and the way her eyes shimmered when she let herself be free.

She rolled over to him, resting her head against his chest, listening to his heartbeat. They talked about their dreams and who they were when the calendar didn't reflect a summer month as they observed the stars in the sky turn to an orange-hued sunrise.

"West!" she screamed, her voice a tone of pure panic. "I have to go!" She stood and ran from the clearing, Weston following at her heels.

"What have we done?" she called over her shoulder, and he laughed. "This isn't funny." She shouted, not slowing her speed. "I told you one hour!"

"It is a little funny!" he called after her. They turned the corner to her site. She stopped short, skidding across the dirt driveway. Jack Savoie stood at the porch steps, red faced and waiting.

"Dad." Her panting, short breaths cut through her excuses.

"You. In the house," he said, pointing to her. "And you" — he pointed to Weston — "leave my little girl alone, you hear? Stay away from her. This 'out all night' bit isn't anything she would have come up with on her own. Every time she breaks the rules, there you are, the common factor. Before she ends up hurt or worse, leave her alone."

"She was never in any real danger, sir," Weston refuted.

"Not yet," Jack said, ushering his daughter into the house, "but it's only a matter of time."

The blue and red lights casting colors on the black sky were interrupted by a bold, white light—the headlights from Kevin's golf cart. Lyla hopped out of it, running toward them. "Camden!" she yelled, kneeling beside her son and Weston.

"What happened?" she asked, cool, collected. For Camden she was steadfast, not a fraction of her distress showing. She practiced motherhood with a steady hand, a flawless show put on for her son, but deep down, Weston knew she was panicking, swallowing back her own fright to keep her son calm.

"I tripped when we were running for the final clue. That's it. It was dark and I tripped." Tears filled Camden's eyes again. "It really hurts."

"I know, baby. I know." She ran her hand across his head, pushing his sweat-slicked bangs from his eyes.

"Ma'am, you're the boy's mother?" An EMT approached and asked. "We're going to take him now. You can come with us." She nodded and watched as the uniformed techs loaded Camden into the back of the ambulance.

Weston reached forward and placed his hands on her forearms. She moved away, keeping a cool breeze between them.

"An ambulance, West? Really?" She crossed her arms and shook her head. "He was already scared enough. I think this is a bit over the top."

"The ambulance covers us as a business, Savvy. It just protects us—"

"So, you took my son out on a late-night adventure I wasn't okay with but gave you the benefit of the doubt and allowed it. He gets hurt and your first thought is how to protect the business? What did you think we were going to do, West, sue you?"

"I had a responsibility to protect the grounds."

Lyla stepped backward, her eyes narrowed, anger glowing in them, as well as a glimmer of hurt too.

"He needed you to stay calm and help him. And you were more concerned with how to protect yourself than my son."

Weston stood with his shoes dug deep into the sand, unable to move. Unable to speak. Even if he did, it would probably be wrong. He seemed to always make the wrong choice when it came to Lyla Savoie.

"Is that everyone?" the EMT said, looking out of the doors as Lyla entered.

"Let me come with you," Weston pleaded, guilt forming in his stomach like a storm.

"I've got this, Mr. Accardi. You have a business to run." Lyla took her seat, and the EMT closed the door between them before Weston had time to refute her words.

Chapter Twenty-Two

Lyla

The hospital was freezing, kept at a cool sixty-eight degrees that spread goosebumps across Lyla's arms. Or perhaps her knotted nerves had caused her skin to crawl all this time and she hadn't noticed until then.

Camden's eyes were heavy, his lids fluttering closed but popping open every few minutes. She sat down on the edge of the bed and wrapped her arms around him. He rested his head against her.

They were called back to an exam room, where a doctor came in to show them Camden's x-rays.

"Good evening," he said with a perfect, practiced-looking smile. "I'm Dr. Jeremy Torrin." He pulled up the images on a large computer screen and showed Lyla where Camden's arm breaks had occurred.

"Two complete breaks," the physician explained, pointing to the screen, "one in the radius, here, and one here, in the ulna." Lyla nodded as he spoke. Camden slept on the exam bed, his arm in a makeshift splint.

Between the pain, fatigue and hospital-given medications, he clearly couldn't stay awake any longer.

"Believe it or not, Mrs. Kenney, this isn't that bad." The kind, too-good-looking-to-be-real-life doctor kept his grin intact, even when telling Lyla her son's broken bone was 'not that bad'. It sent Lyla into an angry spiral, one she had to take deep, calming breaths to pull herself out of. That was the balance of being a mother — staying calm when unraveling would be more natural. In reality, it probably wasn't that bad. But since it was her kid, instinct and reason went out of the window. It was like everything she'd ever learned had dissipated, leading straight to hysterics, because he was her whole world and seeing him in pain made her feel a little less competent — even when it wasn't her fault. *Especially* when it wasn't her fault.

"I know," she said, and she pressed her fingers to her lips.

"Mrs. Kenney, let's keep that splint on for a few days to allow the swelling to take its course. Come back and see us in three days, and we will evaluate for a plaster cast, okay?"

She nodded, taking in all the information, physical and mental fatigue weighing on her chest. A tear trickled down her cheek, small at first, then more followed until she couldn't stop them. She covered her eyes and sobbed, struggling to take a deep breath. She knew this wasn't as bad as it could've been. She understood that things happened, and that as far as injuries went, this was fairly minor. Regardless of bombarding herself with rationalization, she just couldn't control her emotions. She was exhausted.

"I'm so sorry." Her sobs turned to a laugh that wasn't any more under her control than her crying. "I'm just so tired." Her laugh continued to barrel through her, echoing in the otherwise-quiet hospital. Dr. Torrin laughed too. Lyla wiped her fingers under her eyes and took a deep breath, finally resuming a calmer emotion.

"I'll give you a minute, Mrs. Kenney." Dr. Torrin said as he headed toward the door. "Collect yourself. I'll be right outside if you need me."

"Okay," she said as he reached the door. "And, Dr. Torrin?"

Dr. Torrin turned to her, raising an eyebrow.

"It's just Ms."

He nodded and stepped outside, leaving the door cracked only slightly.

It was the first time since Jared's death that she had corrected anyone, presenting herself as a Ms. instead of a Mrs. She'd never been able to bring herself to do it out loud, but it was time. She looked over to the bed where her child slept soundly as if nothing was wrong at all. Perhaps he wasn't the only one who required healing.

"Is this the room Camden Kenney is in?" a familiar voice asked from the hallway.

"I can't answer that," Dr. Torrin said. "Besides, regardless of whose room it is, it is the middle of the night. No visitors. That's the rule."

"I've never been much for following the rules." Weston's never-take-no-for-an-answer voice traveled in the door, followed by it creaking on its hinges. She laughed at his confidence. It was a glimpse of the boy he used to be—a person who'd seemed so far away since his newfound sense of responsibility and conduct had emerged—but in that second, in that comment, that former version of him wasn't so far away at all. Weston stormed across the threshold, heading toward Lyla. He wrapped his arms around her, and she collapsed into them.

"I'm so sorry." He spoke into her hair as he ran his hand over the back of her head and curls. "I'm so sorry."

"It's not your fault, West. He's a kid, a fearless, competitive kid. It was bound to happen eventually."

"But it wasn't eventually," he said, stepping back but keeping his hands on her shoulders. "It was right now, with me. I should have gone with him. I should've been closer by."

"West, stop. I'm sorry about what I said earlier. I was emotional and short-fused. It's...difficult, keeping your emotions in check when it's your child."

Weston walked over toward Camden and leaned into the hospital bed.

"I don't know how you do it," he whispered, whipping his ball cap off his head and crushing it in his grasp. "I don't know how you keep your guard up all the time. The way I worried about him tonight, the way I wondered where he was and if he was okay? It's exhausting. How do you keep yourself going all the time with that kind of weight on your shoulders?"

The corner of Lyla's mouth twitched into a barely there grin. "You get used to it." She stepped toward the hospital bed at the side opposite Weston. He reached forward and took her hand, their fingers interlocked over Camden.

"I didn't... I didn't mean to put the business first." Weston looked away, using his free hand to mess with some machines and devices on the hospital wall that he probably shouldn't have been touching. *Apparently anything to distract himself.* "I didn't think of it like that. I was trying to protect both Camden and Begoa's. If it were any other kid, I still would've called emergency services. It's protocol. It covers us if things go from bad to worse." He swallowed hard. "I know it was an accident, Savvy. But it was an accident that lost us Begoa's Point the first time. I'm just trying to do everything right." His voice was shaking and his hand trembled in hers.

"I know." Her voice cracked. "I know. I get it. And I'm sure…being here…"

"Don't say it, Savvy." His voice shifted from a normal, healthy rhythm to a flat line.

"I just assume it's hard for you to be here right now." She squeezed his hand tighter, walking around the bed toward him without letting go. "I admire you for coming to be with us, even though I know it's the last place you want to be." Her gaze fell to where his artificial leg extended from his cargo shorts. They stood cloaked in a hospital silence — the kind of quiet that was interrupted by the beeping machines from surrounding rooms, ambulances pulling into nearby bays and doctors and nurses chatting as they sped down the hallways. They didn't speak. They didn't have to. They held each other's hand and walked down memory lane together without having to say anything at all. Lyla was about to speak, about to direct the memory to something better, something happier, and Camden's eyes fluttered open.

"Weston!" he cried, foggy but with the most energy he had mustered since his injury. "Did we win? Did my team get the T-shirts?"

Weston looked at Lyla and laughed. Lyla shook her head.

"Yeah, bud." Weston sat at the edge of the bed next to Camden. "You won a T-shirt."

* * * *

Weston drove home from the hospital in a truck that belonged to the campground. Camden slept in the back seat, his head lolling against his mother, who refused to leave his side. Weston kept glancing away from the road, just for a moment, watching Lyla in the rear view then back to the road again. Lyla smiled each time his gaze met hers. No matter which direction he looked, ahead or behind, the thought led directly to a past memory they shared or the hope of a future one he would create with her and her boy.

The truck tires kicked up dirt and rock as Weston pulled into Site 101. He hopped out of driver's side and headed to the rear of the truck, opening the door.

"I'll get him," he offered, taking Lyla's hand and helping her out.

"Just...be careful." Lyla wished she hadn't said it as soon as the words had left her lips. Weston looked at her with sullen eyes, what was left of the light in them dimming as she made it clear that she still blamed him, even just fractionally.

"I will." His voice was as faint as the distant crickets chirping across the grounds.

He leaned in, assessing each move before he made it. He unbuckled the seat belt, careful to pull it over Camden's body without hurting him or waking him, then scooped him into his arms and walked slowly toward the cabin.

Lyla opened the door, and they tiptoed to Camden's room. Weston laid the boy down on the bed while Lyla adjusted his arm so it was propped on a pillow. They shut the door quietly behind them and headed toward the porch. Weston pulled her in close, placing his chin on her head in an embrace that was more silent slow dance than hug. They stayed there for a moment, taking in every minute of the turbulent day and breathing each other in until they both looked up at the sky at the same time, watching as the heavens lit up into a brilliant purple hue that was there and gone again in a flash.

"Heat lightning," she said and brought her eyes to his again. "Do you remember that night?"

"I remember every night." His voice was steadfast, strong — somehow, a promise without ever making one at all. The patio door opened behind them and they turned to see Jack Savoie had joined them on their star-speckled dance floor.

"Dad? What are you doing here?"

"I figured I'd come here until I got word on Camden. How is he doing?" Jack asked. "Is he okay?"

"Just a minor break… He will be fine." Lyla turned toward her dad, Weston's fingertips trailing across her hips as she moved.

"Just a minor break?" Jack spat, irritated. "Seems like an oxymoron, doesn't it?"

"Just calm down, Dad," Lyla patted the air with her palms.

"I will not stay calm." His jaw clenched. "Some things never change, Accardi. People just always seem to end up hurt around you."

"Dad!" Lyla yelled. "That's enough." She reached her arm back and grabbed Weston's hand.

"Why must you continuously protect him, Lyla? Even with everything that happened tonight, you just can't see that trouble follows him like a black cloud."

"That's not true," Lyla said, her voice small. She didn't have any more fight left in her. Not tonight.

"Sure it is. Or have you already forgotten about Charlie?"

There was an excruciating silence between the three of them. Weston was hurt. She could hear it in the way his breathing pattern changed. Before she could argue, before any words worth saying rose to the occasion, Weston stepped off the porch and got into the truck, peeling out of the circle without looking back.

She looked at her father with tears leaving her eyes and traveling down her face.

"You need to go." She looked at her shoes as she spoke.

"I'll stay and help you with Camden," he said, disregarding her words entirely.

"I said you need to go." This time, there was no mistaking her statement. "I don't need your help."

"The boy is hurt, Ly. You're going to need someone, and he's going to need someone to be there for him."

"We have someone, Dad. We have Weston."

"Ly—"

"No, Dad. I shouldn't have asked you to come here." She didn't cry, surprising even herself. Historically, Lyla's anger almost always was synonymous with tears—but not that night.

"Fine. I'll go back to my cabin. I'll check on Camden tomorrow."

"No. The campground, Dad. You need to leave the campground. This is Weston's place because he owns it, and it's my place because it's the place that feels the most like home, and it's Camden's place because he is learning how to be happy here… But it's not *your* place. It's not *our* place—not like it used to be. Not anymore."

Jack nodded, likely giving her a moment to change her mind before he left, but she didn't. He walked down the stairs, and as soon as he was out of sight, she collapsed to the deck boards, finally letting the day weigh her down, lying on the porch and watching as the heat lightning tried to break its way through the force that contained it.

Chapter Twenty-Three

Weston

Weston sipped coffee from a Styrofoam cup, his mood so distant that he didn't even notice the horrible taste he usually complained to Sheila about.

"Have you thought about what I suggested?" Sheila looked over her bifocals, staring at Weston, who yawned into his fist.

"Hmm?" he asked, not awake or inspired enough to keep track of the conversation.

"About inviting Lyla and Camden to lunch with the investors?"

Weston laughed out loud. The twisted look on Sheila's face said that she didn't appreciate it.

"Yes. I thought about it, long and hard. Spent some extra time with them and broke the kid's arm for good measure. Then had a cute little duel with her dad—spoiler alert, her dad shot first. I just walked away and haven't heard from any of them in days. So, brilliant idea, Sheila." Weston clapped his hands together in a mocking applause. "It's not going to happen." He picked up his drink and swirled the coffee in the bottom of the Styrofoam cup.

Sheila stood and leaned into her desk.

"Are you going to behave like a teenager forever? Or just today? Because if you plan on growing up sometime soon, we can reschedule this."

Weston looked up at her, not feeling great about what he had said but not feeling guilty about it either.

"You can't just revert to the punk seventeen-year-old version of yourself every time something doesn't go your way. You've come so far, and you've changed so much."

"Seems like not everyone is in agreement with that." Weston adjusted his hat and sat up, leaning his head against the wall of her office, trying to find answers on the ceiling.

Her voice softened. "You have to leave the past in the past, Weston."

"I try. I try to leave the past in the past. It just doesn't ever leave me."

"Do you regret bringing her here?" Sheila removed her glasses and placed them on the table.

"What?" Weston asked, though he'd heard the question perfectly.

"Do you regret bringing her here?" she repeated the question. Weston rubbed at his jaw.

"Of course not. It's the best decision I've made since reopening this place." Weston nodded, seeing the point Sheila was forcing him to arrive at.

"Jack Savoie has gotten in the way of so many things, so many times. When you were a kid, you had to take it. His word was final. But you're not a kid anymore, Weston. It's about time you stood up for yourself — and for Lyla too."

Weston soaked in her words as he stood to head out of the office.

"Don't forget about the investor lunch, Weston. And for Pete's sake, ask the girl to come with you."

He shook his head and left the office, walking around the campground with no real destination.

He turned the corner to the dirt road that led to his campsite, and when he got there, he wasn't alone.

Camden sat in Weston's usual chair, using his good hand to toss a ball to Achilles.

"Trespassing is a crime, you know." Weston laughed as he approached Camden.

"Call security," Camden quipped, holding the ball. Achilles sat at the ready, waiting for Camden to throw the ball.

"How are you feeling, kid?" Weston pulled up a second camping chair.

Camden shrugged. He dug the toe of his shoe into the dirt and looked at the ground.

"What's going on?"

Camden shrugged again, taking a deep breath before he spoke. "Lonely, a little bit. I can't do a lot of the activities my friends are doing. My grandfather hasn't been around...and... Well...you haven't been either."

Weston rubbed at the back of his neck. "I'm sorry...for everything — the scavenger hunt and your arm and not coming around after."

Camden looked at him with an unenthused expression then broke into an animated yell. "Are you kidding me?" He jumped up from the chair. "That was the best night *ever*. I had so much fun. I made friends, I stayed out late *and* I got a T-shirt."

"And a shiny new cast to match," Weston added.

"That only hurt for like a second." It was a nonchalant response that was borderline believable. Kids were resilient. There was a pause between them, and Weston considered asking about Lyla, but bit his tongue.

"You need to talk to her, ya know."

"I know."

Camden, though? He was intuitive.

Camden held up a small, lime-green walkie-talkie and shook it back and forth, his eyebrow raised and a mischievous grin on his face—a facial expression he'd stolen from Weston himself.

Weston snatched the walkie-talkie from Camden and began pacing around the site. He held down the button, a quick two toned *bing* sounded from the device.

"Sulking moron to Savvy. Come in, Savvy. Do you copy?" He let go of the button and a moment later, his device transmitted a slightly static version of her voice.

"Savvy to sulking moron, what's your twenty?" Her giggle rang loud and clear over her words, no matter how much she seemingly tried to stay serious. Camden laughed too.

"Campsite. I have something to say. You ready?"

Silence, for a moment, then more communication.

"Affirmative."

"I'm not going anywhere, Savvy. Not this time. I don't care if your dad fights me every step of the way. I know I have a way to go to prove that I am in—but I *am* in. If you want out, you're going to have to be the one to leave. I won't do it. So, I guess what I'm saying is, you're stuck with me. You hear me? Over."

She clicked the button but didn't speak. Static filled the line, but nothing else. She'd let go of the transmitter. He could tell by the sudden silence.

"Loud and clear," she finally said, only, it wasn't through the speaker. She stood about halfway up the dirt drive. He sped toward her, lifting her off her feet and spinning her around when their bodies collided. She leaned in and kissed him. Camden laughed, Achilles barked, and for the first time in a story with way too many twists and turns, they were all on the same page.

"I have another meeting I have to go to," he said once her feet were firmly on the ground. "But we're going to do something tonight, all three of us."

"Where are we going?" she asked, tucking a piece of her hair behind her ear.

"Do you remember the best date you ever went on?"

"Of course," she laughed. "It was one of the greatest nights of my life."

"Okay, well. I was thinking something along the lines of that."

She smiled and looked over at Camden, who was still messing with Achilles.

"Want us to walk you to your meeting?" Lyla's happiness still glistened in her eyes.

"I'd like that." He took her hand in his.

"Boys," Weston and Lyla called at the same time, and the boy and the dog came running, the four of them taking off down the path as one unit.

"He won't even let me talk to her," Weston said, skipping a rock across the lake top.

"Do you blame him?" Charlie asked through a bite of a licorice stick. "You didn't exactly make a good first impression. Or second...or third..."

"Yeah, I get it. Thanks." Weston threw another rock at the water, too hard. It sank instead of jumping. "I haven't

talked to her in days. Every time I see her, her dad isn't too far behind. I can't even get close to her."

"You're trying too hard — or not trying hard enough or something. I don't know. I'm not good at this advice thing." Charlie waved the candy vine as he spoke, and Weston laughed, which was a start.

"I just want to get a chance to get to know her more. I want to know everything about her. It's like…all of a sudden, I have all these questions about who she is when she's not here on these grounds. I know it's just because I can't ask them. I want to know who she is in the spring and fall and winter, but I can't. And now I'm going on this weekend fishing trip with my dad. Sleeping on a boat out in the middle of the lake. Some sudden need for father-son bonding or something. I can't talk to her, and now this weekend I won't even be able to catch a glimpse of her."

"Does your two-way radio work out there?" Charlie asked.

"My dad's does. The campground radios work across the entire property, even the lake because of the marina."

"Okay, okay. I'm going to solve all your problems. Just this once, because I like you and I'm hands down the greatest best friend who has ever lived, I'm going to fix your little star-crossed lovers scenario." Charlie sat up straight.

The light bulb brightened above Charlie's head. It was flickering, fighting to stay lit, but it was there all the same. "What did you have in mind?" Weston dropped the remainder of the rocks into the sand. "What's this brilliant plan?"

Charlie stood up, clapping a hand on Weston's shoulder. "She can date me instead."

Chapter Twenty-Four

Lyla

A boy she had never seen before knocked on the sliding door of the cabin. It was rare to not recognize a face around here. Even if she didn't know the name, most people were at least recognized after the amount of time spent on the campgrounds.

The boy was about her height, had clean-cut brown hair and kind eyes. He wore braces and a nervous smile.

"Can I help you?" she asked as she opened the sliding door. The boy held out his left hand, flat, palm up. On it, in messy, smudged handwriting, was a note.

Just go with it.

She smiled so bright that it almost lifted her off the ground. Someone was up to something. Her father approached from behind.

"What's this about?" he asked, crossing his arms over his puffed-out chest.

"Sir, I'm Greg Langley." The boy certainly did put on a lovely show. Entertaining even, since she didn't know what would happen next.

"You're George and Sherry Langley's boy?" he asked, rubbing his chin.

"Yes, sir." He reached his right hand out and shook his hand in a visibly firm grip.

"I've met your father a few times on the golf course. Good man… Has all great things to say about you. What brings you here?"

"Well, sir, I wanted to ask for the chance to take your daughter to the movie they're playing on the beach tonight. It starts at nine, and I could have her back by eleven." Lyla wondered how many times he had rehearsed those words while hoping her dad hadn't looked at the program. There was no movie on the beach scheduled for that night.

"What do you think, Lyla?" her dad asked. "Do you want to go?"

Lyla nodded a quick, excited yes and her father agreed to let her go. She grabbed a light jacket and returned to the door at a run.

"Let's go, Craig," she said, linking her arm with his.

"Greg," her father corrected with a raised eyebrow.

"Uhh, yeah. That's what I said." She smiled an innocent, angelic grin at him and walked away, hopeful that she hadn't overshadowed the boy's shining production by fumbling her only line.

As they turned the corner, Charlie stood outside the circle and applauded Greg's performance. He handed him a twenty-dollar bill, and Greg waved as he took off, payment in hand.

"What are we doing, Charlie?" she asked. Charlie linked his elbow in hers.

"Going out, of course." She giggled as they walked. "Just because Weston is out on some boat somewhere and can't take you out on a date doesn't mean I can't."

221

"I think he will have something to say about that." She continued to laugh at Charlie's antics and smooth answers.

"Oh, he does," Charlie reached into his pocket. He pulled out a walkie-talkie and hit the side button, a beep sounding before he spoke.

"Stealthy sidekick to sulking moron. Come in, sulking moron." Charlie let the button go, and Lyla stifled a laugh with her hand. "Sulking moron, do you copy?" Charlie yelled into the speaker.

"Affirmative," Weston's silky voice finally responded. "How goes the mission?"

Charlie held the radio to her and pressed the button.

"Mission complete," Lyla said.

"Well, it's not complete yet," Charlie said. "We haven't reached our final destination."

They proceeded down the main road and walked around the back of the snack bar.

"It's closed," Lyla said, confused. Charlie reached into his pocket, which was apparently as deep as Mary Poppin's bag, full of surprises at each turn. He shook a set of keys in front of her. "Perks of being the owner's son's best friend. Or dating him, in your case."

"They just…gave you the keys?" she asked as he opened the door. She was hesitant to step over the threshold.

"Gave is a loose term," he said, reaching forward and grabbing her forearm in a playful manner, pulling her toward the snack bar. She obliged, passing the 'employees only' sign.

"Question numero uno," Charlie spoke into the radio then put it down, drum rolling both his hands on the counter.

"What is your favorite kind of ice cream?" Weston asked over the speaker.

"Hmmm." Lyla pressed her finger to her mouth and thought about her answer. "I really like root beer floats."

Charlie's mouth gaped open. He leaned into the counter and shook his head, picking the radio back up.

"If I date her for you, does that mean I get to break up with her for you?" Charlie asked, letting go of the transmitter button.

"Hey!" Lyla said. "What's so wrong with that?"

"Root beer float is not ice cream," Charlie retorted, followed by Weston chiming in with the exact same sentence.

"Pick an ice cream, Savvy," Weston's voice floated over the static airwaves. "Then any and all of the toppings that you want. Make it a good one."

Lyla dug out a scoop each of three different ice creams then eyed all the possible topping options, pulling out each container one by one and adding a new sugary addition to her bowl.

Charlie walked over to a radio on the wall and powered it on. Music blasted from its speakers.

"Shouldn't you be a little more inconspicuous?" Lyla asked. "What if we get caught? Or do you have a plan for that too?"

"Oh, I have a plan," Charlie said. "If they catch us, I'm going to tell them this was all your idea. I'll tell them you threatened my life."

Lyla guffawed, practically spitting ice cream through her nose. "I'm sure they will buy that."

"I love this song." Charlie turned up the radio and began dancing like a fool across the snack bar floor.

"Weston," Charlie said into the radio without pausing his out-of-date dance moves. "Your girlfriend is going to dance with me."

"She is not. Don't you touch her." Weston replied, but there was a chuckle in his voice that suggested he wasn't jealous or threatened.

"I don't dance." Lyla leaned into the counter.

Charlie swayed and pirouetted toward her, inching closer as he tried to convince her to join him on the sticky dance floor. He held down the transmitter button, singing —

poorly — to Weston. She grabbed a can of whipped cream and aimed the nozzle at his face. "Come any closer and I'll pull the trigger."

"You wouldn't." Charlie let go of the radio's call button.

"She would." Weston's voice rang through. And without missing a beat, she plunged her finger down and covered Charlie's face in a steady stream of whipped topping.

"Weston." Charlie licked around his mouth. "We're going to have to call you back later."

"Uh oh." Lyla took off to the other side of the snack bar, trying to evade Charlie's attempt at retribution.

It was the first night of a beautiful friendship. Lyla learned that in many ways, dating Weston meant dating Charlie. They were a package deal. Where Weston was, Charlie could be found and vice versa. And though the remainder of the night was spent answering a series of questions from Weston and getting to ask some in return, she got to know Charlie too.

Weston stood on the opposite side of the sliding door, knocking on the glass with the back of his hand.

It was odd, seeing him knocking on the door of a home he owned in more ways than one. Camden was using the bedroom Weston had grown up in—the one that used to be decorated with posters of cars and professional baseball teams, the one with the dart board no one ever used and a lifetime's worth of cargo shorts always covering the floor, never folded or put away.

Lyla slid the door open and took both Weston's hands, guiding him into the house and into an up-onto-her-tiptoes kiss.

"Ready?" he asked as they parted.

"I am, just waiting on Camden."

As if on cue, Camden came running out of his room wearing his newly acquired 'Camp Champ' T-shirt and a lime-green arm cast.

"I like the shirt, Cam." Weston held out his fist and Camden bumped it with his good hand. "I wouldn't wear it tonight, though."

Camden looked at Weston with an inquisitive arched eyebrow and confused frown.

"I just don't want it to get ruined," Weston added in response to Camden's disappointment.

"Ruined?" Camden's eyebrow held its curious arch.

Weston reached into his pocket and pulled out a single blue ribbon with gold writing, just like the ones that composed Lyla's personal collection. Camden took the ribbon and flipped it over, reading the back.

"Largest sundae." Camden said out loud. "Whoever builds the largest sundae is going to win?" His voice raised an octave, excitement caused his words to run together.

"Whoever can build the biggest sundae...and eat it all!" Weston added with one palm up. Camden leapt for the high five.

"That ribbon is *so* mine!" Camden exclaimed as he ran out of the door.

* * * *

Weston unlocked the door to the snack bar and held it open for Camden and her to follow. Even though Weston had the keys and owned the property, Lyla still had butterflies in her stomach like they were doing something wrong—the same feeling she'd had when she'd come here with Charlie all those years ago.

Weston slid back the covers of the deep freezers that the ice creams were kept in. As Camden pointed to each flavor he wanted to use in his never-ending sundae, Weston pulled out the large five-gallon buckets of ice cream and placed them on the ground, since Camden was too short to lean into the chests.

Weston grabbed a large box of clear cling wrap from a nearby shelf. Lyla and Camden both stared at him, puzzled.

"Let's see the arm, kiddo." Weston pulled the shrink wrap away from the roll. Camden propped his casted arm on the counter as Weston wrapped the clear, protective sheet over the cast, following the path of the fiberglass, leaving Camden's fingers free but his cast covered.

"What are the rules?" Camden asked, bouncing up and down on his toes, picking an ice cream scoop and Styrofoam to-go container from the counter. "It's a competition, so there has to be rules."

"He is *so* your kid." Weston turned to peer over his shoulder, and Lyla. "You're not going to let the kid win?" Weston asked, a slight pull at the corner of his mouth.

"Absolutely not." She waved the ice cream scoop in the air. "You heard the boy, West. Give us some rules."

Weston shook his head with a laugh and cleared his throat.

"There are three rules. Rule number one... I'm going to set this timer for seven minutes. Remember, the goal is to build the biggest sundae."

Lyla pointed two fingers at her eyes then directed them to Camden.

"You're going down, Mom." Camden leaned forward like an athlete ready to make a play.

"Rule number two." Weston clapped his hands together. "The timer will reset for fifteen minutes after the sundae is assembled. Whoever eats the most of their ginormous sundae in that time without throwing up or getting a brain freeze wins the ribbon."

"And rule number three?" Lyla tilted the ice cream scoop like a microphone toward Weston's lips.

"Rule number three is..." he dragged out the words then called out, "boys against girl!" He grabbed the ice cream scoop from Lyla's hand and began digging into buckets, him and Camden roaring with laughter while Lyla clamored to find another scoop.

"Don't think I won't use my hands, West!" she said over their laugh. Weston handed her scoop back over, probably knowing from past experience that the threat was very real, then found an additional scoop for himself.

"Go, Cam, Go!" he urged as Camden piled scoops of double chocolate over scoops of mint chocolate chip and rocky road. "Don't forget toppings!"

Lyla and Camden raced to the topping counter, boxing each other out like basketball players going for a rebound. Weston stepped in between her and her son while shoveling scoops of sprinkles onto their sundae and blocking Lyla's path to the topping buckets.

"You never did know how to beat me without cheating," Lyla jested. Weston looked over his shoulder, one eyebrow raised, then tossed a scoopful of walnuts onto Lyla's sundae.

"You're in trouble now," Camden said. "She hates nuts."

"I know." Weston looked at Lyla. Her jaw was dropped, her eyes narrowed and the timer sounded.

"Dig in!" Weston ordered, reaching for spoons, but Lyla snagged the entire container. Camden acted quickly, grabbing two forks instead. He stuck out his tongue at her.

Camden had a chocolate mustache, a smear of unknown origin across his shirt and ice cream up to his elbows. Lyla's hair was slicked back with a chocolate and whipped cream concoction. Weston's arms looked like they were bruised and bloodied from battle, but the dark spots were just a mix of fudge and strawberry.

Camden reached over and grabbed a can of whipped cream, spraying the contents into his mouth. She couldn't imagine taking another bite, but somehow Camden kept going.

"So, who won?" He sprayed more whipped cream.

Weston handed the blue ribbon to Lyla. She ripped it from his fingers with a loud "Wooo!" Weston high-fived Camden then looked toward Lyla.

"You okay?" Weston asked.

"Yeah, just thinking about the last time we did this."

"I know." Weston's tone took on the same sullen hint as hers. "Charlie would've beat all three of us in an eating competition though."

She smiled at him for a moment. Sadness wouldn't bring their friend back, but retelling stories of the best of him kept his memory alive.

"Who's Charlie?" Camden broke the automatic moment of silence.

Weston turned toward Lyla and swallowed hard.

"He doesn't know?" Weston's voice cracked as he spoke. Lyla shook her head in a long, drawn-out but distinct no. Camden's confused look stayed affixed to his chocolate-stained face.

"A really good friend of ours, kiddo." Lyla's voice cracked. "His name was Charlie Camden. He was a really, really great person."

Weston reached over and grabbed Lyla's hand.

"That's where my name came from?" he asked. Lyla nodded. Then before she could speak again, Camden added another thought. "You said *was*."

Weston's eyes dimmed in a sympathetic downcast, and Lyla closed hers tightly. She couldn't talk. The words wouldn't come out without the tears. She looked at Weston, a plea for her to tap out.

"He passed away when we were teenagers." Weston took over for Lyla. "But before that he was funny, smart, kind and the best friend any of us ever had. He would be honored to have shared a name with you."

Camden nodded, his chest puffed out and face serious, like he was ready to take on the task of filling Charlie's shoes.

Lyla and Weston paced the dock, the wood creaking beneath their feet as it floated on the water. The moonlight lit the center of the lake like a spotlight over an otherwise-dark stage. The water didn't ripple. There was no sign of a boat coming or going, no waves made by a nearby engine or craft.

"They've been gone forever." Panic shook Lyla's vocal cords.

"They haven't been gone that long." Weston said, but Lyla wasn't convinced and the wavering in Weston's voice said he wasn't either.

"We should tell someone." She pushed herself up and started down the dock. Lyla was always the voice of reason. She was trying to let loose a bit, fit into her friend group's 'you only live once' style of existence, but something in her gut said this was different.

"We can't tell anyone, Savvy. Do you know how much trouble Charlie could get in? How much trouble we could get in? We just have to wait until he comes back."

She whipped around, her curls flying in the wind off the water.

"And what if he doesn't come back, West?"

Weston pushed himself up and walked toward her, wrapping his arms around her and pressing his lips into her hairline. Her body shook with worry and her heart pounded hard enough that he must have felt it.

"I have an idea." Weston grabbed her hand and pulled her the length of the dock, the echo of their heavy jog fading over the open lake. He pulled her to the marina office, plowed through the door he had left unlocked and ran to the desk.

"Remember when I went on that fishing trip and we talked over the radio? The radios work over the water. We can call into the boat."

Weston's words collided. Lyla barely heard them but understood what he was getting at. Her heart rate slowed a bit, her hands trying to settle from their tremor. This has to work. Weston searched in the dark room for the radio, knocking the main desk's contents and papers askew.

He grabbed the radio. Wasting no time, he held down the call button, which sounded a high-pitched tune.

"Charlie," he said, breathing heavily into the radio speaker. "Charlie, come on, man. Answer me."

Moments passed and silence remained. Weston slammed his hand on the countertop. Tears pressed in Lyla's eyes.

She took the radio from Weston as if her attempt might have a different outcome.

"Charlie Camden, you better answer this call right now," she threatened into the speaker, tears falling against the radio. "You have thirty seconds, or I'm sending security."

Lyla and Weston stood in the dark marina office.

Weston moved toward the door, holding it open for Lyla.

"Now we have to go find someone to help. I don't know what else to do," he said with a shrug.

As Lyla stepped over the threshold, the radio buzzed and a familiar voice came through the static line.

"Jeez, you two, relax. Live a little. It's gorgeous out here. You're missing out."

Chapter Twenty-Five

Weston

The logs that made up their fire crackled and popped, sprinkling ash and sparks over the dirt driveway at Site 101.

"Tonight was amazing." Lyla leaned into Weston, her back against his chest. "I haven't laughed like that in a long time. It really brought me back to when we were young."

"We're still young, Savvy." Weston wrapped an arm around her waist.

"This place is like our own real-life Neverland. I come here, start aging backward and refuse to grow up."

Weston nodded, resting his chin on the top of Lyla's head. "Doesn't seem like it was all that long ago. We were kids here—no responsibility, nothing we had to do except buy ice cream from the snack bar, participate in the activities and find some way to get in trouble when the sun went down."

"You and Charlie were constantly getting into trouble with the campground security." Lyla laughed. "Remember the year your father refused to claim you were his? Every time security called over the radio or brought you home, he lied and said you belonged to the Camdens."

"We had a lot of good times. That was for sure."

"I remember so much." Lyla shifted so she was lying flat, looking at the stars. "Mostly about you."

"What do you remember?" he asked, Achilles joining them on the blanket and curling up in the space between Weston and Lyla.

"I remember the year you traded your bike for a skateboard, and your father actually almost killed you."

"Not my best year." Weston flipped his hat from forward-facing to backward.

"And the year you decided a Mohawk was a good idea. It wasn't."

"It wasn't that bad. That was before you. I didn't even know you then."

"It doesn't mean I didn't notice." Her lip curled into a shy smile. "You used to go to the snack bar and order a vanilla milkshake with gummy bears mixed in and Dotty always kept frozen Snickers bars for you in the back freezer at the general store."

"She still does," Weston said, and Lyla laughed an echoing sound that drifted above the fire and into the sky.

"Can I ask you something?" Lyla leaned up on her elbow, her head in her hand. She used the other to pet behind Achilles' ears. The way she avoided looking at

Weston made him uneasy about what type of question would follow.

"Do you really not want kids?" Her eyes stayed fixed on the dog between them. Weston could tell this was a question she had been hanging on to for weeks and its weight was wearing her down. "You're just so good with Camden. I mean, it comes so naturally to you. I was just surprised to hear you say it, I guess. And maybe, in a way, a little hurt too."

Weston bit his bottom lip. He'd never wanted kids. Or at least, he didn't think he did. But his comments when they'd reconnected weren't supposed to be hurtful, just honest. He hadn't even known Camden then. Not really, anyway.

"I never thought I'd be a good father." Weston turned and snapped off a twig from a nearby log, feeding it to the flames. "I don't know. I spend a lot of time listening to people tell me how many times I screwed up and how the guy I used to be wasn't anything to be proud of. I guess I just felt like I wouldn't be a good role model."

"You're not the Weston Accardi you used to be." Lyla reached her hand over the dog and rested it on the prosthetic that took up the space where Weston's natural leg used to be. "You've come such a long way. We all have. And Camden looks up to you so much. Whether you like it or not, you're who he wants to be when he grows up."

Weston nodded, a smile he couldn't control growing across his face. Maybe, despite all he'd been groomed to believe about himself, he could fit into a parenting role after all.

* * * *

The hot summer days faded into cool summer nights. Everything was going according to plan. No, better than he'd planned. When he had opened the grounds, he'd expected hard work. He'd known problems would arise. He'd imagined he would endure a tough first year but learn from every experience. The campground was the first love of his life. He'd never expected the other love of his life would waltz back in and complete the dream. From the beginning of his plans to reopen and rebuild, something had always been missing—he was sure of that. Now, with confidence, he knew it was her.

They ran alongside each other in the mornings and spent the nights watching the stars glow in the skies, and he was happy—truly happy—the kind of fulfillment that reopening the campground couldn't have accomplished alone.

Sheila walked into her office, heels clicking against the wood floor. Weston was plopped in her seat, feet up on the desk and a half-moon smile on his face.

"You're...early." She glanced at her watch—twice for good measure—with her jaw dropped in disbelief. "That almost never happens."

"I'm in a good mood." He placed his hands behind his head and reclined the chair.

"That also almost never happens these days." She looked at him over her glasses.

He laughed and removed his feet from her desk. "Sorry about that. This year has been a bit of a roller coaster."

"You've handled it better than I had thought. Your dad was kind of a hot head, as I'm sure you remember. Never with us, but with the business in general, his fuse was about as long as a toothpick."

"Yeah," he recalled, "I do remember. Anyway, what's on the agenda for today?"

"Lunch tomorrow." She motioned for him to move, and he obliged. She took her seat and flipped through organized folders of paperwork. Sheila pulled a packet of printed forms out, marked with various colored tabs. "This is the list of investors expected to be in attendance." She licked her thumb and returned it to the corner of the pages. "And this is what we had in mind as far as what ideas to present to them, what options to discuss and so forth."

Weston scanned the list, nodding in agreement to many of the included items—WiFi or an office space with computers for public use, a small waterplay park, an indoor play area for rainy days, a dog park. His gaze stopped toward the end of the list.

"I don't know about that last one." Weston rubbed his jaw. "It's just not ready yet."

"You don't think anything is ready. You didn't think the campground was ready and look how it's going. It's a brilliant idea, Weston. Probably the one that's going to sell the investors the most, if I'm being honest."

Weston rocked his head back and forth from one shoulder to the other, mentally weighing his options on revealing some information regarding one of his newer ideas. It was a project that he'd started long before he'd even begun plans for the rest of the campground. It was ready and he knew it was, but something in him kept pulling him back from letting this new idea become a reality.

"Okay," he said, "I'll have it ready to showcase. But there's something I have to do first."

* * * *

Lyla sat on the beach, her chair laid flat, allowing the sun to kiss her skin. Camden was building a large sandcastle fortress not too far from her spot, dragging buckets full of water from the lake's edge to his construction site with his good hand and his casted arm secured in a plastic cover.

"Good afternoon." Weston plopped down in the sand next to Lyla.

"Good afternoon. How'd the rest of your morning go?"

"You mean after you obliterated me on our run...again?"

Lyla nodded and laughed.

"It was good. I had some work to get done and a meeting with Sheila." Weston watched as Camden shoveled more sand into the buckets. "What do you have planned for tonight?"

"Camden is camping out at a friend's house for the night. For some reason I cannot figure out, he actually wants to tent camp. I don't really have anything specific in mind for myself."

"I wanted to show you something. A concept piece for one of the new amenities we're going to pitch to the investors. Can I borrow you for the night?"

Lyla rolled her eyes. "Investors," she said as she let out an exhale. "You're going to modernize this place and it's going to lose all its Neverland-esque charm."

"Can you at the very least come see it before you decide you hate all my ideas?"

Lyla stole Weston's hat from his head and pulled it down over her curls.

"I suppose." She smiled and returned her face to the direction of the rays. "Can I run something past you?"

Weston nodded and rested his arm on the side of her chair.

"I think I was a bit too hard on my dad." Her lips twisted into a regretful pout. Weston ran his hand across his forehead and into his hair. "I mean, I told him to leave the campground. That's a bit harsh."

Weston looked at Lyla, his eyebrows rising a bit to give space for his eyes to widen.

"What?"

"Savvy," Weston didn't know how to approach the topic, "your dad hasn't left Begoa's. He's still here."

Lyla sat up, leaning forward in her chair. "You're sure?"

"Positive." He ran his hand over his hair. "I've seen him at the golf course a few times."

"And you didn't feel like you should mention it to me?" A hint of annoyance cloaked her words.

"I've interfered many, many times with you and your father. I can't be involved with decisions involving the two of you anymore. You're going to forgive him and be close to him or you're not, but I can't be a factor in it. Besides, I kind of figured one of you would've reached out to the other by now."

"Why's that?" She looked at him from under long lashes.

"You two never stay mad at each other long. You say your piece then move on. It's just what the two of you do."

Lyla took in all the information.

"Anyway," Weston stood up from his spot, shaking the sand from his shorts. "I have some things I need to set up for tonight. Finishing touches. I'll see you later?"

Lyla nodded, but her mind was elsewhere, her expression leaving it clear that she was still torn about her father.

"Savvy?" Weston said, and she looked up at him with soft eyes. "I told you I'm not going anywhere. If you want to reach out to your dad, I'll support it."

The confusion lifted from her face a bit, leaving her eyes a clear blue that sparkled in the summer sun.

* * * *

Weston arrived at Site 101 when afternoon was morphing into evening. The birds closed out their daytime songs and the crickets started to take over, warming up for what would be an all-night concert. A gentleman at Site 102 waved to Weston with a spatula in his hand as he leaned over a charcoal grill. A family across the way held hands with their heads bowed over a full table of food, while another family at a nearby site threw a football around, playing two-hand touch in the dirt road. That was one of the most beautiful things about this place. In any direction, there was a family who believed and behaved differently but belonged all the same.

Weston turned into the site driveway. The clothesline was pulled from a post alongside the deck to the corner of the house. On it, newly tie-dyed T-shirts hung in the sunlight. Camden's freshly laundered 'Camp Champ' T-shirt drip-dried to the left of the colorful handmade shirts and, to the right, a beautiful white sundress with a sunflower pattern across the skirt. Weston admired it from where he stood, picturing how beautiful Lyla would look in it. In all their shared years at Begoa's, he'd never seen her in a dress. She had an unbreakable bond with shorts and sneakers.

"I'd offer to let you borrow it, but I'm not sure it's your size." Lyla came out, startling Weston. He jumped backward but tried to recover as if he were unfazed by her sudden appearance. She leaned into the edge of the sliding door as she spoke. "Camden and I stopped at the craft fair in the square this afternoon. Mrs. Bennington had that hanging from her tent and insisted it was made for me." Lyla tossed her curls back in with dramatic flair.

"She was right." Weston stepped toward her and took her hand in his. "Ready?" he asked.

"Let me just get my bag." Lyla skipped into the cabin, grabbing a small backpack and returning to close the door and follow Weston down the stairs.

They walked hand in hand down the main road and through the square where the snack bar was serving the dinner rush—the line a mile long. The beach was almost empty. The chairs, umbrellas and coolers had been packed up, and only a handful of people remained. Some were desperate to soak in that very last ray of sun as it lowered itself to cool off in the lake, while others played bocce ball in the vacant space that had previously been occupied by hundreds of families. Their footprints trailed behind them as they passed the mini golf course and the overturned canoes on the sand, which had been retired for the evening.

Lyla grasped Weston's hand a bit tighter as they turned onto the road that led to the docks.

"Are we going to the marina?" Her voice sounded hopeful that the answer would be a resounding no.

"No." Her grip on his fingers eased a bit. "Past it."

"There isn't anything past the marina." Lyla's voice was sure and steadfast. She wasn't wrong—she very rarely was. She knew these grounds as well as Weston did himself, maybe better.

"There wasn't anything beyond the marina. But there could be. There's so much waterfront space, a quiet area and such a beautiful view. There's so much wasted space that someone could be enjoying."

The dirt path they had walked on ended abruptly and became a mossy green forest floor in a harsh line that separated the road often traveled from no road at all. Weston moved as if he could see a walkway that she couldn't. There were large trees all around, the foliage seemingly getting thicker by the inch. Large bushes covered in tiny blue specks crossed the area they had chosen as their path. Lyla reached for a berry at the end of a protruding branch.

"They're just like the faux berry bushes at that beginning of the pathway to the clearing." She squashed the berry in her fingers. Weston smiled as she turned toward him, her curls helicoptering around her shoulder as she turned. "These are actual blueberries!" Her voice carried in the echo between the thickly settled trees. "Real, wild Maine blueberries. Right here on the grounds. Who knew?" She stepped away from the bush, leaving the rest of the tiny purple-hued berries intact.

They traveled farther, Lyla looking over her shoulder every few feet, surely mentally measuring how far they'd ventured from the grounds.

"Almost there," Weston whispered, reading her mind.

He veered right, pulling her to follow. As they moved beyond what seemed like the emerald green end of the earth, sand and water came into view. A small strip of beach met crystal clear lake water. The area was almost untouched, no sign of human interruption as far as discarded trash or ashy logs left from fires. Someone had been there, though. A bridge extended from the edge of the sand over the rippling water and connected to a similar untouched piece of land on the other side of the inlet.

"It's gorgeous." Lyla ran her hands across the banister. She turned her head over her shoulder and looked at Weston.

"Thank you. It wasn't easy, but the work was worth the reward."

"You..." Lyla started, shaking the handrail but it remained sturdy in her grasp. "You built a bridge?"

"Surprising, right? Usually I'm burning bridges — and here I am building them."

Lyla turned around and rolled her eyes at him, he smiled in return. "Is this what you wanted to show me?"

Weston moved forward and placed both his hands on her hips. He led her backward until they were both at the center of the structure. He checked his watch, and she waited, looking around to figure out what secret he was keeping. He held up five fingers, then four. He tucked another finger down, leaving two remaining pointed to the sky. He lingered on the last one, his timing off by a half-second. When he closed his fist, a stream of water sprayed up from the lake where a fountain placed beneath the water's surface powered the display. The leaping water show sprayed upward, arched at the top then rained down to meet the water again.

Lyla looked up at to the highest arch of the fountain, the water's reflection sparkling in her eyes. Weston didn't watch the water move and fly, but instead watched her. He focused on the way she lit up and her smile danced.

"I can't believe you did all this." She spoke to the sky, never looking away from the fountain.

Weston took her hand and flipped it over, placing his hand flat against hers. Her gaze trailed down his arm and to their fingers. When he pulled his away, one brand new penny sat in her palm.

"Make a wish," he said. "Make it a good one."

She turned the penny in her fingertips then closed her hand around it tight. "Can I save my wish?" Her cheeks blushed a light pink. "There's nothing else in the world I need right now."

She looked up from under her long, dark lashes, and Weston leaned down to kiss her.

"So," she whispered as they parted, "you asked me to bring an overnight bag. Are we sleeping on the bridge?" She laughed, and he shook his head. He placed both hands on her shoulders and turned her around, leading her to the other side. Their feet met the sand, which turned to forest and foliage once more, and just beyond a new row of wild blueberry bushes, a large, tan, dome-shaped tent sat in a cleared-out space in the middle of the woods.

"West." The name was a whisper. That one syllable, though quiet, held the weight of a million words. True awe came out in it. She couldn't speak anymore. There was clearly nothing else worth saying. The goal had been to leave her speechless and he'd succeeded.

"Come on in." He led her toward the door and opened it, allowing her to enter first.

This was no ordinary tent. Its thick canvas walls protected its occupants from insects and weather. The space was vast, allowing enough room to stand and walk around, even accounting for a true, full sized bed. The frame was made from hand-cut logs, and the mattress it held was covered with what appeared to be homemade blankets.

The structure was built to look like a tent but function like a cabin. It had running water and a fully working fireplace.

Lyla paced the area, twirling with her arms out beside her as she looked around.

"Do you like it?" Weston asked. Her seal of approval was all he needed to move forward with such a huge undertaking. He wanted to offer more on the campground, a place to stay that was more than just a standard cabin. A place parents could rent out for a night to get a much-deserved break from their rambunctious children or an area that could be used for teen birthday sleepovers and so much more. But going forward with plans of this magnitude meant modernizing Begoa's, which so far Lyla had vocally voted against.

She turned to look at him and her eyes appeared dazzled with amazement.

"It's like a dream," she said breathlessly.

"Oh, wait, one more thing." Weston stepped past her, heading toward the bed at the center of the room.

"There's more?" Her voice raised an octave.

Weston stood on one of the logs that made up the bedframe and reached toward the top of the tent, undoing three tied sections of canvas. The fabric broke away from the ceiling, unrolling downward to separate the bed from the rest of the room.

"Come here," he said from inside the sectioned-off area. She giggled as she made her way inside, but her laughter was cut off, silence taking its place as she walked in and looked up.

A clear section remained where the canvas had been covering a skylight that gave them an uninterrupted view of the starry sky above. She stepped forward, gazed at the sky then turned to lay on the bed.

Weston lay down next to her with his hands behind his head, watching the sky, the ceiling above him a snapshot of a perfectly clear night, full of a bright moon and scattered stars.

They were quiet for a while, in a way that let the silence do all the talking.

"He would be so, so, so, unbelievably proud of you, you know," she whispered.

"Charlie?" Weston spoke to the ceiling.

"Your father." Lyla found his hand and squeezed tight as she said the words.

Weston looked around the room at the intricate décor as he thought about the possibilities of expanding the area around them and making similar tents with different themes and ideas. He thought about the bridge and the symbolism it held — bringing together old Begoa's and new Begoa's in perfect harmony. He looked at the woman beside him, smiling, perfect and proud, and in that second, he knew he was succeeding. He was finally doing something right, and for the first time since he'd started the plans for reopening the grounds, he knew it was the right thing to do, that everything would be okay and he could finally accept that he'd grown up to become a man his father would have been proud of. Beyond that, he'd *become* the kind of man his father had been.

"West?" Lyla asked after a lengthy silence. "I need to know why Begoa's closed. I know you don't like to talk about it. I know it was hard for you. But it was hard for me too. This place was my whole world. It was here and I was here, each and every summer, my whole life—then it was just gone. There's a story there and you're the only one who knows it."

West sat up and ran his fingers across the stubble that covered his jaw line.

"That's not true, Savvy. You know the story."

"Jeez, you two. Relax. Live a little. It's gorgeous out here. You're missing out."

Weston ran inside, Lyla trailing closely behind, and grabbed the radio, slamming his finger into the button. "Charlie, this isn't funny anymore. Get back here right now. We were worried about you."

"There's nothing to worry about." Charlie said through the speaker. "You would know that if you hadn't backed out at the last second."

Weston looked at Lyla, shifting from worry to relief to regret – the last a result of not following his friend out on what could've been the adventure of a lifetime.

"You're in Sal's office, yeah?" Charlie asked. "Get a set of keys, start up a boat and come find us. It's a gorgeous night. I'm not coming back in there until you come out here. Trust me. I'm doing you a favor. I'll see you soon." Charlie cut off the radio to a dead quiet.

"I don't have the key to the box Sal keeps all the spare keys in. It's on the keyring Charlie has."

Lyla's eyes widened in surprise. "You're kidding me, right?" she asked. "You can't just take a stranger's boat, West."

"Savvy, what other choice do I have?" Weston pulled off his baseball cap and ran his hands into the roots of his hair.

"We have to go get him. It might be the only way to reel him back in."

Lyla reached into her pocket and pulled out a set of keys, dangling them in front of her.

"My dad's boat key is on the cabin key ring."

Weston's gaze followed the keys as they swung back and forth, hypnotizing him into a smile and a sigh of relief.

"We will be quick. I promise." He stuck a pinky out and she did the same, linking hers around his. They kept their fingers locked, holding tight to that everything-will-be-okay kind of promise as they returned to the docks and climbed aboard her father's boat.

Weston pulled the boat away from the dock and sped into the center of the lake. Lyla wrapped her arms around herself, and the air whipped her curls into straightened tangles. Weston looked around as he drove, searching for a sign of another boat anywhere else on the water. There was no one else he could see. He cut the engine, the boat floating and rocking on the remaining waves they had created as they sped over the open water. Lyla reached forward, placing her hand on Weston's forearm as he continued to grip the steering wheel. She stood from her seat, stepped in between him and the steering wheel and wrapped her arms around his waist. They stood there for a moment in silence, their heads both shooting up at the sound of another boat's engine echoing, getting closer by the moment. He moved his hands to her arms.

Lyla's frightened pulse accelerated under Weston's grasp at her wrist. If another boat was approaching, it had to be either Charlie or the cops. There was no third option.

The light from the boat grew brighter as the vessel approached, painstakingly slow. Neither he nor Lyla took a breath, each of them paralyzed with fear that the oncoming boat was an authority figure about to effectively end both of their lives as they knew it.

The boat pulled up next to them, the driver turning a flashlight toward himself to illuminate his face. Charlie laughed into the artificial light.

"Well, it's about damn time." He wrapped his arm around his little blonde co-captain.

"You guys missed out!" she squealed, her valley-girl voice in full effect. "It's so gorgeous out there. Way out that way, away from the lights of the campground and the town, you can see stars like you've never seen before."

Weston turned toward Lyla and shrugged. She let her head fall backward, looking to the sky for an answer. When she returned her gaze to Weston's, she nodded yes and her smile turned to one that matched the one he felt himself wearing.

"Want to race?" Charlie asked.

Suddenly, Weston was years younger, standing in a dirt circle across from a boy holding two remote control cars asking him the very same question.

It was the very first and very last question Charlie Camden ever asked Weston Accardi.

"I didn't realize how far the land came out into the water," Weston said, remembering, his eyes still affixed on the clear panel in the canvas. "We turned around the bend heading toward a small inlet and the land jutted out farther than I expected. I hit that strip of land at that speed and lost control. Flipped the boat into Charlie's boat. Totaled both of them."

He swallowed hard, fighting back fifteen years' worth of tears he'd been holding on to.

"When I came to, when I realized what was happening, I was pinned at the leg between both boats. I wasn't sure I could move at all, but all I could think about was you. I couldn't see you. I didn't know where you were...or...if...you were..." Weston couldn't control his emotions anymore. Tears streamed down his cheeks.

Lyla flipped over onto her stomach. "Shhhh," she said in a calming whisper, "I'm sorry. We don't have to talk about it."

"We do. We've needed to talk about it every day for fifteen years. We just never got the chance. Now we have it. It was a few days later before I was coherent enough to understand what was going on. Between the surgeries and medications and everything else, I wasn't thinking clearly. By the time I was functioning enough to really understand everything that had happened, your dad had already transferred you to a major hospital closer to your home."

Lyla wiped tears from her eyes. "I don't remember much," she admitted, "but I remember hearing the EMTs saying one of the males was DOA. I didn't know until the following week which one of you it was. It was the most excruciating seven days of my life. But I couldn't think about it. I had to know, but I didn't want to know because neither of the answers was going to be easy to hear."

Weston ran his hand down the side of her head, playing with her hair as she spoke.

"My injuries were nothing compared to yours," she added. "Severe concussion and I had a lot of breaks — shattered my pelvis, and after multiple surgeries and physical therapy, I was fine. It was months later, but I came here to see you, and everything was boarded up. Just gone, just like that. Like Begoa's never existed at all."

Weston nodded.

"My parents didn't really have a choice, you know?" He tensed, his breathing changing to a short, nervous puffs. "It was my fault, Savvy. We took those boats out. We raced when we had no idea what we were doing. There was so much bad press surrounding that accident...that mistake...that reservations started dropping off almost instantly. Ratings went way down. Plus, my hospital bills weren't even in the ballpark of cheap and my recovery was costly and time-consuming. They didn't have a choice but to consider giving it up. And at first, they weren't going to. They were going to try to find a way to get it up and running again." Weston took a deep breath and looked to the sky for assistance in getting through the rest of the story. "But this lawyer showed up and served my parents with papers. It was a lawsuit against them and the campground that put the final nail in the coffin. Eventually they settled, but they gave up everything for it."

"Charlie's parents..." she said in a statement, not a question.

Weston hesitated then sat up and turned away, pulling at his fingers, doing anything to distract himself and not look at Lyla's flooding eyes anymore.

She sat up on the bed at Weston's back and wrapped her arms around him from behind.

"I'm so sorry, West. I'm so sorry." A tear dripped from her jaw to his shoulder.

"I was driving the boat."

"I gave you the key," she whispered against his ear. He turned over his shoulder, and she sat back, allowing the space to grow between them before speaking again. "It was not your fault, West. It was mine."

Chapter Twenty-Six

Lyla

The time she'd spent with Weston had offered more transparency than just the skylight above the bed. They'd talked the whole night, airing out old grievances and putting the pieces of a complicated puzzle together but making it through all the year's obstacles and arriving at a clarity both had craved since the accident all those years ago.

They trekked back over the bridge and through the wooded area, walking down the path toward the main grounds, where they paused for a moment at the marina. They held hands as they looked out over the water, neither of them saying a word until they left and continued on their way.

"Have you been on a boat since?" she asked, her sandals flipping and flopping in a rhythmic pattern as they walked. He shook his head.

"Not even once."

"Me neither," she added. "Well, not a motored one. Canoes and kayaks, I can handle." Camden keeps asking to go out on one. I'm running out of excuses not to."

Weston and Lyla entered the main square near the snack bar and general store, where Camden waited at a table with some of his friends. He bounced off the seat, ran toward them and launched himself forward to hug them both. Lyla took advantage of the embrace, keeping him close to her slightly longer than usual. Someday, he would outgrow the desire to hug her in public, so for that moment, she held tight and prayed that time would just slow down.

"Are you hungry?" She ran her fingers across his brown hair. "We could go back to the site and I'll make breakfast."

Camden shook his head. "Joey's dad cooked us food. We were going to play flag football on the beach. Is that okay?"

Lyla nodded. "Just be careful. You only have one good arm as it is."

Camden laughed and ran off with his friends.

"How about you?" She reached for Weston's hand. "Can I tempt you with bacon and eggs and frozen waffles?"

"Frozen, huh? Almost impossible to say no to…" He turned to her, letting go of her hand and placing both his palms at her hips. "I would love to, but I have to go get ready for the investors' tour and lunch."

"Right, right!" Her voice was a mix of anxiety and excitement on his behalf. "That's fine. I have a few things to do. I might go up to the welcome center and snag Sheila's computer for a minute."

Weston fake-coughed the word 'hypocrite' then followed it up with a dramatic display of more coughing and banging his fist against his chest.

"I know. I know." She put her hands up in forfeit then laid them on his chest. "I don't like being tethered to it all the time. But there is something I have to do."

Weston nodded and pressed his lips to her forehead. "I'll walk you there."

* * * *

Lyla moved the mouse across the Begoa's Point mouse pad and the computer slowly awakened. Eventually the screen cooperated, and she clicked into the Internet icon to log into her email. Hundreds of emails, mostly junk, filled her screen. She moved the advertisements and clutter to the small trash can at the bottom of the page and they disappeared, leaving her screen filled with emails that were work-related reminders, autopay receipts for her bills and a few from her group of other moms and friends back home.

Though they were bold and marked new, all uniform and ready to be read, a single email stood out from the rest—one from her mother-in-law, Donna Kenney.

Lyla,
How are you doing, dear? I do hope all is well. It's been a bit since we've had time to chat. Your father mentioned that you were able to visit that old campground in Maine you always went on about. How wonderful!

And Camden, I hope that he is well too? I understand he had a minor injury, but boys will be boys! His father went through more casts at that age than I can even recall.

Do you have any plans for the Fourth of July this weekend? I'm sure the campground does something exciting!
Nothing new to report here. Please, do check in soon.
Donna

Lyla's heart clenched. Surely she wasn't expected to stay single forever, but she and her mother-in-law were very close. Would she be happy that Lyla had moved forward and found someone to spend her days with? Would she be offended? A mix of both?

But Lyla knew Donna. She would even consider her a close friend. Her instincts told her that deep down, Donna wanted what was best for her and Camden, even if it took some getting used to. She typed back a quick reply.

Donna,
The campground has a parade, fireworks, a barbecue on the beach and more. If you're free, you're welcome to join us. I would love to see you and I know Camden would love to spend some time with you.
Hoping to see you soon,
Lyla

Lyla scrolled through a few more emails, and just before closing out, a new alert filled her inbox.

Lyla,
Consider me there. Send me the details. See you this weekend.
Donna

Lyla added a few attachments and details to a response and sent it back, closed the screen and allowed the computer to resume its nap.

* * * *

The campground was buzzing, everyone out and about decorating their cabins in red, white and blue paraphernalia, getting ready for the weekend's festivities. She walked down the road, opposite to the way she would take to go back to Site 101, and found herself standing in the driveway of the new-build Weston had put her father up in for his stay — a cabin that should have been long checked out of by now but wasn't.

She rested her foot on the step to the deck, hammering her fingers against the handrail. Lyla had made the conscious decision to walk all the way there, but now that she'd arrived, she questioned why she was doing it. Maybe Weston was right. This was what she and her father did. They were both stubborn, never willing to give an inch or meet in the middle. But everyone else was changing, so why couldn't they? Then again, Lyla had been here before. How many last times would there be before it was truly the last time? How many times could they drop their relationship before it shattered beyond repair?

Lyla turned away, the dirt crunching underneath her shoe. She stepped forward, but the sound of the door opening glued her to her spot.

Jack placed two cups of coffee and a newspaper on the table, took a seat and motioned for her to follow suit. Lyla took the stairs and walked across the deck as if it were a plank leading to treacherous waters below, but there was no turning back now.

They sipped coffee under the sappy pine trees and let the campground soundtrack do all the talking. Kids laughed and played. Music sounded from various campsites. Animals were running through the bushes behind the cabin.

"Donna is coming up." Lyla tapped her fingernails against the ceramic mug.

"Great." Jack kept his eyes forward. "She's only about two hours from here."

That was Jack Savoie—always filling the voids with obvious remarks instead of steering the conversation in a way that would prove he was capable of real emotion. Lyla didn't want to spend the entire day here playing 'beat around the bush', so she dove in headfirst.

"Weston and I talked about the accident last night— really talked about it for the first time." She swallowed hard, the sound as loud as her speaking voice. "I feel like everything is so clear now. I had so many questions. I mean, I had heard different accounts from different people, but not anyone who was there. It was always this black hole in my memory, like the day didn't exist at all."

"I would think that's for the best. Perhaps you should've just left it forgotten. Sealed away." He cleared his throat and took another sip.

"I can't change the past, Dad. And I'd say I've learned a lot from it. I turned out okay, despite everything. But I still wanted to know what happened."

Jack placed his coffee down and reached his hand across the table, placing it on hers.

"I know we don't always see eye to eye. But I want you to know that I thank my lucky stars every single day that I still have you. Every day, Lyla. A parent shouldn't ever have to bury their child, Ly. I thought I'd lost you that day and I don't ever want to feel that way again."

He removed his hand and picked up the newspaper, unfolding it and scanning its print.

Lyla smiled. He'd allowed himself to be vulnerable. For exactly ten seconds, but ten seconds of kindness from Jack Savoie was a lottery win of its own.

She stood up from her chair, wanting more but intending not to push him away with an overload of questions and emotions. She reached the stairs and turned, just for a moment.

"Hey, Dad?" she asked. He peered at her over the papers edge. "Why'd you stay?"

"I knew we'd figure this out eventually. We always do."

She grinned as she hopped off the final stair and headed down the dirt paths that led to Site 101.

Lyla turned into her campsite and jogged up the steps. A small green envelope with the Begoa's Point logo on it was taped to the sliding door. She pulled it from the glass, sliding a finger under the seal.

Investor Lunch at one at the lakeside restaurant. I'd love to have you by my side. Bring Cam.

Lyla smiled and her cheeks warmed. Something about being on the arm of the owner of her favorite place in the world for such an important meeting tickled her in an indescribable way. Wes wanted her there and she was proud.

She went inside and checked the clock. It was already noon. She had only a bit of time to wash away her usual campground casual and transform it into presentable poise — and she knew just what to wear.

Lyla left her curls down, hanging around her tan shoulders. She pulled the sunflower dress over her head and adjusted the skirt around her hips. It fit like it was tailored to her. She hardly recognized herself — not just because of the dress, but the whole package. The happiness. The feeling of being whole again. And home again.

She slid her feet into decorated sandals and applied a pink shimmer lip gloss to her lips. It was the only cosmetic she had with her at the campground.

Where is the boy? She peeked a head outside the sliding door, hoping to catch a glimpse of him running by with his friends. The wind had picked up, causing her styled curls to find their way back to their usual unstyled look.

She paced around the main living room quarters of the site, hopeful that he'd make it back so she could take him to lunch too. With only moments to spare, a sweaty, heavy-breathing version of Camden ran into the cabin.

"Hey!" she exclaimed as he entered, "I was hoping you'd come along. Weston invited us for an important lunch at the restaurant. He wants you to come. Go wash up and hurry. We're going to be late."

Camden beamed an excited smile as he ran toward the bathroom. The water sounded and a few moments later, a slightly cleaner boy emerged through door.

"Better?"

"Passable," she said. "Change your shirt and let's go."

Chapter Twenty-Seven

Weston

The meeting wasn't going as planned. Weston couldn't say the right thing no matter how hard he tried. What did he know about running a business? Nothing...that was what. There he sat in the restaurant in a T-shirt and cargo shorts, in front of a group full of suits with their ties done so tight that he wondered how they could breathe. He was out of place in his own home — not to mention he'd just made them follow him to an undisclosed location, off map, through the woods and across a handmade bridge. And it was the windiest day of the summer so far.

One thing was for sure... They didn't have quite the same reaction to the idea of the new-style tents that Lyla did. Most had been picking pine needles off their shoes when Weston had opened the ceiling for the big reveal. It was not the reaction he had hoped for. *Not even close.*

Over the lunch table, each time an investor asked Weston a question, he either spoke in rambling, roundabout answers that made no sense — not even to him — or made a joke that was poorly received. The crickets at this table were louder than the ones that lived on the grounds. Weston wiped his brow. He needed something to wow them. Something needed to change in the next few minutes, or they were going to leave the grounds for good, not giving it a second thought, never mind a dollar.

A balding gentleman leaned forward. He wore thick glasses and a tie that had some color and life versus the solid neutrals of his businessmen friends. "Mr. Accardi," he began, adjusting his napkin over his lap. "Why this venture? Why a family campground?"

Finally, a question Weston could respond to without tripping over a pre-rehearsed answer or Sheila bailing him out.

"I grew up here, sir. And I just don't mean because I lived here." Weston sat up straight, talking with his hands the way he did when he was nervous. "I grew up here. I learned here and explored here. I was part of teams and competed individually. I learned the value of family and memories and moments. I laughed here. I fell in love here. I made friends here and I lost them here. But this place built me then rebuilt me. It was my turn to rebuild it."

The investor nodded and wrote something down with a gold-plated pen.

"But you're not married yourself? No children?" Every eye turned, giving Weston the floor and their full attention, probably for the first time since they had arrived. Sweat beaded across his forehead.

"Well," he said, letting out a deep breath.

"That situation is changing." Sheila said, placing her hand on Weston's arm, cutting him off before he had the chance to speak. "Weston has found love, right here on the grounds. It's the most amazing 'star-crossed lovers' story, truly. You have to hear it." She nodded quickly and smiled, and the men and women across from him leaned in. This had their attention. But Weston remained unsure. His situation was still new, still fragile. His story with Lyla wasn't supposed to be the selling point of this meeting. He hadn't wanted that and thought he had made it clear.

As he decided what words to use, what stories were his to tell, the door opened, a small voice echoing through the otherwise empty restaurant that had been closed for this particular event. Camden stumbled in, standing up straight and adjusting his posture once he saw all the well-dressed adults at the table. Lyla stepped in behind him, placing her hands on his shoulders and ushering him forward. Weston's mouth parted, unsure why she was here or what was happening, but it only took him a moment to figure out that she had been invited — just not by him.

"I'm so sorry we're late." She approached the table. "Hi, I'm Lyla and this is my son, Camden." Camden waved with his casted arm, garnering a light chuckle from the tough crowd. It was more than Weston had gotten all day. She leaned forward, shaking many outstretched hands and laughing with the investor guests as if she had been their friend for years. She was brilliant. Perfect.

And Weston was furious.

He wrung his cloth napkin in his hands and made a tight-pressed snarl as he looked over at Sheila, who was beaming.

But she was here and there wasn't anything that could be said or done at this moment that wouldn't take the meeting from bad to worse, so he rolled with the punches as they were thrown.

He stood from his chair and walked toward her, placing his hand on her lower back and kissing her cheek before pulling out her chair then Camden's.

"Weston was just about to tell us how you two met," one of the gentlemen said, suddenly interested in the meeting he had been yawning through since he arrived. "But perhaps you could kick off the tale." The other investors nodded in agreement, a wave of interested whispers floated over the table.

"Oh, we met when we were just kids." She wore a smile that touched both ears. "We always knew each other, played the same games and competed in the same tournaments on the grounds, but we didn't get close until our teen years. But those summers, they were wonderful."

"Just the summers?" a woman asked. She was obviously invested in the story, though Weston felt that might be the only thing she'd be investing in.

"We actually didn't keep in touch during the year." Lyla shrugged. The investors did a collective eye-widen, jaw-drop dance at her words. "We were young. Besides, Weston's parents weren't much for technology. Weston still isn't. It's one of the charms of being here. Poor cell phone service leaves us less tethered to the wires and more tethered to our families and the world. Maybe I have a naïve or narrow view, but I think it's the best thing about coming here."

She paused, and a few of the investors took a sip of their ice waters.

"You were right, Sheila," one of the gentlemen said, drying his lips with his napkin. Weston raised an eyebrow.

"Well, I'm sure you know we had expressed some concerns," the man continued, "but Sheila assured us that you weren't just the single, lonely woodsman we see on the TV and in the interviews. You're a family man now. That's a good look for the grounds, you know. A family campground of this size and demand should be run by someone with family values. We didn't see it in you before, but we didn't know you were hiding such a beautiful woman and child."

Weston's focus traveled to Lyla's, but she stared blankly ahead, her usually sun-kissed complexion fading to a pale white.

"Lyla," another attendant added, "tell us what you think of Weston's plans for development. Do you have a favorite part? Something you're looking forward to seeing?"

Lyla's glare met his for a moment. His eyes were pleading, apologetic even, but hers? They were distant, lost somewhere between angry and disappointed.

Her voice wavered but she answered, and her response was nothing short of perfect. She played the role perfectly — no matter how upset she clearly was to find out she'd been inadvertently cast for it.

"Did he show you the Star Hut?" She cleared her throat. Whispers and under breath questions filled the room.

"The new campsite over the bridge that we walked to earlier." Weston didn't attempt to hide his frustration. "Yes, they've seen it."

"Star Hut." A woman nodded as she said it. "Now that changes everything. Has a nice ring to it."

Waiters and waitresses appeared, placing lobster, steak and chicken in front of each person according to what they'd ordered. Weston had never been more thankful for food. Chewing meant a reprieve from debating and selling. He was no longer in the mood to talk to anyone in the room except Lyla. The look on her face as she pushed a piece of broccoli around her plate said she wouldn't be talking to him anytime soon. She wouldn't even look at him then.

At the end of the lunch, Lyla stood at one side of the table, investors shaking her hand with goodbye salutations. She flashed her pearly white teeth and was as kind as could be, giving them all her attention and keeping strong eye contact as they rambled on. Some of the attendants said their goodbyes to Weston at the other side of the room, but she was far more attentive than him. His gaze wandered over their shoulders to watch Lyla steal the show, clearly putting on a brave face when inside she was probably fighting crippling confusion.

"We will be in touch, Weston," the balding guy said, shaking Weston's hand as he left the room.

Every potential investor had gone except for one who insisted on continuing a lengthy conversation with Weston, no matter how many times Weston tried to cut it short. Apart from them, only Lyla, Camden and Sheila remained.

Weston was tuned in to Lyla, completely ignoring the sentiments the lingering businessman was sharing with him.

"Camden, why don't you go find your friends and enjoy the rest of the day?" Lyla ruffled her hand in his hair and sent him on his way.

"Lyla," Sheila said, "you were just perfect. I've been telling Weston for weeks you were the solution. The golden ticket. This couldn't have gone any better. And the boy? That was just the cherry on top. Well done."

Sheila pressed her hand to Lyla's shoulder then left the restaurant. Weston fumed as he heard the words come out of Sheila's mouth. There was no confusing Lyla's emotions now. She was the very picture of seething. She turned on her heel and stomped out of the door.

"Sir, I'm so sorry." Weston pushed past the investor, cutting off any further conversation. "I have to go," he added, chasing after Lyla.

"Savvy," he called out as she stormed down the beach with a vengeance that matched the hurricane-force winds that blew her hair and dress in a fury. "Savvy. Just stop, please!"

He jogged after her, the sand flying around his shins and ankles, both from the particles he was kicking up and some the wind was carrying. He closed the distance between them and grabbed her hand.

"What, West?" she snapped, turning toward him like a tornado in the already-gusting wind. "It all makes perfect sense now. Crystal clear."

"What's clear?" Weston yelled back. "Fill me in, because whatever epiphany you've come to hasn't quite reached me yet." He dropped his hands, slapping them against his thighs as they fell.

"Suddenly the timing just all seems so perfect." Tears spilled over the brim of her eyelids.

"Timing?" he whispered, the wind drowning out the word. "Timing of what?"

"All of it. I don't hear from you for fifteen years. Nothing. No call. No letter. Silence. For a decade and a half. And you open this campground. You get us off the waitlist. And now all of a sudden, we're talking again after half a lifetime of nothing? The invite for today taped to my door —"

"No," he said, adamant, firm, quite literally digging his foot into the sand as he said the word. He was piecing together what Lyla was implying and she was all wrong. "That's not how it is at all."

"Of course it's not, West." She wiped the tears from under her eyes. "What other reason could there possibly be? You don't show up for fifteen years and here you are, stringing me right back along in perfect time to help you build up your image as this family-friendly guy you need your investors to see you as. You even said you never wanted kids! This isn't just about me and you anymore, West. I have Camden to think about. He will not be a pawn in your business game."

Her voice cracked as she hollered over the wind, her hair blew around her face and stuck to her tears.

"I didn't invite you here today. This was not some carefully crafted plan to use you and Camden as a ploy to get more financial interest. You have to believe that."

"That still doesn't answer any of the other questions. As usual, you give me bits and pieces of information but never the whole story."

Weston crossed his arms over his chest, holding himself together as everything unraveled around them.

"You could've ruined me in there, Savvy. If you were so mad, why play along? Why not speak up and say it was all a setup?"

"Because, Weston," she said, sounding out the syllables in his name, "I am capable of putting others first. This is the place I love, run by the man I love." Just like that, she said the word he had been holding on to since the last time he'd heard the same sentiment more than a decade ago. He would've given anything to hear her say it—but not like this. Not now. "I gave you some credit about not reaching out to me that first summer. But you let years go by without even trying. And now I'm sitting at a table full of people in suits being portrayed as the sob-story widow who found love again so you can expand your business. What am I supposed to make of that?"

"I couldn't contact you, Lyla." Weston called to the sky. His fists clenched at his sides, the words he'd been fighting back burning on the way out. It was the first time he used her given name, maybe ever. "Not because I didn't want to. Not because I forgot about you. I couldn't."

Her eyes softened, giving him time to elaborate.

"I legally couldn't contact you after the lawsuit went through." He ran his hand through his hair. The wind softened a bit, allowing for a quieter conversation. "The campground closed. My family was legally bound to not contact you after the settlement."

"What in the world does Charlie's parents suing your parents have to do with me?" she cried, but her voice trailed off at the end of the question. She already knew.

Weston moved toward her, closing both her hands in his. She stared over his shoulder, probably putting all the fragmented pieces together one by one.

"Do you really think your father retired as early as he was able to on a teacher's salary alone?" His quiet whisper of a voice shook as he spoke, low and serious. "If you want to know why this campground closed, if you want to know every detail, you're asking the wrong man."

He stepped backward, putting space between them for the wind to blow through. "As for why now, why you're here? You're still asking the wrong person."

Weston turned and walked down the beach, leaving Lyla with the only answers he could give her.

Chapter Twenty-Eight

Lyla

Lyla's feet pounded against the cement as she stormed up the campground streets toward her father's cabin. He was sitting in his usual spot in the corner of the deck with a book open in his hands.

"Lyla? What's wrong?"

Tears threatened to pour out, but she controlled them. She'd always hated that she was a person who cried when she was mad. It made her feel small and emotional.

"Everything," she finally said, crossing her arms.

Jack pushed his glasses into his receding hair and stood, tossing his book onto the table. "Weston told you."

"*You* should've told me!" she screamed, her voice carrying, birds retreating from the tree branches above them. Campers stuck their heads out from their sites, but she didn't care who was around. *Let them listen.*

"You know how hard it was for me that summer. You know what I went through and how distraught I was when this place closed down—and it was your fault!"

"Lyla," Jack said.

How can he remain so calm? She shrieked louder and louder and he stayed unruffled, his emotions in typical working order.

"I waited for him." Those were the words that broke the dam and caused a flood of tears that couldn't be stopped. "Every single day I waited, thinking Weston would reach out. I talked to you. I cried to you...and you let me! You let me carry on and wonder and wait. You could have saved me a lot of tears and you didn't. You've been lying to me every minute since that accident."

"I did what I had to do to protect this family after that mistake." He hissed the word, a subtle reminder that this was no 'wrong place at the wrong time' accident, but rather an incident that was a direct result of a poor decision she'd made.

"You've made your feelings about my choices abundantly clear. But we've all paid for it, time and time again. Charlie lost his life. Weston lost a limb. I lost the person I loved most and the place I loved most. And maybe the first two are my fault. Those losses are my burden to carry." She hammered her finger into her chest as she fell on her sword, taking her portion of the blame. "But the last two? Those are on you. You took that love from me."

Jack leaned into the deck, the railing shifting under his weight. "Lyla, please. Can you please, for one minute, just listen?"

"You've had fifteen years' worth of chances to tell me the truth and you didn't."

"I'd like to start now."

Lyla gave in, desperate for answers, leaning on the same railing. She stared at a missing rhinestone on her sandal strap rather than look at her father.

"Starting with the most minor issue, that boat was brand new. Insurance didn't want to cover the cost to replace it or what we owed because of the situation. It wasn't exactly your standard accident, so right off the bat we were upside down. Our health insurance was barely helpful, and your hospital bills, Ly? They were astronomical. I missed so much time at work during your rehab and healing.

"Everything just kept piling up and we were so far behind that I wasn't sure how we were going to get out of it. But the other girl that was on the boat with Charlie? Her father was a lawyer. He reached out and he said we had a case. There were so many rules broken — the marina not being properly locked up or guarded, the way some of the reports had been filed. There were enough inconsistencies and glaring problems that he suggested we could take action and benefit from it.

"At the time, it was an attempt at keeping us afloat, to help regain some of what we lost. I didn't realize it would get so far, so in-depth. But the girl, Christy? She was largely uninjured. They didn't have any damage to fight for funds for — not personal injury or property damage, so he really just helped me. I didn't have a choice, Lyla. My option was to lose our favorite vacation spot or lose everything else. There was never a second thought about what I was going to do. I had to do what was best for this family. Whether you see it or not, I made the right choice."

Lyla took a deep breath for the first time since the investor lunch. The day had been a rollercoaster composed of only straight downhill drops and upside-down turns. Her heart was torn. She wanted to be mad at her father, but as a parent, she could see it from his side. He'd been in an impossible position because *she'd* put him in one.

"You should have told me." Her voice was calm, her energy tank depleted.

"It wouldn't have helped." He wrapped an arm around his daughter, and she leaned her head against his chest. "For what it's worth, I am sorry. I'd be lying if I said it hasn't eaten away at me every single day."

She nodded and stayed in place, letting her father hold her, allowing that like-a-kid-again feeling to linger for just a few moments longer.

* * * *

The cabin, though mostly clean since its partial renovation, now had to be the cleanest it had ever been. Lyla buried herself in tedious chores for two reasons — first, to avoid the main square and beach at all costs. She wasn't ready to see Weston — or anyone else for that matter. Second and maybe the more stressful reason, her mother-in-law was expected to arrive in the next few hours. They got along great and Donna wasn't the judgmental type, but she was extremely organized and appreciated the art of a deep clean.

Lyla wiped her brow with the back of her forearm as she swept the floors, which were apparently made of sand. No matter how much she tried to sweep it outside, more appeared, spontaneously multiplying by the second. The early July sun beat down on the roof, raising the temperature in the cabin. A curl was slick with sweat on her forehead, and the back of her shirt stuck between her shoulder blades.

She was physically and emotionally exhausted. The bags under her eyes held carry-on luggage of their own. Sure, she had been wrong to lay into Weston about keeping secrets and maintaining his distance from her all those years ago, when in reality he wasn't the one she should have been mad at. That storm began and ended with her father, and they'd managed to weather it, but there was still a part of her that felt Weston wasn't being honest. If the lawsuit prevented Weston from contact with her, why contact her now? *He let all those years pass and suddenly, when he's in a position where he needs to look like a man with a family, now the legality goes by the wayside and gets tossed aside like an old newspaper?* It didn't make sense to her, and as much as she wanted to believe Weston's intentions were noble, she didn't. There wasn't enough evidence that said he'd brought them there for any other reason than potentially benefiting his business.

Camden exited his room while tossing a football in both hands, regardless of his cast. He headed toward the sliding door, opening it without acknowledging her at all.

"Uhhh, hello?" Her voice carried to the outside. Camden stepped inside and gave her an uncharacteristic agitated look. "Excuse me?" she asked, though he didn't say anything, she knew when her child was thinking disagreeable thoughts. Camden didn't answer. "Are you going to talk to me?" She leaned the broom against the counter.

"Are you going to talk to Weston?" he snapped back without missing a beat. The words knocked her off balance, causing her to step right into the sandpile she had swept up.

"That's not really any of your business." She swept the sweat-sticky curl from her forehead and put on what she hoped was her best stern-mother face.

"It is, though, isn't it? We've spent every day this summer with West and Achilles. Did you think I wouldn't notice they haven't been around?"

Lyla shifted her head to one side, a sadness weighing her to a downcast glare. "Weston and I have a lot to figure out, Cam."

"You love him, Mom. And he loves us. What else is there to figure out?"

Never in his life had he spoken to her the way he did now, but the thing was, he was wise beyond his years and not wrong — not in the least.

"He used us, Camden." The sentence came out harsher than she'd intended. Her voice turned to an exasperated sigh as she said the words out loud. "Why else would he have brought us here? Do you think it's coincidence that he chose now to reconnect? There is no other explanation." She ran her hand across her hair line, taking a deep breath and letting it out.

Camden stared at her with his lips parted. He ceased throwing the football.

"What?" She leaned into the counter.

"There is an explanation, actually," Camden whispered. An expression she recognized as an admission of guilt crept into his eyes.

He retreated into his room, leaving Lyla by herself with her shoulders in a confused shrug. He returned, slowly unfolding a piece of paper and shaking it out to flatten it at its creases.

"It wasn't a coincidence," Camden said as he handed over the paper accompanied by a photo of Weston and Lyla from a lifetime ago. "This wasn't Weston's idea, Mom. It was mine."

* * * *

Lyla sat at the welcome center in a golf cart, reading and rereading the letter in her hands.

If there is anything you can do to move us off the waiting list, I'd be thankful. My mom deserves to smile again – the way she smiled in the photo I sent with this letter.

Lyla smiled and cried, laughed and sat silent and still, emotion after emotion hitting her in waves. Her son—her generous, kind, warm-hearted boy—had written this letter and given her a gift she hadn't known she needed. Then there was Weston—grown, changed, responsible, imaginative, supportive—and she'd screwed up. She'd blamed him for so many things. She'd blamed him for everything. And he hadn't deserved any of the scrutiny she'd laid onto him. Lastly—and maybe the part that was breaking her heart the most at this moment—Jared.

Jared had been gone for a long time, and though her grief wasn't new or near the surface, it still existed, lying dormant, peeking its head out at unexpected and uninvited moments, with no warning of when they were coming and no indication of how long they'd stay. Today, she imagined, the sudden onslaught of emotions was mostly due to sitting in a golf cart, waiting for her former mother-in-law to arrive on the grounds.

There were three versions of Lyla. There was the kid version—the one who'd spent her summers on this campground dancing like no one was watching and competing in activities because at that age, winning was everything, and those ribbons she'd won were worth more than the ten cents it cost to print them. She'd fallen in love, for the first time, with a place and a person. Then there was life circa Jared. She'd grown up, matured, finished a degree program, walked down an aisle and promised 'until death do us part'. And then it had. And now, slightly older and maybe wiser, with a child of her own, she was back at her favorite place in the world. But it wasn't like coming full circle. It was like moving backward, but in the best way—revisiting the parts of her that made her who she was, reminding her that it was okay to let who she was be a part of who she was becoming.

She folded the letter and slipped it into the pocket of the capris she'd chosen to wear to greet Donna. She had read the page so many times that the edges of the paper were folded and frayed, the creases threatening to separate each time she origami-d the paper back into its pocket-sized shape. She tapped her foot against the floor of the cart, and she pulled on her fingers as she watched each car turn into the parking lot, perking up to look at each one but slouching down into the seat again each time it wasn't who she was expecting.

A silver Mercedes SUV pulled into the welcome center, disturbing the dirt of the parking lot. A dusty cloud rose around the car as the tires spun, settling to the earth again shortly thereafter. The sleek body of the luxury car looked out of place amongst the old Jeeps and large pick-up trucks.

A tall woman with shoulder-length deep brown hair stepped out from the SUV and walked to the back of the vehicle, waving to Lyla as the lift gate powered open. The golf cart's small engine murmured to life as Lyla turned the key, pulling it up directly behind Donna's car to help with her bag.

"Lyla, darling." Donna opened her arms wide. Lyla hopped out of the golf cart and welcomed the embrace. "I've missed you. You look wonderful."

"I've missed you too."

At first, when Jared had passed, it had been hard to be around her. He was so much like his mother in both appearance and character that almost everything she said and did had been a reminder that he was gone — most specifically, though, their laughs. They shared a silly, hearty, made-their-whole-body-shake cackle. At first it had caused Lyla pain to hear it from Donna's mouth, knowing she would never hear it from Jared again, but in time she'd learned to appreciate the small connection she still had to him. Of all the things she missed, his laugh hovered at the top. His mother being able to recreate it so accurately was a curse turned blessing.

Lyla grabbed Donna's Louis Vuitton duffle and pulled it from the trunk.

"Oh, I can get that." She reached for the handle, her manicured hand resting on Lyla's. "I'm not that old, you know. Not yet."

Lyla handed the bag over as requested and returned to her seat at the driver's side of the golf cart.

"Ready for the grand tour?" Lyla jammed the cart into reverse.

"The way you've talked about this place, the way you describe it, I feel like I've already seen it!" She laughed Jared's laugh as she spoke. "I can't wait to put an image with each story."

Butterflies danced deep in Lyla's abdomen. She wanted Donna to love the grounds the way she did, but Begoa's Point was certainly not Fiji or The Maldives or wherever her fancy CEO title had allowed her to visit most recently. Having Donna at Begoa's was like introducing old friends to new friends and praying they loved each other.

Donna placed her purse — which matched her duffle bag — on her lap.

Truthfully, apart from a small addiction to shopping and high-end accessories, most people probably wouldn't peg Donna as a wealthy woman. She didn't talk about money the way some who had it did. Lyla hadn't even known that Donna had climbed her way to the top of one of the largest software and data management companies in the country until after she and Jared had been married.

She lived in a sensible house, something reasonable for just one person. It was a two-bedroom, two-bath with a farmer's porch on a street that ended in a cul-de-sac.

Lyla reversed, and the four tires of the cart dug into the dirt pathway.

"Where's Camden?" Donna asked as they drifted down the main road.

"I'm not sure." Lyla admitted, accompanied by a sigh. "We're not seeing eye to eye at the moment."

Donna laughed. She reached into her purse and pulled out a lip balm, applying the liquid to her full lips as she spoke. "If he and you are anything like Jared and I were, this is only the beginning of that. We were great friends, but we butted heads frequently. He will come around when he needs something."

Lyla laughed. *Ain't that the truth.* It wouldn't be long until he needed money for the snack bar or permission to participate in an event, and suddenly his strike would come to an end.

"Where's the first stop?" Donna held on to the metal rod at the side of the golf cart and looked around.

"The bar." Lyla smiled.

"Now this is my kind of place." Donna did a little dance in her seat, the excitement in her voice echoing into the cloudless sky.

Chapter Twenty-Nine

Weston

The sound from each plucked string of his ukulele rang into the sky as he tuned the old instrument. He lay on the ground outside of the camper, staring at the treetops, fingerpicking spontaneous chords but not playing any one song in particular.

Achilles ran to and fro, playing tag with some innocent creature Weston couldn't see — probably a squirrel or chipmunk, but Achilles could make friends anywhere.

Every site was filled. The waitlist hadn't moved an inch. The activity schedule was packed, the staff alternated shifts twenty-four-seven, and somehow, this was the quietest the campground had ever been.

He hadn't been down to the main square in days, avoiding everything and everyone, hibernating in the dead of summer. He couldn't see Sheila. He wasn't calm enough yet to make that encounter with a reasonable head, and he'd probably fire her on the spot if he approached the welcome center now. The thing was, he couldn't. She had been right. He disagreed with her actions and choices, but the outcome was exactly as she had said—the investors had been far more interested in the expansion project once Lyla and Camden had become involved. Without Sheila, those interested phone calls wouldn't be happening.

His heart clenched, thinking about Lyla's words. She'd accused him of using her for capital gain. If she thought he was capable of that, how much did she know him? Had she seen and recognized a change in him at all? She was the one who'd said, *'you are not the Weston Accardi you used to be,'* and yet, there she was, treating him like the careless, selfish boy he had been all those years ago.

He was not that man anymore. He had proved it time and time again since Lyla's arrival here, and for what? So she could throw it all away over a misunderstanding he had nothing to do with? He'd said he wouldn't leave her—not again. And still, even in his angered state, it was a promise he intended on keeping. The thing was, he was ready for her. All in. Playing for keeps. But she needed to be ready for him— and she wasn't.

Weston dropped the ukulele to the dirt, the bang from the impact with the ground echoing in the sound hole. He pulled his hat low over his eyes. There was so much to be done, but his energy level hovered on empty.

Footsteps approaching the campsite brought Weston out of his pity puddle and back to the real world. He slid his hat off his face and used it to block the sun, squinting one eye closed as Camden entered the site.

Weston looked at him, not saying much and not knowing what to say. He couldn't read him. Was he as mad as his mother? Did he even understand what she was mad about? Then again, Weston didn't really comprehend the latter—but that was a matter for another time.

Weston watched him for a moment, giving him the opportunity to say why he was there or if there was something he needed.

Camden stared at him, a football tucked underneath his casted arm, his 'Camp Champ' T-shirt on dull display.

"You want to play catch?" Camden asked. Uncomplicated, like nothing had ever happened.

Oh, how much simpler things are in the minds of children. Scraped knees healed. Broken bones mended. Arguments came and went in the time it took to blink, with no explanation or debate.

Weston sat up slowly, the campground spinning around him for a moment as his equilibrium settled into place. Camden offered his uncasted hand and pulled Weston to his feet before tossing the football over his shoulder and running down the dirt pathway, going for a long pass.

* * * *

It took a lot of internal wrestling and force to get Weston to go back to the welcome center, but work had to be done. Even though it was the last thing he wanted to think about, he had to know if this expansion project was being bankrolled or steamrolled.

He marched into Sheila's office and closed the door behind him, anticipating some conversation that might become more heated than the campground on a sweltering July day.

"You're still mad." She didn't look up from the calendar she was writing on.

"You deliberately did what I asked you not to. I told you I didn't want to involve her in this, and you did it anyway." Weston tried to keep his voice calm, but it had a mind of its own, gaining volume with each word spoken. "And I was right. She was upset. She still is. I don't know what happens now." Weston's voice fell into a saddened mutter.

He missed her. The last few days on the grounds without her had made him realize that this place wasn't the same without her by his side. That it wasn't just the grounds that made him happy, but it was sharing them with someone who loved the place as much as he did. He paced for a moment, stopping and staring out of the window. A family was in the welcome center parking lot. A mother, a father and a little girl on a purple bike with tassels on the handlebars bonded just outside the welcome center. The father kneeled next to the bike, nodding as he spoke directly to the little girl. He tapped her helmet then readjusted his position to a crouch, pumping the bicycle along.

He started running, keeping pace with the bike, but then let go. She kept pedaling, her little legs pushing the pedals as if she were trying to take off to the moon, then she stopped. She turned over her shoulder and waved to her parents. The father jumped into the air and clapped, landing and wrapping the mother in a celebratory hug. The little girl pedaled back and joined them. Their excitement was tangible. From here, through the thick panel of glass, watching from afar, Weston could feel their excitement and love and joy, and he wanted to feel that way too, no matter the cost.

He knew in that moment that these extravagant ideas he had, these frivolous additions to an already fully functioning campground, were an expensive attempt at filling a void that couldn't be filled by more reservations or a red line on a revenue chart moving in an upward trend. The thing this campground was missing was her. *She* was the missing piece.

"You can be mad at me all you want, Weston." Sheila peered at him over her glasses. "I was putting this business first, which is what you should've done. And you know what? I was right."

Weston turned over his shoulder, waiting for a further explanation. She handed him a piece of paper — a list of investors who had called asking to speak with him about a second meeting. He couldn't tell Lyla about the offers, because accepting them would prove her right — and she wasn't.

There were real offers, real financial backing available to take his dreams and make them reality.

But those weren't his dreams anymore.

Weston ripped the paper into confetti and sprinkled it on Sheila's desk. "Tell them we decline. We don't need their backing — not like this, not this way."

Sheila stood and slammed her hands against the top of the desk.

"Weston, you need that backing. It's the only way to get everything you wanted."

"You're wrong." He looked out of the window at the family once more, the little girl flying like she'd been riding that bike her whole life. "If I take it, I'll lose everything I ever wanted."

* * * *

Dark clouds formed above, blotting out the sun and leaving the grounds dim. Weston ignored the telltale signs of oncoming, unforgiving weather and laced up his sneakers, popped buds into both ears and ran down the path toward the main area of the campground. Small drops of water started to fall from the heavens. He put his face to the sky, allowing the precipitation to mix with the droplets of sweat on his skin and run down his cheeks and jaw. He inhaled deeply, taking in the clean, crisp aroma that only oncoming rain could provide.

Running in the rain was Weston's preference. He found it clarifying, eye-opening. With a lot to think about and large decisions to be made, there was nowhere more appropriate to be than sprinting down his usual path, cleansing rains washing over him, opening his mind to decide whether he should do nothing and keep Begoa's exactly as it was or move forward and find a way to expand and enhance the existing amenities. Then there was Lyla.

He believed Lyla loved him, but he also believed that love scared her. She hadn't mentioned any relationships since her marriage, and in many ways, Weston thought Lyla was looking for any excuse to pull back, to avoid committing to him—and Sheila had handed her one on a silver platter.

Weston reached the marina and sat on the dock, lay backward and watched drops of rain fall in slow motion from the sky.

He had to find her. He had to tell her that he'd declined the investors' proposals and ensure she knew and understood that all of this turbulence was a misunderstanding—even if she wouldn't listen. She'd already spent years with the wrong impression of him, hanging on to a version of him where he was the villain for leaving her with no explanation. This time, if she were going to leave, she would do so with the whole story and the option and ability to make her own decision as to how that story ended.

Chapter Thirty

Lyla

The beach was empty, and consequently, the bar was too. Donna and Lyla were Mark's only two patrons, but it didn't stop them from having a great time. The clouds filled the skies, their deep rumble competing with the bass of the music from the speakers above the bar.

"I'm sorry the weather isn't better." Lyla tapped her fingers to the beat of the song playing.

"Oh, dear, I didn't come here for the weather. You're more than enough sunshine for me." Donna elbowed Lyla lightly. "So"—Donna added, keeping her elbow going, bumping it into Lyla's—"tell me everything."

Lyla watched the clouds darken. Her gaze followed their collective mass all the way across the lake. At the other side of the lake, almost as far as she could see, the wall of nimbostratus ended, and a bright blue strip of sky interrupted by yellow rays was visible—a clarity just beyond the quandary.

"There isn't much to tell." Lyla rested her head in her hands, twirling melting ice around the bottom of a plastic cup.

"I don't believe that." Donna laughed. "Not for a second."

Lyla's heart pounded, just as loud as the music and on par with the thunder. Her hands sweated, the moisture on her palm becoming one with the condensation on the cup. She could have tried to bury the lead, to continue to change the topic, but it would make for a very long weekend. Donna could see right through her. Any time she'd ever tried to keep anything from her, she'd figured it out.

When she had been pregnant, Donna had known before she did. Multiple times, Donna had asked her if she was and Lyla had said no. At the time, Lyla hadn't known. But a few weeks later, when the lines had showed up on the test stick, Lyla had been in disbelief—but Donna hadn't been. She had known all along. It would be a large waste of energy and resources to try to lie to Donna, so as hard as it was, she didn't.

"Well, there's this guy."

"I knew it!" she exclaimed, her bar stool rocking back on two legs. "I want to know all about him."

Lyla placed her hands on the bar top and took a deep breath.

"You're... You're not...mad? Sad? Upset? Anything?"

Donna took a sip of the drink in front of her and placed it back down. Her face fell from its usual permanent smile to an uncharacteristic line.

"Of course, I'm sad." Her voice was quiet, straying from the volume it usually boasted. "I wish you and Jared had gotten more time than you did. It makes me sad to think about you two not having more moments together or growing old together, but let's face it, Lyla—"

Tears clouded Lyla's vision. Her mother-in-law didn't have to finish the sentiment. She knew what the abrupt sentence ending implied. *Let's face it, Lyla. We're not ever going to get those moments.*

Donna tapped the fingers of one hand on the bar top and dragged the other underneath her eyes, wiping away the hint of a tear.

"There are some things I want you to know about my Jared." Donna's voice trembled. "But you need to tell me something first."

Lyla looked up at Donna, their eyes meeting in an unbreakable way that showed she wasn't just asking a question, they were both listening to the answer.

"This man..." Donna said, placing her hand on Lyla's. "Do you love him?"

* * * *

Puddles formed outside the campsite, the blondish dirt turning to a thick brown paste. For the sixteenth year, the calendar had ticked by, page by page, until May had become June and June became July. July faded into August, and August? It flew by, spiraling downward like water in a basin where someone had pulled the plug. This was the downside of summer at Begoa's. It always ended.

Her father pulled the pots and pans from their places in the cabinets, the clamoring sound echoing through the small kitchen as he tossed them into a yellow plastic tote.

Lyla sat on the couch, her feet in canvas sneakers resting on the coffee table, a loose hooded sweatshirt hanging over her shoulders. She chewed the aglet at the end of the drawstrings as she watched the rain pour over their SUV.

"I could use some help, you know." Her father slammed a colander into the tote. He wiped droplets of sweat from his brow, but Lyla stared ahead, ignoring his suggestion.

Sixteen years. Sixteen times of packing up these same totes with the same camping supplies and packing them and unpacking them under the roof of the same cabin. Everything was exactly the same. Well, almost everything. This year, while they packed up every item, ensuring nothing was forgotten, Lyla realized the most important thing would be left behind.

"I have something I need to do." Lyla jumped up, sprinting toward the door.

"Lyla Joyce Savoie," her father hollered into the rain as her feet hit the deck, "you have one hour before this SUV leaves or you'll be stuck here all winter."

Lyla pulled her hood over her ears and smiled. Stuck in Begoa's? It was a dream, not a threat.

She ran down the main road to the marina. She looked around, but there was no one, no boats pulling in or out. Even Sal had abandoned his post at the service desk.

She retreated from the slippery docks, running past the vacant mini golf course, down the untenanted beach. The swings from the playground swayed forward and back in the rain, empty and unused. Her feet carried her in flight to the basketball court. It had collected inches of rain at various places on the blacktop, but she was the only one standing on it. She stood at center court, her face tilted to the sky to kiss the rain in the same spot she'd shared her first kiss earlier that year with Weston Accardi. She turned and kicked a puddle, and droplets of water rocketed off her toe and through the air.

She checked her watch. Forty-six minutes had passed since her sixty-minute warning. Time was waning, the final countdown, and here she stood, entirely by herself.

She took off once more to check the only place she hadn't visited yet – but possibly the most obvious. She cut across the main square, past the snack bar and down the main road, turning into Site 101. Weston sat on a camping chair on the deck under a brightly colored beach umbrella, watching the clouds roll past.

His eyes lit up when he saw her, the kind of light that brightened the dreary day.

"I didn't think you were going to say goodbye." He stood from the chair, stepping into the sheets of rain.

"I'm not going to say goodbye." She moved forward, taking the steps toward him slowly, one at a time.

"What are you going to say then?" The rain slicked his hair to his forehead.

She skipped forward, throwing herself into him. He steadied them both as they kissed. She cried, but the rain masked her tears. He rested his forehead against hers, their eyes exerting a magnetic pull. "I love you," Lyla whispered. Weston paused, blinking away rain from his lashes. He said nothing back. Lyla's heart went from tachycardic to flat line as they stood in silence.

"I just thought..." she panicked, expecting a better response. "You don't have to – "

He placed a finger to her lips, and a light 'shhhh' escaped from his. He smiled and leaned toward her again.

"You win again," he said through a half-smile, "I was going to say that. You said it first. Think there will ever be a time I beat you to anything?"

"It's not likely," she said, and his lips were on hers again.

She looked at her watch – seven minutes before the search parties were called.

"No goodbyes?" he asked as they parted.

"No goodbyes." She turned on her heel and walked down the steps. It was the hardest walk she had ever taken.

"Savvy?" She turned to look back over her shoulder, waiting to see what Weston would say.

"Until next summer." He winked and she turned away, giving herself over to the rain as she ran back toward the site that was their summer home – only, summer was over.

"I do." Lyla nodded, the tears retreating and a smile taking their place. "I do, very much."

Donna squeezed her hand.

"I know how much you loved my son. He knew how much you loved him. But you know what he always said?"

Lyla shook her head, listening to Jared's mother speak on his behalf.

"He always said that he knew you loved him, but he wasn't what you loved most."

Donna's voice wasn't angry or spiteful. In fact, she was laughing. Lyla was confused. She had loved Jared with everything she was made of.

"He said this place was your one true love." Donna looked around as she spoke. "And he dreamed, Lyla. He dreamed of the day this place reopened its doors and he could bring you and your children here. He knew you'd left your heart here, and if he could have opened this place himself so you could have found it again, he would have. I can promise you that."

A single tear streamed down Lyla's face. She held tight to her former mother-in-law's hand.

"You can't be alone forever, Lyla – and neither can Camden. You both deserve to have happiness and life after Jared. And if this is the place that brought you that, if this is the place you found love again, well, it's kind of a sign, isn't it? Don't ignore the signs, Lyla."

Lyla leaned in, hugging Donna and using her shirt to catch the tears that fell from her eyes.

"Now, dear." Donna pulled away and dried her eyes, returning to her proper self. "I came here for a vacation, and I love this song!"

"It's raining." Lyla watched the water drip from the bar's roof.

"It will pass, Lyla. It always does."

Donna stood and dragged Lyla outside the protective bar cover and into the rain, kicking her shoes off in the damp sand. She threw her arms in the air and danced, leaving circles of footprints behind.

Mark leaned over, turning the speakers up to full blast. Lyla joined Donna on the sand, dancing to the music Mark played.

She and Donna laughed and sang, enjoying the moment and each other, not concentrating on the past and with no idea what would happen next.

Lyla looked around the campground. It was beautiful, but it was aged. Weston had done what he could to update it, relying on this first season's successes to allow further updates. With the backing from investors, he'd take this place into modern territory, where it deserved to be.

He had the chance, and she stood in his way. She didn't know where he was at this moment, what he was thinking or if he'd even want to see her after what she'd accused him of. But she could admit she was wrong—twice. First, this wasn't Weston's fault...any of it. Secondly, he should fight for those investments. This place deserved to be the best it could be. *Weston* deserved to have this place be the best it could be. The next time she saw him, wherever she found him, she would give him all her support and encourage him to take any offers he may get.

Donna took Lyla's hands, shuffling her back and forth. They must have looked silly on acres and acres of completely empty beach, dancing and playing like the world had stopped and they'd kept going. Donna lifted Lyla's arm over her head, and she dipped to turn under it. As she made the full turn, Lyla paused and she stared toward the bar. Staring back at her, leaning into the wall of the tiki hut, Weston looked back at her, watching her dance through the storm.

"Is that him?" Donna leaned into Lyla's shoulder.

"Yeah," Lyla whispered, "that's him."

Chapter Thirty-One

Weston

He had almost given up for the day — stopped his search and headed back to the site for the evening, but something had caught his ear then his eye. Despite the cloud cover and less-than-ideal conditions, dance music blared from the bar. Upon hearing it, Weston decided he would pop in and check on his old friend, who was almost guaranteed to have little-to-no profitable business in this weather. When it rained, most of the patrons opted for the indoor bar located near the restaurant. As Weston headed in Mark's direction, he noticed movement on the otherwise vacant beach. Two women were dancing under the heavy rainfall — not just in it but with it.

He leaned into the hut's corner beam, watching as Lyla and a woman he had never seen before left everything on their sandy dance floor. They held hands, shuffled around and sounded off a head-thrown-back laugh that could be seen even if it couldn't be heard over the rain.

He fell in love with Lyla all over again in that second. He watched her as she spun in the rain and he thought back to the very first kiss they'd shared, the very first summer they'd introduced each other to what first love was. She was his entire past. She was his whole future.

He smiled as she took the woman's hand and twirled. Halfway through her spin, she paused, Lyla's gaze finding his. The other woman paused too and in a simultaneous second, all three of them smiled.

The two women walked to the bar, stepping under its tiki top, seeking solace from the downpour.

"Lovely weather we're having." Weston reached out his hand and took the unfamiliar woman's hand in his own. "Weston Accardi."

"Donna Kenney," she responded. Weston fought the surprised expression that tried to find its way to his face, opting for a kind grin instead.

"It's very nice to meet you, Donna."

"Same to you," she added. "I think I see a lonely bartender who needs some attention." She sashayed toward Mark at the other side of the bar.

"West," Lyla began. She ran her hands down her face, wiping the remaining raindrops away. "I'm so sorry. I was wrong about everything."

Weston shook his head, willing to share the blame for the misunderstanding.

"I should've told you everything." He reached for her hands. "I thought about telling you the whole story so many times."

"Why didn't you?"

"It was a very confusing time, Savvy. When the lawsuit went through, I knew I had to keep my distance. My family had already lost so much. But now, that's so far in the past. My dad is gone. The grounds have reopened. When I saw your name on that letter… I don't know. I figured that regardless of all the red tape we had to cut through, this was where we were meant to be. I wanted you here. I figured the rest would stay in the past where it belonged."

"I should have heard you out after the luncheon. It's funny… This summer, I had thought about what it would be like to hear you talk about me and Camden as if we were your family. But then when I finally heard the words…I was scared, I think."

"I'd like you to hear those words too." Weston trailed a finger down her cheek and jaw. "But not like that. Under different circumstances. When we are ready."

Lyla rested her face against his hand, nodding into it. "How did it go, anyway?" she asked. "Did you get any offers?"

"A few —" He started, but she cut him off.

"West! That's great!"

"I declined them," he admitted, her excitement fading to a confused silence. "The gain wasn't worth the loss."

She blushed, and a shy smile raised her lip up at one corner. "I'm honored, but that's crazy! You should have taken them. Expanding this place is your dream. And they are really good ideas, all of them."

"I'll still do it…all of it." He squeezed her hands tightly in his. "Just on my own terms. There will be another way. I can feel it."

She nodded. She believed in him. He could see it in her eyes.

"I'd really like to start over, Savvy." Weston held her close to him. "There's an event this weekend for the Fourth of July. It's open to Begoa's employees and their families. Just a small thank you from me to them for all their hard work."

Lyla nodded, soaking in the details as Weston spoke. "I'd really like you and Camden to come — for real, this time." He winked, and Lyla laughed.

"I would." She cast her eyes down and out as she rejected the offer. "But my mother-in-law is here for the weekend. I can't just ditch her."

Weston looked toward the bar where Donna leaned in close to Mark, the bar between them, but barely.

"Bring her along. Mark will be there, and it looks like they're becoming fast friends."

Lyla looked in the direction of the two flirting over the bar and pressed her fingertips to her lips, a laugh escaping through her hand. She gave him a yes, looking up at him.

"That sounds perfect." She stood on her tiptoes as Weston leaned down to meet her in a kiss.

* * * *

Weston stood with Achilles by his side on the dirt road where the campground met the marina. There was a track under his feet from all his pacing over the dirt road. He was nervous, both for himself and for her. But this was right. It was time.

Lyla, Camden and Donna all strolled down the path toward him. He swallowed hard and slammed his hands into his pockets, rocking back and forth on the balls of his feet. Camden ran ahead from the group, kneeling down and ruffling Achilles' fur in his hands.

"Hello, ladies." Weston tipped his baseball cap toward them.

"So, what are we doing?" Lyla asked. Weston took her hand and led the group down the remainder of the path. They walked over a mulch-covered hill to a crushed gravel walkway — a brand new addition to the marina area. The rocks crunched beneath their feet. As they reached the bottom of the hill, Lyla stopped short, taking in the scene in front of them.

A large, two-decker boat sat at the edge of the water, about seventy people already aboard. Music played loudly off the stern, echoing over the lake. Mark waved from the corner of the second deck as they approached. Donna adjusted her large-brimmed red, white and blue hat and waved back.

"A boat!" Camden yelled, running to the dock and jumping with both feet onto its deck without waiting for the group. Achilles followed the boy without hesitation.

"West," Lyla whispered, but she didn't finish the sentence.

"I know," he said. "Me too. But just come look at something."

They approached the boat, standing at the stern. In large, gold lettering filled in with a pristine matte black, the name 'New Beginnings' was tattooed across the white fiberglass of the boat's back end.

"It's gorgeous, West." She looked over the massive vessel, scanning each inch and feature.

"We said we would start over. I think this is how we do that." Weston stepped forward, reaching out his hand. "Are you ready?" he asked.

She hesitated, pressing her teeth into her bottom lip. She looked over the boat one more time then reached out her hand, taking his and following Weston onto the immense craft.

As the sky fell to a darkened sheet, all the occupants of the boat found their selected spots — some in chairs, some on blankets and some standing at the sides of the deck. Camden lay on a blanket with Achilles. Donna was off somewhere on the first deck dancing with Mark, but her laugh could be heard despite the music, echoing out over the water and traveling to the top deck, where Weston and Lyla stood. She gripped the railing at the side of the boat, and Weston held his arms around her.

From where they stood on the boat at the center of the lake, they could see the outline and lights of Begoa's Point as it shrunk smaller and smaller while they drifted farther away from it.

"I forgot how beautiful it was out here," Lyla said, leaning her head back into Weston's chest. He nodded, his jaw rubbing against her curls. He surveyed the campground from this view. Half of his dream was just over the water, shining bright at the edge of the lake. The other half of the dream was in his arms. *Finally.*

The first burst flew toward the sky, shattering into a thunderous sound that announced the beginning of the fireworks show. A second group of fireworks quickly followed, their explosions coloring the sky overhead and brightening the lake below.

Lyla tipped her head, staring straight up, watching the man-made lights join the stars in a shimmering detonation as the show progressed. She did not shy away from them the way she used to.

"I love you, Savvy." Weston turned her body towards his. "I always have."

Her eyes reflected the illumination in the sky, the purples, the blues and the reds shining against her pale blue irises.

"I was going to say it, you know." Lyla laughed.

"There was no way I was letting you beat me to it." Weston placed his palms at each side of her face. "Not this time."

"I love you too, West."

He pressed his lips to hers, a sharp whistling of rockets taking to the sky above them. Thunderous bursts erupted overhead, the ending of the show backdropping their passionate kiss.

Camden clapped and Achilles barked, certainly for the finale of the firework display, but Weston and Lyla parted and laughed. They stepped forward, crashing down on the blanket, flanking the dog and the boy where the four of them lay and stared at the show's ending, while their own beginning unfolded.

* * * *

The calendar read August once again. Another summer had come and gone. Lyla stood at the center of the new bridge, overlooking the untouched inlet's crystal-clear water. She tapped her fingers on the wooden railing and stared at the fountain, holding the penny Weston had given her more than a month ago.

The bridge shifted as a second person placed their weight on it. Weston approached her, wrapping his arm around her as he reached the center of the bridge.

"How was the meeting?" She leaned into him.

"We discussed what expansions we would be tackling over the winter." He stared at the fountain as the water danced through the air.

"The expansion?" Lyla asked, skeptical but excited. "I thought you declined the funding?"

"I did." Weston smiled. "I told you things would work out. Someone who vacationed here wrote us a letter and offered a fairly substantial amount of money. They asked to stay anonymous."

Lyla jumped up and down, and the thud each time her feet hit the bridge echoed across the water.

"So, what now? What are you going to expand first?"

"First, the star huts. They are going to be a huge hit. I just know it."

Lyla's eyes lit up, and her excitement glistened in her eyes.

"Second," he said, holding up two fingers. "I think this place needs to be open all year round. Think about the snowmobile riders and ice fishers that could use a place like this. We could open the cabins to a winter crowd." He pressed his palms into Lyla's upper arms. "Think about Christmas at Begoa's Point."

"I couldn't think of anything better." A smile pressed into her cheeks. She turned the penny in her fingers.

"What do you have there?" Weston asked, holding the back of her hand in his. She held the penny in a flat palm.

"My wish." She closed her hand around the cent.

"Technically." He raised one finger. "That was *my* penny. It could be my wish."

She raised an eyebrow at him and pulled her hand away.

"I'll tell you what." She stepped past him, turning back to look at him over her shoulder. "I'll race you for it."

"To the Begoa's sign?"

"To the Begoa's sign."

And he took off with her by his side down the paths they had always known, the very paths that had led her back to him.

Want to see more from this author? Here's a taster for you to enjoy!

Consistently Inconsistent: One Motion More
L A Tavares

Excerpt

The locked, guarded door and shiny new mark on my already scarred record are laughable penalties. The real punishment is the *smell* in these small quarters—body odors, stale alcohol. One thing is for sure... There are no VIP suites in New York police stations.

More like a bench than a bed, the slab of flat ceramic I lay on is uncomfortable and determined to punish me with back problems that will last longer than this overnight hold.

My eyes snap shut each time I try to open them—an involuntary response to block out the outdated fluorescent light overhead. I press the palms of my hands into my eye sockets and run my fingers through my overgrown hair. Sure, the lights don't help my already throbbing head and the sleeping arrangement is a far cry from comfortable, but the atmosphere is 'welcoming'. I purposely bent the rules just far enough to win myself a one-night, all-inclusive stay at the nearest precinct.

Quiet. No crowds. No screaming fans. Nowhere for me to be, no way for me to screw up. Most people would find the locked doors, silence and lack of company alarming. Not me. For me, it's tranquil. A vacation. Maybe that's why I frequent the sin-bin so often.

"Hey there, sunshine," a plump guard says, opening the thick-paned glass door so it swings into the hallway. He leans into the metal door frame, holding a large stick of beef jerky in one hand, tearing off a chunk between his teeth and chewing so I can hear it.

"The doors are a nice upgrade," I say through a yawn as I knock on the glass. "They were bars when I was here last."

He gnaws on the dried meat, unamused. "There's someone here to pick you up," he says as he chews, spewing small chunks of meat and saliva as he speaks.

"Aw, so soon?" I bring myself to my feet and stretch — every muscle protests. "Guess I'm not twenty-one anymore, eh?" I ask.

"Maybe you should stop trying to be," he says. His stone expression remains as such.

"Noted," I add, and salute him as I step away from the cell, turn around and head toward the station's lobby to retrieve my sunglasses and cell phone before heading out of the doors.

Blake — my bass guitarist and lifelong best friend — leans against a car I've never seen before, opens the back door and gets in without waiting for me to approach him. He slides to the opposite side of the hired car and I slide in next to him, closing the door as the driver pulls away from the curb.

"How bad this time?" I ask, one side of my mouth lifting at the corner.

"You really don't remember?" he asks.

"No. That was the whole point." I drop my phone into the breast pocket of my shirt and place my sunglasses over my eyes.

Blake tilts back the top of a box of Marlboro Reds, a flagrant disregard of the *No Smoking* sticker adhered to the car's dash. The lingering tobacco smell of the car tells me he's already broken that rule.

"Never fear," I say, elbowing him in the arm. "Social media and the news will remind me, I'm sure."

"If Cooper doesn't kill you first," Blake adds, cracking the window and fishing for a Bic in his breast pocket. His words come out draped in a mix of his slightly faded South African accent and the dialect he has picked up during his years in the States.

Blake moved into my house at a time when his mother couldn't provide for him anymore—right as we started tenth grade and, truthfully, his appearance hasn't changed much since I met him in junior high. He looks almost the same way now as he did then, down to his stupid blond-tipped faux hawk and slightly spaced teeth. Only now, the tall, slender physique he boasted back then has morphed into a 'definitely enjoys beer'-type body. Though, the same could be said for me.

The car arrives back at the venue where we are set to have our second show in a back-to-back schedule.

We enter the building and Blake walks ahead of me by about five strides. I am in no condition to keep up. He turns a corner, disappearing from view. As I turn the same corner, Cooper, our band's manager, is standing there waiting for me. Startled, I jump out of my boots and my stomach takes a drop it can barely handle. I swallow back whatever threatens to make a reappearance.

"Jeez—" I start, but he has no intention of letting me talk.

"Leave," he says, his eyes an even deeper brown than they usually are, enhanced by the dark bags beneath them. "Go find food, water and a shower. Whatever it is you need to do to clean up and be ready for today."

"I'll be ready, Coop. I always am."

"You should be grateful we have a show today because I can tell you—no, I can *promise* you—if I didn't need you today, you would still be sitting in that cell." Cooper paces the width of the hallway, pausing every few moments to make a hand gesture my direction, as if he can't walk and shake his fist all at the same time. "You're lucky the cops here are fans of yours, you know. There will come a day where just *being* Xander Varro doesn't get you what you want. Your status won't get you out of everything forever. The sooner you understand that the better."

"I had a few drinks. I was having a good time—"

"Drunk and disorderly, disturbing the peace, resisting arrest." Cooper starts listing off, using his fingers to keep track of all the misdemeanors. "This band can't keep a publicist because they're tired of covering for you. You can't keep yourself out of the negativity and the spotlight. You're dependent on drama. You're going to be a father, for crying out loud. When do you plan to grow up, Xander? When is enough, enough?"

He's right, but I'm too proud to admit it. Cooper's growl shifts to a hushed pause, allowing me to say my piece or apologize, but I don't do either, so he continues, filling the silent void.

"This isn't just about you, you know. Your band counts on you. Your fans count on you. *I* count on you.

Someday your kid will count on you, and you are becoming the kind of guy who can't be counted on." His pacing comes to a halt and his eyes soften. His voice quiets, falling so calm that I would almost prefer the yelling. "You have it all, Xander. Everything. Stop *trying* to throw it all away."

I nod, a silent response, even though I know Cooper wants more from me. It's all I have to offer.

"Just go, Xander," he says. "Come back when you're ready to be on that stage and not a second sooner."

"Can you send a car to take me back to the hotel?"

"You can walk."

I laugh at his joke, but the sound becomes a scoff when I realize he's serious. I nod without enthusiasm and turn toward the door, slamming my bodyweight into the metal push bar though the signs clearly indicate Emergency Exit Only.

The hotel is only just over a mile away, but I'm still annoyed. These boots definitely were not made for walking. My feet are throbbing by the time I arrive at the lavish hotel doors. The lock clicks as I hold the key card to the door of the hotel room that I was supposed to be long-checked-out of. I lay on the bed longer than I should, ignoring the clothes and other items strewn across it. A red light blinks at the base of the landline phone the hotel provides, most likely a wakeup call ordered by Cooper or a message about the late fees incurred as a result of the ignored check-out. I almost delete it without listening, figuring whatever message it holds is either now irrelevant or I just don't care what it has to say.

But I click it, and my girlfriend's voice is on the other end. I smile at first, listening to her words.

"Hey, it's Mariah."

But the smile fades to a flatline. Why would she call the hotel and not my cell phone?

"I have something to tell you."

* * * *

The brilliant spotlights above the stage beam hot against my skin as if the sun itself made a front-row appearance at the show. Sweat soaks my long hair, my shirt sticks to my skin.

Thousands of people are packed wall-to-wall into the venue. A mosquito would put us over capacity. The crowd is just feet from me, yet their profiles are indecipherable. The bodies become blurred as they jump and dance at the front of the stage. The crowd melts together to form one jumbled image.

With a wrinkled forehead and my eyes shut tight, I will my vision to clear, but it's not enough. The words she left me with can't be unheard.

'I lied to you.'

Stumbling back across the bowing floorboards of the stage, I stagger, but fight to keep myself upright.

'I'm sorry. I was holding on to something that wasn't there and hasn't been there for quite some time.'

The band still plays, strumming their guitar strings and keeping time on the drums, but I can't concentrate on the words I am supposed to be singing while hers still play wildly in my head.

'I knew if I called your phone, you'd answer, but if I hear your voice, I know I'll never tell the truth.'

This feeling — the chest tightness, the rapid pulse — it's foreign to me. I don't recognize this kind of distress.

'When I told you that I was pregnant with your baby, I was just trying to give you a reason to stay. But it's not true.'

My mouth goes dry again, paralyzing my tongue against the back of my front teeth. Everything around me moves in slow motion, like quicksand.

I should be entertaining this crowd. The only thing I'm entertaining is spiraling thoughts.

The baby that never was.

The conniving woman who screwed me over.

The fastest way to get out of playing a show tonight and be anywhere but here.

The members of the band shout to me—maybe *at* me—but their muffled voices sound miles away. A high-pitched ringing sounds at both ears, overpowering the thousands of voices that fill the venue. Blake stands in front of me, asking if I'm okay.

I'm *not* okay.

The lights are glaring, the music is flawless, the crowd is thunderous but I am broken. The microphone falls through my clammy palm, hitting the stage and bouncing with harsh echoing thuds and horrid feedback. I make my way toward the wings of the stage. I can't look back—and I don't.

Proof of this disaster is better than likely already uploaded to every available social media platform shared by one person, then the next—gone viral.

Like a disease.

The magazines and tabloids, they will slander my name with assumptions of drug use. *Xander Varro Performs While Inebriated at New York Venue.*

They think they know me.

They don't know a damn thing.

The truth is…. Well, it doesn't matter what the truth is. The truth doesn't sell like the bullshit does. This isn't drugs. This is a feeling that tears through my chest cavity like rot in old walls. This is unrelenting anger that robs me of my breath. The lyrics to a song I wish I had never written in the first place, had dismantled me in a way that I never would have anticipated. Blindsided me, much like Mariah had.

This is panic.

Everyone tried to warn me about her.

All the signs were there.

Warning. No lifeguard on duty. Swim at your own risk.

And I did.

I dove in head-first every damn time, catapulting myself into deep, troubled waters — a treacherous mix of her crooked lies and mouth full of deceit. I filled my lungs with air and held it as I treaded the waves of fables she was known for.

And now, I'm sinking like an anchor in waters I never should have navigated in the first place.

There is no mistaking the sound of the crowd beyond the stage now — their disgruntled outcry a mix of boos and jeers, openly expressing their demands for our return to stage. I don't blame them for being this vocal. Had we been nearing the end of the show, we could have passed this off as a cutoff point and returned to the stage for an encore, but we had just started our set. "What do you want to do, Xander?" Blake asks, sweat beading across his brow. "Are you okay? Do you want to try to get back out there?"

Blake's eyes are trained on mine. Without blinking, I stare at him. He's my best friend, my brother, really — but there wasn't much going on between his ears.

More often than not he wears this absent expression with his eyes frosted over and his lips parted like someone asked him a question he doesn't know the answer to. That's the face he wears now, only no one asked him anything, and I wish he would just shut up.

"I need to get the hell out of here," I mumble. Leaving the band behind me, I stand and half jog the length of the backstage area. Eager to escape, I slam my bodyweight into the first door I see, with no idea what sits on the other side.

Hundreds of pairs of curious, demanding eyes await. I stand frozen in the doorway. There are only two things separating me from the crowd — a thin fabric barrier and a few security guards who may not even be tall enough to ride large rollercoasters.

A guy who stands about six feet tall or so — only about an inch or two shorter than me — steps around the barrier with two other men flanking closely beside him. The two security guards closest to me step forward, posing about as much threat as a Nerf gun in a bad neighborhood.

"I paid for a show. I came to see a show. I expect a show," the disgruntled fan says, flaunting a pierced tongue. His friends yell a resounding agreement.

"Fuck off," I hiss, turning away from them. That should have been the final word. At least, that was my intention, but he spits in my direction. I urge myself to keep walking and forget this jackass exists — but I can't.

Not tonight.

My conscience is as lopsided as a seesaw with only one passenger, encouraging me to turn and give this guy a piece of my mind. The security detail instructs me to 'Let it go', which I kindly disregard, shaking free of his grasp on my arm.

Security is on my heels as I approach the man, who somehow seems bigger than he did a few moments ago. His back is to me, but he yells over the house music, bragging to a group in the crowd as if his disgusting behavior were something heroic.

I tap him on the shoulder and he turns toward me.

"How's this for a fucking show?" I say through clenched teeth and throw my body behind a well-timed right hook. Either my knuckles or his jaw emits a distinct *crack* as the two connect, but there is no time to think about which it was. He lunges back at me, grabbing the front of my shirt.

The security staffed by the venue floods the area, separating me from my opponent and the gathering onlookers.

A salt-and-pepper-haired security guard pushes me backward a few steps as the other guy is escorted from the venue. He looks back at me with fury in his eyes. I curtsy, holding the edges of an invisible skirt, then give him the middle finger as the security detail drags me backstage.

TOTALLY BOUND

Home of Erotic Romance

Sign up for our newsletter and find out about all our romance book releases, eBook sales and promotions, sneak peeks and FREE romance books!